Date: 1/31/12

LP FIC SALA
Sala, Sharon.
Blood trails

BLOOD TRAILS

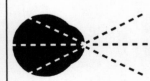

BLOOD TRAILS

SHARON SALA

THORNDIKE PRESS
A part of Gale, Cengage Learning

GALE
CENGAGE Learning™

Detroit • New York • San Francisco • New Haven, Conn • Waterville, Maine • London

Copyright © 2011 by Sharon Sala.
The Searchers Series #3.
Thorndike Press, a part of Gale, Cengage Learning.

Thorndike Press® Large Print Basic.
The text of this Large Print edition is unabridged.
Other aspects of the book may vary from the original edition.
Set in 16 pt. Plantin.

LIBRARY OF CONGRESS CATALOGING-IN-PUBLICATION DATA

Sala, Sharon.
   Blood trails / by Sharon Sala. — Large print ed.
     p. cm. — (The searchers series; #3) (Thorndike Press large print basic)
   ISBN-13: 978-1-4104-4333-5 (hardcover)
   ISBN-10: 1-4104-4333-7 (hardcover)
   1. Women—Identity—Fiction. 2. Murder—Investigation—Fiction.
3. Large type books. I. Title.
PS3569.A4565B575 2011
813'.54—dc23   2011032338

Published in 2011 by arrangement with Harlequin Books S.A.

Printed in the United States of America
1 2 3 4 5 6 7 15 14 13 12 11

It is true that the sins of the father
are often visited upon the child.
We come into this world through pain.
Pain is a constant throughout our lives,
whether from a brief physical pain, an
enduring emotional pain, or a damaged
soul that cannot heal.

Having to also endure the shame
of someone else's transgressions is
without doubt the hardest, and the
most unfair. Bearing a damaged
name is one pain too many —
a pain no child should suffer.

I dedicate this story to the innocents,
whose only sin was to carry a name
with a shame not of their making.

ONE

Missoula, Montana

The ranch house was quiet — too quiet. It should have been filled with energy and activity — voices, snippets of conversation and laughter, the scent of something good baking in the oven.

But Andrew Slade's death had been the beginning of the end of what had been. There was nothing to be done now but look toward what was — or, in the case of his three daughters, what *could* be. The revelation he'd dropped on them at the reading of his will had torn the family apart.

His oldest daughter, Holly, was the only one of them left at the ranch now, along with Robert Tate, Andrew's best friend and ranch foreman — and the love of Holly's life.

But Robert — Bud to his friends — didn't know about Holly's feelings, and she was so used to keeping them a secret that revealing them now in the midst of so much turmoil didn't seem possible.

Her sisters, Maria and Savannah, were already gone. They'd jumped into the search for answers to their pasts without hesitation, while Holly had lingered. She couldn't wrap her head around what she'd learned without getting sick to her stomach. Even now, when she should have been making travel plans, she was still at the Triple S — still wavering as to what she should do and replaying the video that had ripped their world apart when they'd gathered in the office of their lawyer, Coleman Rice, and seen it for the first time.

She sat now within the quiet of the family den while a log burned and popped in the fireplace behind her, her gaze fixed on the television, and re-watched the video. As soon as it ended, she played it again. Andrew's image and voice were a source of comfort, but at the same time they fed her grief.

"Hello, my daughters. Obviously, if you're seeing this, I have passed on. Know that, while I am sorry to be leaving you behind, my faith in God and the knowledge that I will be with my beloved Hannah again is, for me, a cause to rejoice. However, what I have to say to you is something I've dreaded your entire

lives, and I'm ashamed to say I chose the easy way out and left it for you to hear after my passing."

Holly held her breath. This time she knew what was coming, but the words were still impossible to absorb.

"My darling daughters . . . you need to know that I am not really your father, Hannah was not really your mother, nor were any of you ever legally adopted."

Holly jumped when she felt a hand slide across her shoulder, then swallowed past the lump in her throat to keep from crying when she realized it was Bud. Somehow he'd come in and she hadn't even heard him.

"There is more. You are not sisters."

Holly hit Pause, then clasped Bud's hand as she turned around. "Did you need me?"

A dozen thoughts of what he might say slid through Bud's mind, but the one that mattered most was one he'd never said. Yes, he needed her: in his heart, in his life, in his bed . . . forever. "Not really, honey. I just came in to see if you were okay."

Holly's shoulders slumped. "Obviously I'm not, or I wouldn't still be wallowing in this."

Bud slid onto the couch beside her and took her hand.

"Let it play out and then we'll talk."

Holly hit Play. Andrew's voice filled the silence between them.

"By now, I suspect your grief at my passing has turned to shock . . . even anger. I understand. But what you three need to understand is . . . I believed with every fiber of my being that, as I was following my calling as an evangelical preacher, God led me to each of you at a time when you needed me most. There are journals that I've left with Coleman, one for each of you. Everything I know about your past is in there, along with why your mothers put you in my care.

"Maria, you were the first one. You were born Mary Blake, in Tulsa, Oklahoma. Your mother had a hard life. She was, for lack of a better word, an escort at the time of her death. You were four years old when you witnessed her murder. As she lay dying, she begged me to take you and hide you. The details as to how it all happened are in your journal. To my knowledge, her murder was never solved.

"Savannah, you are actually Sarah Stewart, from Miami, Florida, and the second child to be given to me. Your mother was dying of cancer and had come to my tent meetings to pray for healing. By then Maria had been with me for nearly six months. You were barely two. You and Maria hit it off immediately when

*your mother came to hear me preach, and
she saw the bond between you two. On the
last night of the revival, she came to me in a
panic. She and your father were not married,
but he had never denied you, and he played
an important role in your life. According to
her, he was also a member of a very rich,
powerful local family, and he had informed
them of his plans to marry her. The night she
came to me, she was sobbing uncontrollably.
Your father had been killed in a car accident
early that morning, and already she had
received a threat on your life. Aware that she
had only weeks to live and no one else to
whom she could turn, she begged me to take
you and raise you with Maria. So I did. It was
then that I began to understand I was being
led down this path by a power greater than
my own.*

*"Holly, you are my oldest, but you came to
me last."*

Holly started to cry. Bud let go of her
hand and put his arm around her shoulders,
holding her close as the video continued.

*"You were born Harriet Mackey and were
five when you and your mother showed up at
a revival I was holding in St. Louis, Missouri.
She seemed troubled, but I thought nothing of
it. At one time or another we are all troubled
by something or someone. On the fourth and*

last night of the revival, I thought everyone was gone from the church. Maria and Savannah had gone to sleep in the pastor's office, and I was on my way to get them when your mother showed up at the door with you and a suitcase. Her story was staggering, but at that point, I didn't question God's plan. What you need to know is that she did not give you away. She was convinced that her husband, your father, was a serial killer the Missouri police had been hunting for nearly a year. She feared what the notoriety would do to your life when all was revealed, and that you would be branded as a killer's daughter. She was going to turn him in, and then come and get you and start over in a new place. Only she never came after you, and no one was ever arrested for the murders. I fear she paid for her bravery with her life.

"As I said before, Coleman has journals for each of you. I've written down everything I know. As to whether you go back to find your roots or not, that is your choice, but I caution each of you to remember, your lives were in danger then. They could be again."

The video ended. This time Holly turned off the TV, then covered her face.

Bud took her in his arms and began patting her back as he'd done countless times before when she'd been a child.

"I'm sorry, Holly, so sorry this is happening."

She didn't answer. The only thing she was capable of at the moment was tears, and Bud knew enough to let her cry it out.

He'd been a young man, barely out of his teens, when he'd come to work for Andrew Slade, but over the years he and Andrew had become best friends. He'd adored Andrew's girls from the start, and they'd returned the feeling. He wasn't sure when he realized his fondness for Holly had turned into something more.

Holly was twenty-five now, finally old enough for his thirty-nine years. But there were too many years of familial friendship between them for him to hope their relationship could become anything more.

Finally Holly pulled out of his embrace and reached for a handful of tissues.

"Sorry. You'd think I'd be past this by now."

"It's okay. Indecision is troubling enough on its own, without all this other crap to deal with."

Holly laughed through tears. "That's what I love about you, Bud. You always cut to the chase."

Bud's gaze was fixed on her mouth. Her lips were slightly swollen from crying and begging to be kissed. It was all he could do to back away.

"That's me — To-the-Point Tate. And speaking of getting to the point, I came to tell you not to bother making lunch for me. I've got to take some of the hands over to the high country, and find the rest of the cows and new calves."

All of a sudden Holly had found a task that she could handle.

"There's no need going without anything to eat until night. There's a full platter of fried chicken in the refrigerator, and at least a dozen leftover biscuits. You can at least take that for you and the boys."

Bud grinned and then kissed the side of her cheek. "You're the best."

Holly's pulse surged. If she'd turned her mouth just the tiniest bit to the left, that kiss would have landed squarely on her lips.

"Give me a couple of minutes to pack it up for you."

"I'll grab a couple of six-packs of Mountain Dew, and we'll be good to go. The boys and I thank you."

Holly flew to her task, feeling a brief moment of respite from all her confusion. This home was where her heart was, and its heart was the kitchen — Holly's favorite room.

Within minutes Bud and the food were

gone, and Holly was once again alone, only this time with a better attitude.

She got a couple of cookies and a can of Pepsi, and went back into the den to get her journal — the one Andrew had left for her alone.

She'd read it through a dozen times over in the past three days since learning the truth, and it still hadn't gotten any better. How did one go from being the oldest daughter of a respected Montana rancher to the only child of a suspected serial killer? The knot in her stomach drew tighter as she picked up the journal and took it to her room. She crawled up onto her bed with the Pepsi and cookies, and once again read the words that had officially ended her happy world.

You were born in St. Louis, Missouri, as Harriet Mackey, the only child of Harold and Twila Mackey. It was while I was preaching at a week-long revival that I first met your mother. She came every night and sat in the front row with you close by her side. I remember thinking her expression seemed sad, even haunted. It wasn't until later that I fully understood why. As for you, you were a very quiet child who played with Maria and Savannah during the services every night, and often fell asleep with them, tumbled up on top of each other like a bunch of worn-out puppies who'd played too hard.

The last night of the revival, your mother was back, but this time she was also carrying a suitcase, along with you. It wasn't until the services were over that I fully understood her intentions, but by then I'd already accepted that God was leading me to these desperate women who had nowhere else to turn. Your eyes were red and swollen and you kept clinging to your mother's arm. When she explained what she wanted of me, you didn't flinch or weep . . . as if you already understood the need.

What you must understand is that, unlike Maria's and Savannah's mothers, yours had no intention of giving you away. She was desperate to get you out of the public eye. She claimed that she had recently come to believe that her husband was a serial killer the police were searching for, and who had been leaving women's bodies all over St. Louis for months. The police didn't have a single clue on which to act, but your mother was convinced that her husband, your father, was the man. She said she had evidence. She was going to turn him in, wait for his arrest, and then, after everything died down, she would come and get you. She had plans for the two of you to start life over under another name and in another state. But she never came. And no one was ever arrested. I could only draw one conclusion: that she'd been murdered for her intentions.

Unable to read any more, Holly laid the journal and her food aside, and curled up in the fetal position. She was still shocked that she had no memories of her parents, or of living anywhere other than the Triple S Ranch. According to the journal, she was five when her mother sent her away with Andrew Slade. So what happened? What had she seen that had been so horrible she'd been willing to block out everything, including a mother who loved her that much?

She lay without moving, staring blindly at the photo hanging on the wall in front of her — one she'd always considered her favorite family portrait. Andrew in his easy chair beside the Christmas tree; Maria sitting on one arm of the chair; Savannah on the floor at his feet; Holly on the other arm of the chair, and Bud standing behind them with a hand on Holly's shoulder. It was a pretty picture, but it was a lie. That family was a fake, and the revelation of their births had torn apart what was left of them.

Maria was already gone. She'd flown out of Montana three days earlier on her way back to Tulsa, Oklahoma, where she'd been born. She was determined to regain her memory and find the killer who'd ended her mother's life.

Savannah was on a similar quest. She'd left for Miami, Florida, the day before yesterday to begin proceedings to claim her inheritance and solve the mystery behind her birth father's death.

Unlike her sisters, Holly wasn't driven to find out all the secrets of her past. She didn't want to leave the ranch . . . or Bud. She didn't want to open the Pandora's box of her past for fear she would wind up like her mother — gone without a trace. Yet at the same time, she couldn't quit thinking about her. If she *had* been murdered like the other women in St. Louis all those years ago, Holly had to go back. She owed it to her mother — to all the victims — to tell the police about her mother's suspicions. She could at least do that. Ignoring the knot in her belly, she rolled off the bed and pulled a suitcase from the back of her walk-in closet.

As she began to move from bed to closet and back again, packing for what might turn out to be an extended stay, her nerves began to ease. The simple act of packing had solidified a purpose, which was what she'd been lacking.

Late in the evening, the men returned. She saw Bud drive toward the house as she carried a load of laundry to the kitchen table to be folded.

She heard his truck stop out back, then the hurried sound of footsteps as he hit the porch running.

She frowned. Something was wrong. Concerned, she was on her way to the door when he burst into the kitchen. His face was pale, his lips tight in a grimace of obvious pain. Her gaze slid to his hand and the towel wrapped around it, then to the blood soaking through the fabric.

"Oh, my God! Bud! What did you do?"

"I was cutting the baler twine off some hay bales and got caught in the middle of a dispute between those two damned herd mares. My knife slipped."

"Is it bad? Let me see."

"I'm okay, honey. I'll just wash it off, wrap it up and —"

Holly wasn't buying it. "Come with me,"

she said, and led him into her room, then through to her bathroom. "Can you take your coat off without getting blood all over it?"

"Don't worry about the blood. It's my work coat." The towel fell into the sink as he began to slip one arm from a sleeve.

Before his coat was off, Holly saw the gaping wound on the palm of his hand. "Oh, no, that's going to need stitches. Leave your coat on. I'm driving you into Missoula."

"Well, hell."

"Does it hurt much?" she asked, as she grabbed a fresh towel and wrapped it tightly around his hand.

"It's beginning to."

Holly saw a muscle jerking in the side of his jaw; his skin was pale and clammy. Shock.

"I'm so sorry." She cupped the side of his face. "Let me get my coat and the car keys, and we'll be ready to go."

Bud flinched at her touch, and tried not to give himself away. Needing to keep an emotional distance between them, he glanced through the doorway to the suitcase on her bed.

"Looks like you're busy packing. I can get one of the men to drive me."

Holly turned on him, her eyes blazing.

"You'll do no such thing!" She grabbed her coat from the closet and her purse off the bed, and led him back through the house and into the garage.

"We should take the work truck," Bud said, as he hesitated beside the door of the family Lincoln. "I'll get blood on these seats."

Holly ignored him and opened the passenger door. "Sit," she said briefly, then leaned over and buckled him in.

She was so focused on hurrying that she didn't hear his swift intake of breath as her hair brushed across his face, and even if she had, she would not have recognized it as the bone-deep want for Holly Slade with which he lived.

Within minutes Holly was on the highway and speeding toward Missoula.

"There's no need to speed," Bud said.

Her lips were pressed tightly together, her eyes narrowed against the glare of the sun coming through the windshield. She glanced quickly at Bud's hand to see if blood had begun seeping through again, then back at the highway.

"You've lost a lot of blood. What if this had happened after I was gone?"

"Then one of the men would have driven me into town," he said, and looked away,

21

suddenly interested in the passing scenery.

Knowing she was going back to where she was born and into such a dangerous situation was making him crazy. If he'd been paying attention to his business instead of thinking about her, he would have had the presence of mind to get out of the way of the mares and not been cut at all.

Holly's fingers gripped the steering wheel even tighter as she drove. Even though it was an improbable title, she considered herself the caretaker of the Triple S. She didn't want someone else usurping her place, which was just another reason she'd told herself she shouldn't go.

She made the drive to Missoula in record time, took the street leading to the hospital and then made the turn leading to the emergency room. She was out and opening Bud's door before he could unbuckle his seat belt. Again she leaned in, hit the button and released the catch.

"Lean on me," she said, and slipped her arm around his waist to steady his steps.

He felt helpless, which made him angry. "There's nothing wrong with my feet."

"You've lost a lot of blood," Holly argued.

"I'm not going to pass out."

"You don't know that," she muttered, as they walked into the E.R.

The receptionist looked up.

"We need a doctor. He's bleeding badly," Holly said.

The receptionist offered her a clipboard with a personal history chart and insurance info to be filled out.

Holly glared. "I'm sorry. You must not have heard me. He has been bleeding like this for the past twenty minutes. That bloody towel on his hand is the second one he's soaked. We need a doctor, not a medical form."

The receptionist frowned, but got up from her chair and hurried through a pair of swinging doors, then returned with a doctor.

"Thank you so much," Holly said, and pointed to the clipboard. "I'll help him fill that out while they're stitching him up."

Still irked that her rules had been challenged, the receptionist handed her the clipboard without comment.

Holly didn't care if she'd ruffled some feathers. Her focus was on Bud's welfare as she followed him into an exam room. Within minutes the doctor and a nurse had his coat off and his shirtsleeve rolled up, and the nurse was cleaning debris from the cut while Holly dutifully filled out the questionnaire, asking Bud questions when she didn't know the answers.

It was the first time she could remember seeing him helpless and in pain, and she didn't like it. He was always the go-to man. It shocked her that he could be felled so easily, which led to thoughts of the only father she'd ever known, Andrew. Once she'd thought the same of him, but fate had proven her wrong. One minute Andrew had been talking and laughing, and the next he had dropped dead of an aneurysm.

Now she was back in the same hospital where Andrew had been brought, only this time it was Bud on the examining table. Even though this injury wasn't life-threatening, it panicked her to think she could ever lose him, too.

As she sat watching them work, her focus was on Bud, and it was as if she were seeing him for the very first time.

Nearly forty, he was a man in his prime at six feet three inches tall, with dark straight hair and even darker eyes, and angular features. Holly caught herself staring at the sensual cut of his lips, then at a mouth that was often curved in laughter. He caught her staring and winked.

Holly blinked. Just for a second she'd let herself pretend he was hers to admire. It startled her enough that she blushed and actually looked away, then wondered why. It was just Bud being Bud and trying to lighten the moment. He couldn't know how she felt. It didn't mean anything.

Twelve stitches later they left the emergency room, stopped by the pharmacy to get a prescription for pain pills filled and then headed home. As the city limit sign disappeared in the distance behind them, the panic of the trip to the hospital also disappeared.

"Are you okay?" Holly asked, looking for signs of pain or stress on his face.

Bud knew she was rattled. "I'm fine, sugar. Stop worrying. It's not the first time I've gotten stitches."

"I guess, but it's the first time I was the only one around to see it."

Bud reached across the seat to give her arm a quick squeeze. "The past week has been hell for all of us, and this didn't help. I'm sorry."

Holly shook her head. "No, don't apologize for anything. It's not just Dad dying, or your accident. It's everything we found out about our pasts. I am scared and mad, but at the same time I feel this huge sense of obligation to go back to my place of birth."

This was the first time he'd realized how torn Holly was about leaving. The other two had seemed driven to leave the ranch. He had assumed Holly felt the same. Knowing she did not made it even harder for him to let her go without telling her how he felt. The urge to spill his guts about his feelings was on the tip of his tongue, but instead of giving in, he offered a simple solution to her fears.

"You don't have to go alone."

Holly grimaced. "Yes, actually, I do. I can't explain it, but I know that much is true."

Bud's frown deepened. "I don't agree. Of all Andrew's daughters, your story scares me most. Your father was a suspected serial killer, Holly. You go back there and stir up old secrets, what's to keep him from coming after you?"

"We don't even know if he's still alive. If he is, he probably moved years ago. I don't expect him to be an issue. I just feel like it's my duty to at least tell the police what my mother believed to be true. I don't have huge expectations of finding out what happened to her, but I have to at least go through the motions."

Again Bud wanted to tell her what she meant to him, that he couldn't sleep for worrying about where she was going, and again he tempered the urge by reaching for the bottle of pop Holly brought him when she had his prescription filled and taking a long drink. The Pepsi burned the back of his throat as he swallowed. After a second swallow, he had his emotions under control.

Still distracted by the accident and her upcoming trip, Holly didn't notice Bud's unusual silence the rest of the way home. It wasn't until she was turning off the highway onto the ranch that she realized he hadn't said a word in miles, but she chalked it up to pain.

A hawk that had been sitting on a nearby fence post took flight. Holly watched until it disappeared into the sun, then shivered. It was like a visual analogy to the women who'd been victims of that years-ago killer. One moment they'd been alive, and the next they were gone. It was an obscenity that her birth father could possibly be the killer. She wouldn't let herself think of what that made her. Not now. Not yet.

She pulled into the garage and killed the engine. For a few seconds they sat within the silence of the car without speaking. Then all of a sudden they both spoke at once.

"Why —"

"When —"

Holly grinned. "You first."

27

Bud tried to smile, but it just wouldn't come. "When does your flight leave?"

"Nine-fifteen tomorrow morning."

"I'm driving you."

"But your hand . . ."

"Is still attached to my arm, which will come in handy when I drive you into Missoula to catch your damned plane," Bud said. "Thank you for driving me. I need to go check on the men."

Holly blinked away tears as he got out of the car and walked away. He sounded angry. But that didn't make sense. He was probably in pain and didn't want to admit it.

She gathered up the sack with his pain pills and what was left of his Pepsi, and went into the house.

Holly was packed. The suitcase sitting by her bedroom door was a potent reminder of what tomorrow would bring. She still had tonight to get through and didn't want to waste it on regrets. Her place in this house was grounded in the everyday realities of life.

After her stepmother, Hannah, had died, she'd become the caretaker, the housekeeper, the cook. Like her sisters, she'd opted to live at home during her college years and had stepped into the role of "lady of the house" without an issue.

Bud was due back at any time. This was the last time she would get to cook for him for a while, and she was determined to make his favorite foods. He would be on his own when it came to laundry and meals until she returned, although she'd arranged for a local cleaning service to come out once a week and clean house.

The roast she'd put in the oven a couple of hours ago was done, as were the vegetables she'd put in with it. She'd just taken a chocolate pie out of the oven and set it on the counter to cool. The meringue was a thing of beauty, with the peaks browned lightly to a golden perfection. Now all she had to do was make a salad and the meal would be ready.

She glanced at the clock. It was half past seven. The sun had already set. She walked out onto the back porch to look toward the barn, then beyond to the stables to see if she could see Bud's truck. No luck.

She shivered as a blast of cold air whipped around the side of the house. Spring was here, but Montana weather had yet to catch up with that fact. She had turned to go back inside when she heard the sound of an engine and saw the lights of Bud's truck coming out from behind the barn. Instead of going inside, she wrapped her arms around her waist and waited for him to reach the house.

Bud's mood was glum until he looked up and saw Holly standing beneath the porch light. At that moment everything that had been dragging him down, from the pain in his hand to the knowledge that she was leaving tomorrow, disappeared.

The wind was cold, whipping her hair about her face. She wasn't wearing a jacket over her jeans and sweater, and yet she stood there waiting, like a beacon in the dark — waiting for him. The surge of emotion that swept through him was so strong that his vision blurred.

God.

He'd never thought it possible to love anyone as much as he loved her. All he could think as he drove toward the house was that he had to get through this night and see her off on her flight without losing it.

By the time he parked, Holly had come off the steps to meet him.

"How's your hand?" she asked, as she opened the driver's side door.

Bud tweaked her ear. "You are such a mother hen."

Holly grinned. "So shoot me. I'm just practicing for the real thing."

Bud stumbled. The thought of someone else being the father of her children was physically painful.

Holly grabbed his elbow, then slipped an arm around his waist to steady him. "See? You do need a keeper."

Bud gritted his teeth to keep from sweeping her into his arms. "As long as it was you, I guess I wouldn't mind."

Holly snorted softly. "You say that, but we both know you're not the kind who'd ever stand for that kind of help full-time. Supper is ready. I hope you're hungry."

"I'm starved," he said. "I just need to wash up."

They walked into the house arm in arm, as they'd done a thousand times before, and without speaking of it, both knew that this might never happen again in just the same way. Andrew Slade's death had changed everything. It remained to be seen how the future would unfold.

"Lord, something smells good," Bud said, as he eased his sore hand out of a glove, then shrugged out of his coat and hung it on a peg by the back door.

"Pot roast and vegetables," Holly said. "You wash up while I make the salad."

Bud paused. "That's my favorite meal."

"I know. It's why I made it," Holly said. "No telling what you're going to eat until I get back."

"I can cook, but nothing like you do," he said.

Holly smiled. She wouldn't turn down a little praise for a job well done.

Then Bud saw the dessert.

"Oh, Lord. Is that a chocolate pie?"

Holly's smile widened. "Yes."

He gave her a quick hug.

"Thank you, sugar. I'm already spoiled, but I do appreciate it."

Holly didn't give herself time to think about how it felt to be standing in Robert Tate's arms. The emotions it conjured were too scary to consider.

When he left, she busied herself with slicing the roast and putting the food on their plates. By the time he came back, she had their plates on the table and coffee in their cups.

Bud waited until she'd taken a seat and then chose the chair directly across the table. Surely to God they could get through one meal without coming undone.

Two

Bud scraped the last bit of chocolate and meringue from his plate, and popped it in his mouth.

"Holly, that meal was amazing."

Holly beamed. Being successful at something was satisfying. She'd planned to have a catering business one day, which had led her to pursue her business degree. She had the degree, but had left the dream on the back burner.

"Thank you. I have Mom to thank for that, you know."

Bud laid down his fork and leaned back in the chair, watching the smile on her face spread to her eyes. It was good to see her smile, even if it was just for a few moments.

"What were you . . . about twelve or thirteen when Hannah died?" he asked.

"Thirteen, almost fourteen, but I had seven precious years under her tutelage. Everything I learned about being a woman

I learned from watching her with Dad. She adored him and us so much. I thought we were the luckiest family in the world to have her for a mom."

Her voice trailed off as memories overwhelmed her. Before she knew it, her eyes were full of tears. Unwilling to break down in front of Bud again, she jumped up and began clearing the table. When he stood up to help, she quickly waved him away.

"No, no, for once you're definitely excused. You don't need to get your bandage or your stitches wet."

He'd had a glove on it all day, but reality about what came next was beginning to set in.

"Shoot. How am I supposed to shower?"

As the problem solver in the house, Holly had a solution. "No big deal. I'll put a plastic bag over your hand and tape it down with duct tape. It will keep the water off your hand at least long enough for you to shower, okay?"

Bud grinned. "You are definitely Andrew's daughter. Every vehicle on the property carries duct tape, WD-40 and baling wire."

Holly grinned as she pointed at a chair. "Sit. I'll help you get your boots off."

"I've got a bootjack in my room."

But she wasn't having it. She stood with

her hands on her hips, waiting for him to acquiesce.

Bud had seen that look of determination on her face too many times to think there was any point in arguing. He sat down and lifted a foot.

Holly grabbed the boot, deftly pulling it off and then set it aside. "Next," she said, and snorted softly when he rolled his eyes. "You're such a fake. You like this, and you know it."

When she bent back over to pull off his other boot, his gaze slid to her curvy body. "Yeah, I like it," he said, then reluctantly looked away.

"There you go," Holly said. "Get your shirt off, and then I'll tape the plastic bag over your hand."

Bud sighed. He'd spent years thinking about getting naked with Holly, but not like this. He unbuckled his belt, then unsnapped the first snap on his Levi's before pulling his shirt out of the waistband, while Holly dug through the cabinet for a plastic bag, then went into the utility room for the duct tape.

As she walked back into the kitchen she stopped short, as if she'd just been punched in the gut. Surely she'd seen Bud Tate without a shirt before, and it wasn't as if he was completely nude. But her knees went weak at the thought of that much man without a stitch of clothes.

Afraid that he might suddenly read her mind, she lifted her chin and strode toward him with purpose.

"I'm just sick that you've done this right when I'm going to be gone," she said, and slipped the bag over his bandaged hand, then tore off a strip of duct tape and fastened it around his wrist.

Bud caught her hand before she could move it. "As long as you promise to come back, it doesn't matter."

Holly looked up. The expression on his face made her heart skip a beat.

"Of course I'll be back," she said, and laughed to hide her discomfort. "So if you need any more help, just let me know." She went back to clearing the table to keep from jumping his bones.

Holly was ready for bed but still couldn't settle. The suitcase by the door might as well have had a flashing red light on it. It was a silent reminder that she was about to leave the safety and comfort of the Triple S for an uncertain future. She slipped her feet into her house shoes, grabbed her robe and left her bedroom.

The house was dark. She glanced down the hall toward Bud's bedroom. The light was finally out, but she didn't need lights to make her way through this place. Little had changed in the past twenty years except Holly herself. She walked the long paneled hallway that led into the great room countless times, but the journey never ceased to move her. There was something very stately yet comforting about the open timber beams and the massive rock fireplace at the far end of the room. The deep colors of oxblood and chocolate-brown in the leather upholstery were accented with Native American rugs and pottery. Family photos, as well as work by some of Andrew's favorite Native American artists, were hanging on the walls. It was a familiar, well-lived in house, but with Andrew's death, it felt as if the heart of it was gone.

Holly could hear the tick of the old grandfather clock, as well as the occasional pop of a dying ember in the fireplace from the fire that had been burning hours earlier. She could almost imagine Andrew sitting in the easy chair there, with his feet toward the fire, dozing, with the unread newspaper still in his lap.

The knowledge that she would never see him again was heartbreaking. He'd been the anchor in their world for all their lives and then gone so quickly it didn't seem real. And yet it was a painful reality they all had to face.

She moved to the windows and looked out into the night. The sky was cloudless, the stars countless. A half-moon cast a blue-white glow onto the dark vista before her. She shivered, and in that moment realized she was no longer alone.

"Are you okay?"

She turned. Bud was walking toward her.

"Yes. I just couldn't sleep."

He slid an arm across her shoulder and gave her a quick hug, something he'd done a thousand times, and yet for some reason tonight it felt different.

"Change is hard, and everything is changing, isn't it?"

She nodded.

"It won't be forever. You'll see. It's just that Andrew's death revealed a lot of secrets. As soon as you and your sisters get answers, you'll all be back."

Holly sighed. "It's just me. You know how I hate change."

Bud laughed softly and gave her another quick squeeze. "Yes, I do. I remember you wearing a pair of boots a size too small for almost three months because you liked them so much and didn't want to tell Andrew you'd outgrown them."

Holly chuckled. "Oh, my gosh! I'd forgotten that. How old was I? About twelve?"

"Thirteen. You were thirteen. I remember because Andrew bought you another pair just like them for your thirteenth birthday."

"I can't believe you remembered something so silly."

"I remember lots of stuff about you."

Holly started to smile, but Bud wasn't smiling. He just kept looking at her, as if he were waiting for something. Suddenly she shivered, then looked away, unwilling to acknowledge that there might be anything beyond the obvious in his statement.

Bud knew she was uneasy, and the last thing he wanted was to scare her. It was time to change the mood.

"I think here's where we decide to raid the refrigerator," he said.

Grateful for the change of subject, Holly laughed. "You just want more chocolate pie."

"Damn, woman. You know me too well."

They walked into the kitchen, laughing and talking, turning on lights as they went. Pie was eaten. Dishes went into the sink. And the emptiness in Holly's heart was momentarily filled. They parted company in the hallway, with Bud giving her a quick kiss on the cheek.

" 'Night, sugar. Sleep well. You've got a long day ahead of you tomorrow." And then he went into his room.

Holly sighed as the door closed behind him. She could still feel the imprint of his lips on her face as she crawled in bed and closed her eyes.

The single lightbulb dangling from the ceiling cast a yellow-orange glow in the basement, but she was headed straight toward a brighter line of light beneath the door to Daddy's workroom. The room they weren't allowed to go in. She could smell the scent of fresh-cut wood mingling with another, less appealing, scent. Something was dead. Maybe a mouse caught in one of the traps. She could hear her daddy working methodically, sanding the wood to a smooth, satin finish, then hammering, hammering. She opened the door.

"Daddy?"

He spun, a look of shock, then rage, spreading across his face as he realized he was no longer alone.

"Get out, Goddammit!"

Holly gasped, then sat straight up in bed. Her heart was pounding so hard that at first she didn't realize her alarm was going off.

Her stomach lurched, and for a second she thought she was going to be sick, but as the crazy dream passed, so did the feeling.

"Lord. That's what I get for eating pie right before I go to bed," she muttered, as she shut off the alarm and began scrambling out of bed.

This was a momentous morning, and she had a plane to catch.

After that, time flew.

A quick shower and choosing clothes for the road. A hasty breakfast, and a last-minute checklist to make sure she had everything she needed. All too soon, they were on their way to the airport. It only added to Holly's panic. Her gut instinct was still telling her not to go. She didn't want to leave the ranch — *or* Bud.

Despite Holly's insistence on driving, Bud had ignored her and gotten behind the wheel. The bandage was still on his hand, but the pain wasn't too bad if he didn't put pressure on it. He couldn't put into words what he was feeling, but fear topped the list.

He'd read everything he could find online about the murders linked to the man the media had dubbed the Hunter. He tried not to think about that man also being Holly's birth father. After what he'd learned, the only reason he hadn't ignored her demand to go alone was because so many years had passed and no new murders had been linked to the Hunter. Knowing that, he couldn't help but believe the man was either dead or had long since moved on.

The fact that the woman he loved still didn't know how he felt — might never know — left him with a sick, empty feeling, as if his life were on hold. The only thing he did know was that he wasn't going to be the one to mess up their relationship. If all she ever wanted from him was the brotherly, family-friend relationship they had now, then so be it.

He glanced at the clock on the dashboard, then increased speed. Check-in at Missoula International Airport wasn't usually an issue, but he didn't want to add to her nervousness by making her have to run for her gate. Then he noticed her digging through her purse and wondered if she'd forgotten something.

"You doing okay?" he asked.

"Yes, just double-checking," Holly said. "Remember, I left my hotel information on the notepad in the kitchen. Don't forget to take extra food to the barn to feed that old mama cat, since she's due to have babies soon. And have the hands do the heavy work until your hand has healed. If —"

Bud interrupted her. "Dang it, Holly, I am a fully grown man. I can figure this out by myself. Just do what you have to do and quit worrying about everything else, okay?"

Holly tried a smile, but the anger in his voice was unsettling. She couldn't bear to leave him on a sour note.

"Are you mad at me about something?"

He sighed. "Lord no. I'm just feeling sorry for myself and worried about you, okay?"

"Okay," Holly said, and settled back.

When they finally reached the airport, Bud drove up to the departure area, popped the trunk and got out to help.

The chill of the early-morning air was sharp. Holly shuddered as she stepped out of the car and shouldered her purse, but she wasn't fast enough to beat Bud to the trunk.

"I can do it," she said when he started to lift her suitcase out of the trunk. But he ignored her and hefted it out with one hand. "Okay, I'm duly impressed at how strong you are."

Bud sat the suitcase on the curb and then turned around to face her.

Holly started to tease him but was suddenly silenced by the look on his face. Then she saw him take a deep breath, and within seconds the expression was gone and his familiar smile was back in place.

"Don't come inside with me," Holly said. "I'm afraid I'll cry in front of everyone when it's time to go."

Bud's heart dropped, but he made himself smile. "So, am I going to get my goodbye hug?" He opened his arms.

Holly walked into his embrace and laid her cheek against his chest, struggling against the urge to cry as he wrapped his arms around her and hugged her close. For a second she thought about throwing herself on his mercy and begging him to love her.

"I'm going to miss you," Holly said, as she leaned back to meet his gaze.

Bud saw her lips part, and the urge to kiss them nearly felled him. Instead, he made himself smile again.

"I'm going to miss you, too, sugar. Promise me you'll be careful, that you won't take crazy chances . . . and that you'll call me. With all three of you gone, I swear to God I'm going to get ulcers."

Holly grinned. "I will. I promise." She stood on her tiptoes and kissed his cheek. " 'Bye, Bud." She pointed at his bandage. "And be careful."

"I will if you will," he said, then glanced

back at the traffic. "I'm going to have to move."

When he walked away, Holly began to panic, but she couldn't let it show. Instead of throwing herself into his arms and begging him to take her back home, she smiled.

"Drive safely," she called after him. "I'll call as soon as I get to the hotel."

"Call my cell in case I'm not in the house. I don't want to miss you."

"Will do," Holly said, and then rolled her suitcase to the curbside check-in as Bud got into the car.

She turned around and watched until he was out of sight, then took her place in line and told herself it was the chill of the wind making her eyes water, not a fresh set of tears.

Lambert — St. Louis International Airport
The flight across country had been mostly monotonous. She'd tried to sleep, but she'd never been able to sleep sitting up. She'd read a few chapters in the book she'd brought with her but had no idea of what she'd read. The journal was in her bag. She could have read it again, but for some reason she didn't want anyone watching her read it for fear she might cry. That was all she felt like doing. The closer she got to her

destination, the more uneasy she became. When they landed, she was on the verge of tears with no explanation, but she blinked them away as they began to disembark.

Out of nowhere, a shudder ran up Holly's back as she stepped off the plane. A little startled, she looked up the walkway toward the terminal, fearing something ominous awaited her just beyond the doorway. Then she chalked up the moment to exhaustion and stress, and moved forward.

But the feeling of uneasiness stayed with her all the way through the terminal, while she reclaimed her suitcase at baggage claim, even after she picked up her rental car. It felt as if every instinct she had was telling her to run, to go back where she'd come from, but Andrew hadn't raised his girls to be quitters.

Her budget rental car was minus GPS, so after a quick study of the city map provided by the rental company, it became apparent that the airport was farther outside the city than she'd expected. As she left the airport, she began watching for the access road that would take her onto Interstate 70, then got on it and headed southeast toward the city.

Her hotel reservation was at the Jameson-Regency near the Arch. According to her directions, the hotel was on Chestnut Street just off I-70 and across the highway from the banks of the Mississippi River, so she drove with a careful eye on the traffic, while still watching for landmarks and street signs. As she drove, she kept looking for something that felt familiar, but it didn't happen.

She had no trouble finding the hotel, but only because she knew where she was going from the map. She'd seen the Arch, St. Louis's most famous landmark, from miles away. It, of course, did look familiar, but only because she'd seen it countless times in photos, not because it was something she remembered from childhood.

When she reached the hotel she dropped her car off at valet parking, then let the bellman take her suitcase and followed him into the hotel. The vivid colors of the lobby furnishings and the white marble walkway leading up to the registration desk were a big change from the hardwood floors and wood paneling of the ranch house. She remembered reading about the hotel's recent renovations online when she'd made her reservations. The place was beautiful, even elegant, but if she'd had to choose, she would have picked the warm wood and Native American art back home.

Once she'd checked in, she followed another bellman to the bank of elevators, then up to the sixth floor.

"Room 663," he said, as he took her key card and ran it through the lock.

Holly tipped him as he left, then locked herself in and moved to the windows overlooking the Mississippi. The current was slow, the water dark. At that point, another shiver ran through her.

"What the hell is wrong with me?" she muttered. "Please, God, don't let me get sick. That's the last thing I need, okay?"

She turned her back on the view and began unpacking. It was a constructive task that needed to be done, and she needed to stay busy to keep from thinking about what lay ahead.

As soon as she finished, she grabbed her phone. She'd promised to call Bud as soon as she got to the hotel, and she needed to keep her promise or he would worry. Just as she began to punch in the numbers, she dropped the phone. It hit the carpet with a muffled thump. When Holly reached to pick it up, she noticed that her hands were shaking. She sat down on the bed and once again started to make the call, but the numbers suddenly blurred before her eyes. Angry that her emotions were so out of control, she swiped at the tears and retried the numbers. Halfway through, she hit a wrong digit.

"Dammit."

She tossed back her head and took a deep breath, but it turned into a sob. She shoved her hands through her hair in a short, angry motion, then swiped the tears from her face as she jumped to her feet and began to pace.

"What's wrong with me? Am I having a breakdown? Is there something in my subconscious warning me I made a mistake in coming back?"

There was a full-length mirror on the back of the bathroom door, and when she caught her own reflection she was shocked by what she saw. It was the same heart-shaped face she'd looked at all her life, the same thick auburn hair, the same green eyes.

But her skin was pale, her eyes wide, as if in shock. There was a muscle jerking at the corner of her mouth, and she felt like throwing up. She laid the flat of her hand against the mirror . . . hand-to-hand with a stranger, both of them mute.

Then, suddenly, Holly wasn't looking in a mirror, she was looking down into a darkened cellar. A man's face appeared abruptly at the bottom of the stairs, like a ghost that had failed to completely materialize.

"If you tell, I'll make you sorry."

Her cell phone rang, and the image disappeared. Holly shuddered. Had that been a memory, or something out of a waking nightmare born of stress and despair? She stumbled back toward the bed and grabbed it like a dying man reaching for Jesus.

"Hello?"

"Hey, sugar, you're there. I was beginning to worry."

Holly crawled up onto the bed, holding the phone close to her ear as she struggled to regain her composure.

"Hi, Bud. I was just about to call you. My flight was good. I've only been in the room a few minutes."

"Are you okay?"

She shoved a shaky hand through her hair. "Yes, yes, I'm fine, just tired. You know what traveling is like."

"So what time is it there?"

She glanced at her watch, which she'd turned ahead when they'd landed. "It's just after six."

"Okay, you're just an hour ahead there. You girls are giving me hell, trying to keep up with so many different time zones. You're going to make me gray before my time."

Holly ignored the fact that she was nauseous and made herself laugh.

"That's what Daddy always said."

There was a moment of silence, then Bud

answered, but in an odd tone of voice.

"Only I'm not your daddy."

Holly's stomach knotted. "No, of course you're not, but don't blame us if we compare you. You were my father's shadow. It stands to reason some of him would rub off onto you."

She heard what sounded like a sigh, then a chuckle.

"I can't deny that," Bud said. "So what are your plans?"

"Sleep. I think I need to sleep. Then I want to look around for a day or so. I keep thinking I should remember something, and I figure the more I can remember, the better I'll feel about going to the police."

"Don't forget to eat," Bud said. "And be careful. Most of all, be careful."

"I will. Love you," she said.

Another awkward pause, and then she heard, "I love you, too," before the line went dead.

Her unrequited feelings for Bud were old news. She didn't have time to feel sorry for herself with so much left to do. Even though her heart told her a different story, Bud was just Bud — an almost brother, the ranch foreman and now part owner of the Triple S, and she was on a quest for her truth.

She went down to dinner, choosing a

place in the restaurant called Annie's Kitchen. With her love of cooking and all things homey, it seemed the perfect choice. Maybe the crazy thoughts would disappear. Lord knows she needed to get on the path of rational thinking.

After she ordered her food, she took her journal out of her purse. Like her sisters, she'd read it from front to back a dozen times already, and the more she read, the more memories she resurrected. She flipped past the journal entries regarding her first years with Andrew to an entry regarding her first date.

The day you came in and told me Joe Don Rooney had asked you out was a real shock for me. I'd always thought of the three of you as my little girls. That really made me adjust my thinking. You were excited and, at the same time, oddly apprehensive. You kept asking me what you should do if something happened and you weren't comfortable with Joe Don. You said over and over that it wasn't ever safe for a girl to be alone on the street, that bad things — really bad things — could happen. It made me wonder if you'd known about your mother's suspicions regarding your father, or if it had to do with just know-ing about the murdered women who'd been the Hunter's victims. When I pressed you for a reason as to why you were so sure something bad would hap-pen, all you could say was that you "just knew."

Of course, the date with Joe Don turned out fine, and when I asked you later if you were nervous when you were with him, you rolled your eyes and gave me one of those looks for which women are famous. It made me laugh, but at the same time, it set a fear in my heart that you were suppressing memories far darker than I'd realized you might have. I don't know how to explain it, but, my darling Holly, I fear for you most of all. Be careful. Be aware. I fear you have seen terrible things — so terrible that it was worth forgetting the first five years of your life.

Holly shuddered as she leaned back and looked up. The dining area was buzzing with hungry customers. She wondered how many of them were living with secrets — secrets that could be as deadly as the most fatal of diseases.

THREE

When she got back to her room, the message light on her phone was blinking. It was from the front desk telling her she had a delivery. Surprised, she told them to bring it up, then spent the wait time wondering what it was and whom it was from.

Although she'd been listening for it, when the knock finally sounded at the door, Holly jumped. After a quick look through the security view, she opened the door to find a bellman with a vase of red roses.

"Oh, my!" she said, as the bellman set the flowers on the table. She handed him a tip, closed and locked the door behind him, then dashed back to see who the roses were from.

She pulled out the card, quickly scanning the few words of text.

Remember, you're not alone. I'm only a phone call away. Bud.

Bud — ever faithful Bud. She burst into tears.

She crawled onto the bed with the card still clutched in her hand and curled into the fetal position. Sobs bubbled up her throat as the past two weeks of shock and fear overwhelmed her. If Bud had been standing in the room beside her bed, she would have begged him to take her home and abandoned this search. Something bad had happened to her here. She couldn't remember what, but she could feel it. Bud was the one sure thing still left in her life, but he was halfway across the country, and she was here alone.

She cried herself to sleep.

Sunlight spilled through a pair of kitchen windows into the room. An half-eaten bowl of cereal was still on the table beside a box of Cheerios that had tipped over, spilling part of the contents. Water was running from the tap at the kitchen sink, only no one was there.

A shadow suddenly cut across the path of sun light. Something dripped onto the floor. The shadow moved, then disappeared, leaving behind a trail of bright red droplets.

"Clean it up!" he yelled. "And don't tell your mother or I'll make you sorry."

Holly woke abruptly, then sat up in bed,

her heart pounding wildly against her rib cage as she swept the room with a frantic gaze, making sure she was still alone. A glance at the clock told her it was still hours before dawn. Even worse, she'd fallen asleep in her traveling clothes. With a groan, she rolled out of bed, then headed for the bathroom. A few minutes later she came out, stripped off her clothes, then crawled between the sheets and once again closed her eyes.

"Please, God, take away all the bad thoughts and just let me rest."

It was a simple prayer. She wasn't asking too much and hoped it was heard. Within minutes she was asleep, and when she woke again, sunlight was coming through a gap in the curtains. She rolled over onto her back, saw the bouquet of red roses and smiled.

"Only a phone call away," she said, then threw back the covers and headed for the shower.

Within the hour she had dressed, gathered up her journal and maps, and headed for the elevator. As soon as she got herself some breakfast, she would be ready to face the day.

A return trip to Annie's Kitchen, and an order of coffee and waffles later, Holly read as she ate, scanning her journal for clues as to where to go first.

She had the old home address and phone number that her mother had given Andrew. Out of curiosity, she'd tried the phone number almost immediately from back at the ranch and gotten a "not in service" message, which hadn't been a surprise. She'd checked the St. Louis phone book for a listing for Harold Mackey and come up short. She'd also researched the city of St. Louis and learned that the address of her childhood home was in a part of St. Louis known as The Hill, mostly populated by a large contingent of people who were of Italian descent.

She couldn't help but wonder if that meant she was also of Italian descent, or if it were simply coincidence that they'd lived in the area. She was anxious to find the address, and even more anxious to know if she would recognize it. It was on her list as the first place to visit today.

After talking to the concierge, she had a general idea of how to get where she wanted to go. It wasn't until she went outside to retrieve her car that she realized it looked like it was going to rain. That wasn't good news, but it didn't deter her. She'd been wet before.

She retrieved her car, and then, armed

with her map, drove away from the hotel. She had a brief moment of panic as she pulled out into traffic, as if by leaving the hotel she had willingly crossed over into the danger zone, but the notion soon passed.

When the first drops of rain began to hit the windshield she turned on the wipers, then tapped the brakes, slowing down enough to compensate for slippery streets. She was headed for the high ground south of Forest Park. According to Wikipedia, the official boundaries of The Hill were Manchester Avenue on the north, Columbia and Southwest Avenues on the south, South Kingshighway Boulevard on the east, and Hampton Avenue on the west. It wasn't until she crossed the boulevard that she felt as if she were finally making progress. When she stopped for a red light, she checked her map again just to make sure she was going in the right direction.

A loud clap of thunder sounded just as the light turned green. Hoping it wasn't a portent of things to come, she took a deep breath and accelerated through the intersection. The car behind her wasn't as fortunate. Halfway through the light it was suddenly T-boned by a pickup truck. Even though she was out of danger, she screamed. The shock of seeing the car spinning out of control, then being hit again by a second car, sent her into a panic. She pulled into a parking lot and stopped. Shaking too hard to drive, she said a quick prayer of thanksgiving that she was still in one piece as the sirens of the approaching rescue vehicles grew louder.

She turned off the engine. The rain was loud inside the car as it peppered the roof. And since she wasn't moving until the downpour subsided, she dug the journal out of her bag and flipped through the pages, seeking solace in the sight of Andrew's handwriting. It was as close as she would ever get to talking to him again, and she desperately needed to get a grip on her emotions. She found a passage dated less than four years ago and marveled at the secrets Andrew Slade had been able to hide.

Your real mother, Twila, wasn't very tall. Not nearly as tall as you are, but you have the same color hair — that dark auburn — and the same green eyes. When you were younger, you insisted on sprinkling cinnamon in your hot chocolate. I always assumed it was the way your mother had served it to you, because it wasn't something we did. Of course, once Maria and Savannah saw you having cinnamon, they had to have it, too. After that, it became the norm. That was something you brought with you that you hadn't forgotten, which leads me to believe there's more — much more. I want you to know that I have faith in your ability to get through this. You were a quiet but strong-willed child. As you got older, you have become less strong-willed and more willing to abdicate leadership to others. Go back to your roots, my daughter. Resurrect that strong-willed child in you, because I fear you're going to need her.

The warning made Holly shudder. "Oh, Dad . . . what I need is you."

When a burst of police sirens sounded from the street behind her, she glanced up in her rearview mirror to see the arrival of an ambulance. Police cars had cordoned off the scene, while a policeman in regulation rain gear was directing traffic away from the area to a temporary detour. He stood firmly in the midst of the rainstorm as if it were of no consequence, waving cars right and left.

Holly reached for her phone. It was a little after ten in the morning here, but just after nine back home. Bud would have been up for at least an hour, maybe more.

■ ■ ■ ■

Bud was cursing his injured hand and his pickup in one steady breath while trying to drive out of a snowdrift. Montana's weather patterns were oblivious to the seasons, and the unexpected snowstorm that had blown in late last night was no exception.

He'd sent two separate crews in different directions to feed cattle that would be in dire need of food, while he took care of the animals penned up in the corrals at the ranch. He was almost finished before he realized Andrew's old gelding, Jim Beam, was missing. The horse hadn't been ridden since Andrew's death and wasn't accustomed to so much downtime. It didn't take long to see the unlatched gate and the tracks leading out through the snow to the back pasture, where the herd mares were kept. Andrew had been amused that the horse he'd named after his favorite brand of whiskey could undo pretty much any latch on the place, but right now Bud wasn't laughing.

He'd already called his crew and had no choice now but to sit and wait for them to get back. One man was bringing a tractor to pull him out while the others went after

Jim Beam. Those herd mares didn't take kindly to abrupt appearances of males in their midst, even if they were no longer stallions. The last thing he needed was for them to get in a fight and someone to get hurt. He'd just settled back in his seat when his cell phone began to ring. When he saw it was Holly, the bad day suddenly took a positive turn.

"Hey, sugar! How's it going?"

Holly shivered. Even the sound of his voice made her ache.

"Oh, pretty good . . . considering," she said. "It's pouring rain, and I just missed being in the middle of a bad wreck. I got through an intersection just fine, but the car behind me was T-boned by one car and rear-ended by another. I pulled over into a shopping area to wait for the rain to subside. What about you?"

Bud blinked. He was still trying to get past the "I just missed being in the middle of a bad wreck" comment.

"Oh . . . my morning's not a lot better than yours, I guess. We had a freak snowstorm blow in last night. Got about eighteen inches, with some pretty good drifts, one of which I happen to be stuck in right now."

"Oh, no! Poor Bud!" Immediately she thought of him trying to dig out. "How's your hand? You're not trying to dig out by yourself, are you?"

"Sore, but fine otherwise, and no, I'm not doing any digging. The crew is on the way with a tractor. Where were you headed when the wreck occurred?"

"I was on my way to the part of the city where I used to live. I'm curious to see if I recognize the house, or if it's even still there. Twenty years is a long time. Plenty of time for things to change."

"You're being careful, right?"

"Yes. That's why I'm parked instead of still driving in this mess."

"Well, I'm parked, too, although not by choice. It appears we're quite a pair."

"Looks like," Holly said, although she was slightly taken aback by where her mind went. There were all kinds of ways for a couple to pair.

"Oh, hey, the guys just drove up," Bud said. "Promise me you'll be careful. I don't want anything to happen to you."

"I promise," Holly said. "You be careful, too. When I come home, I expect you to be there waiting and still in one piece."

There was a long moment of silence before Bud answered. "I'll always be here for you, Holly. Love you, honey, and stay in touch."

"Love you, too," Holly said. The sound of the disconnect was too sudden for her peace of mind, but at least she wasn't cold and stuck in the snow.

She glanced up in the rearview mirror again. The ambulance was gone. Wreckers were in the act of towing away the damaged vehicles, and most of the police cars were gone. An accident had happened, and just like that, lives were forever changed. Hopefully they would live to see another day.

Happily, the rain was beginning to subside. Talking to Bud had been what she needed to regain her confidence. After a quick glance at the city map, she pulled back into traffic and continued to weave her way through the streets.

As she drove, an odd thing began to happen. Instead of constantly referring to the map, she realized she was making turns instinctively. And when she found herself on the same street where she used to live, she was stunned. She pulled to a stop at the curb only two houses down from the address she'd been looking for and then killed the engine. Her hands were shaking, and she wanted to throw up.

"God help me," she whispered, as she gazed through the windshield to the craftsman-style dwelling with a porch spanning the front of the house. The longer she sat staring at the house, the sicker she felt.

Disgusted with herself, she either had to get out or drive away, and she had not come all this way to quit. She opened the door to get out, but her legs were shaking too hard for her to stand up. Then she thought of the guts it had taken for her mother to do what she had done. One way or another, she had to do this, so she got out of the car and started walking.

The rain-washed air had a cool, clean scent, and her own footsteps sounded loud in the quiet neighborhood as she moved ever closer to her past. Just as she started up the walk toward the house, the front door suddenly opened. She stopped.

A woman came out and started down the steps toward her car when she saw Holly standing at the end of the walk.

Not wanting to appear threatening, Holly lifted her hand and smiled as the woman came nearer.

"I didn't mean to startle you. I was just revisiting my childhood. I used to live here when I was a little girl."

The woman's expression shifted from guarded to friendly.

"I'm Holly Slade," Holly added. "I live in Montana now, but I wanted to check out the place since I was passing through. I hope I didn't frighten you."

"I'm Loretta Fairfield."

Holly nodded, but her focus was on the house. "How long have you lived here?"

"We bought the house a little over eighteen years ago."

"Who did you buy it from?" Holly asked.

"I don't remember the name," Loretta said, then pointed across the street. "The lady who lives in that blue house has lived here for years. She might be able to help you."

Holly turned to look. "What's her name?"

"Mrs. Pacino. She's older . . . probably in her late sixties, maybe early seventies."

The name didn't ring a bell, but Holly was hoping she might recognize the woman when she saw her.

"Thanks again," Holly said.

"Sure," Loretta said, and got in her car and drove away.

Holly stood on the sidewalk, looking at the big blue house and trying to remember if she'd ever seen it before. Nothing about the property seemed familiar, but then again, twenty years was a long time, and she'd only been five. Not really old enough to retain a lot of memories.

It was time to see if Mrs. Pacino could

help her. She crossed the street and rang the doorbell without hesitation.

A moment later she heard a small dog begin to yap, then a woman's voice scolding. The dog quieted, and seconds later the front door opened.

"Yes? May I help you?"

Within seconds Holly had taken in the woman's diminutive size, her white curly hair and a face wrinkled with lines that only a lifetime of laughter could create.

"I'm sorry to bother you," Holly said. "But I lived in that house across the street about twenty years ago, and I was wondering if you could answer some —"

Mrs. Pacino gasped. "Oh, dear Lord! You're Twila's girl, aren't you?"

Holly tried to smile, but her face felt stiff. She managed a nod.

"I'm Ida Pacino. I used to babysit you years ago. Back then you called me Nonna. Come in! Come in!"

Holly felt weird that she had no memory of this woman. But Ida Pacino wasn't shy. The moment they were seated, she began to chatter.

"Oh, my goodness, honey, I can't tell you what a wonderful surprise this is for me. How's your mother? Where do you live now? Are you married?"

"Uh . . ."

Ida burst into laughter. "Isn't that just like me? I ask all these questions without waiting for an answer. So, Harriet my dear, what brings you back to the old neighborhood?"

Holly was going to have to guard her answers. There was no way she could announce the complete truth of what had happened to her when she had yet to go to the police.

"I go by Holly now, and I have to admit, I don't remember much about my life when I was here. Twenty years is a long time to be away. And that's part of the problem I brought with me. I have very little memory of my past. Twenty years ago my mother sent me away with some friends, with the promise that she would follow soon. Only she never came."

Within seconds, the expression on the old woman's face went from surprise to shock. "No! I can't believe that. This is awful . . . just awful. I always wondered what happened when you and she disappeared." She paused, then asked, "What about your father?"

"I don't really remember him . . . only bits and pieces of things that I think are about him."

"Why did you come back?"

68

"To get answers," Holly said.

Ida's eyes filled with tears. "What can I do? How can I help you?"

"I'm not sure," Holly said. "Can I ask you a few questions?"

"Of course."

"Do you remember anything about my father? When my mother and I suddenly disappeared, what kind of explanation did he give?"

"He filed a missing persons report on the both of you. Said he went to work one morning, and when he came back you were both gone. We all felt terrible for him. I suppose the police worked the case, but nothing ever came of it that I heard. After about a year, he moved away. I have no idea where he's at or if he's still alive."

Holly nodded, although she was surprised to learn about the missing persons reports. Harold Mackey was either an innocent man or the biggest faker of all time. She kept wondering what kind of guts it would take to be the serial killer an entire city was searching for and still go to the police to claim his family had gone missing. She wondered if he'd thought it was funny, almost a taunt. As if to say, *I'm right under your noses, and you still don't know a thing.*

"I don't suppose you remember the last

time you saw my mother?"

"No, not really," Ida said. "I'm sorry."

"It's okay," Holly said. "I appreciate you taking the time to talk to me."

"Of course," Ida said. Then she gasped and slapped her legs. "Oh, wait! My goodness. You said you don't remember much about your life here. My house used to be the place to come for Fourth of July cookouts and block parties and New Year's Eve celebrations. I have several pictures of you and your family taken here at different times. Just give me a minute to go get the albums."

Holly felt a little bit sick as Ida Pacino hurried out of the room. She was excited and at the same time afraid — afraid of her own reaction. Would she see something that triggered her memory? If she did, would it leave her afraid of what was to come?

Ida soon came back carrying a handful of albums, then sat down beside Holly.

"These are the ones from the years you lived here, but I'm afraid we're going to have to go through them all to find the photos I remember."

"That's okay," Holly said. "I'm not on a schedule, and I really appreciate your kindness."

Ida impulsively cupped Holly's chin.

"It's not kindness. Twila and I were more than friends. We were family. I'm just sorry you don't remember."

Touched by the gesture, Holly managed a smile as Ida opened the first book and began scanning the pages. It took a few moments, but she quickly found the first picture of what would become many.

"Here's one! That's you and one of my nieces eating watermelon at one of the picnic tables. It must have been a Fourth of July party, because there are flags on the tables."

Holly could only stare at the photo with a measure of disbelief. There was no denying it was her, but she had no memory of the occasion.

Ida pulled it out of the album and set it on the couch beside her as she turned the page. There were two more pictures, obviously taken at the same party. Ida pulled them, as well. About halfway through, she stopped again, but this time her expression saddened.

"This one is of you and Twila. Look how happy you two were. I just can't believe your mother disappeared without a word like that. It's not like her at all."

Holly knew the old woman was still talking, but the words were fading into the

71

background as she focused on the face of the woman in the picture. Her pulse quickened; her vision blurred. She could almost remember her mother's smiling face bending over her as she was being tucked into bed. How could she have forgotten someone as important as her own mother?

Ida pulled that photo and added it to the small pile, then leafed through the rest of that album without finding any more.

"Here's another album," Ida said. "Let's see what we can find in here, okay?"

Holly nodded.

Ida paused as she glanced up. "Are you all right, dear? I didn't think about how emotional this would be for you."

"I'm fine," Holly said. "Please, could we continue?"

"Absolutely."

Within thirty minutes Ida had pulled more than a dozen pictures. And then she opened the last album and began flipping through pages.

"Oh, good. Here's one of you and your daddy."

Holly didn't want to look, and yet she had to.

FOUR

The moment Holly's gaze locked onto that face, her mind went blank. The man in the photo was the same one she'd seen in her nightmares: the man at the foot of the stairs, the one who'd warned her not to tell. But tell what? What had she witnessed that had been so horrifying that it had made her forget the first five years of her life? Did it have something to do with the murders? She didn't know how much time had elapsed before she realized Ida was still talking.

"He was a real hardworking man, but a difficult man to live with, I suppose," Ida said. "Twila wasn't the kind of woman to quit when the going got tough, though. I can't say what kind of trouble lay between your mother and father, but I'm sorry for what happened to you. It makes me sad. What must you have thought, being abandoned like that?"

"I honestly can't say what I thought,

because until the death just a little while ago of the man who'd raised me, I didn't know I'd ever lived here. Once I got here, some things seemed familiar, but I can't say I actually remember anything."

Ida gave Holly a quick hug.

"Bless your heart, honey. Bless your heart." Then she gathered up the photos she'd taken out of the albums and laid them in Holly's lap. "I want you to have these. Maybe if you look at them some more it will help you to remember."

Holly couldn't imagine willingly looking at the photo of her father again, but the police might want it. She took the photos and put them into her shoulder bag.

"Thank you. You've been very helpful, and very kind."

"You're welcome," Ida said, as she walked Holly to the door. "I would love it if you stayed in touch. Just a card or letter now and then to let me know what's happening in your life would be wonderful."

"Sure," Holly said, as she stepped out onto the porch.

"So where do you go from here? Maybe your old school?" Ida asked.

The idea was intriguing. "Do you know where I went to school?"

"Of course! It was at St. Margaret of

Scotland. Catholic school, of course. I remember how excited you were to start kindergarten. I think Twila had enrolled you in their preschool at one time, but Harold made her take you out."

Holly frowned. "Really? Do you remember why?"

"I never knew, but I remember Twila was upset with him, and then, like everything else, as soon as he got his way he was fine. Anyway, everyone in this neighborhood goes to St. Margaret. It's in the old Shaw neighborhood."

Holly pulled the map from her purse. "Can you show me?"

Ida quickly scanned the map, circled the address with a pen Holly handed her, then gave it back.

"There you go, honey. Happy hunting."

Holly shuddered. "Yes, hunting for my past," she muttered, and suddenly looked over her shoulder, as if she expected her father to be standing in the yard.

As it turned out, St. Margaret of Scotland school was easy to find. Holly drove past it slowly, then circled the block and came back around again before pulling into the visitors' parking lot. She didn't know how much good this would be in helping her find the answers to her past, but she was willing to try anything.

The scent that greeted her as she entered the building was familiar, but not in a way that brought back memories, only in the fact that all school buildings smelled alike. It was a combination of books and chalkboards, plus the bodies of hundreds of children and whatever the cooks were making for lunch.

A middle-aged woman looked up as Holly entered the office. She smiled politely as she gave Holly a once-over.

"Good morning. How can I help you?"

Holly leaned across the counter. "I need some information. When I was five, I began kindergarten at this school. I think I was here for a year before I left. Would it be possible to get a copy of my records? I go by Holly Slade now, but I was enrolled here as Harriet Mackey, daughter of Harold and Twila Mackey. This is the address where I lived."

She slid a piece of paper toward the receptionist.

The receptionist frowned and looked back up at Holly. "You do know we can't give out school records to anyone who walks in without proof of ID?" She looked back at the piece of paper and asked, "How long

76

ago was this?"

"Twenty years."

"Oh, my, I'm not sure where those records would even be kept. Sorry."

Holly sighed. It had been worth a shot. "I understand. I don't suppose there's anyone still here who was teaching back then? Someone who might remember me?"

The receptionist frowned. "Actually, there is. Only she's no longer a teacher. She's the principal now. Her name is Mrs. Baronne."

"Do you think I might be able to speak with her?" Holly asked.

The receptionist picked up the phone. After a brief conversation, she nodded.

"Mrs. Baronne has a few minutes before she has to leave for a meeting. She said she'd be happy to speak with you. Her office is down that hallway, first door on your right."

"Thank you so much," Holly said, and hurried down the hall.

She knocked twice, and then the door opened abruptly. The woman standing in the doorway was tall and stately, with short gray hair and soft brown eyes.

"I'm Mrs. Baronne," she said, and shook Holly's hand. "Come in, please . . . have a seat."

"Thank you for taking the time to talk to

me," Holly said.

"Certainly," Mrs. Baronne said, as she resumed her seat at her desk. "Now, tell me a bit about this search you're on."

Holly told her story, leaving out all the ugly details and mentioning only that she was here for a short while and hoping to reconnect with her past. It wasn't until she mentioned the name Harriet Mackey that she saw the principal's expression change from polite attention to shock.

"You're Harriet Mackey?"

"Yes, ma'am, only I have no real memory of the first five years of my life. As I said, I've lived as Holly Slade for the past twenty years. Trust me, this has been quite a revelation for me to handle."

"I definitely remember the name. You were in Miss Peach's kindergarten class. It was only a few days before the end of the school year when you and your mother disappeared. The police questioned all the teachers and staff. We were shocked by the entire situation."

Holly's heart skipped a beat. "Really? Did you ever talk to my father?"

"Not personally, but I remember reading in the paper that he'd filed a missing persons report on the two of you. Oh, my, oh, my! This is such a shock! What happened?

Where did you two go?"

Again Holly had to be careful about what she said and how she said it.

"That's part of the mystery I'm trying to solve," Holly said. "My mother sent me away with her friends, and in a few days she was planning to come and get me, so we could start a new life somewhere else, only she never showed up. To this day, we don't what happened."

The principal gasped. "How awful for you!"

Holly shrugged. "I guess, but I don't remember the incident . . . or her."

"Not at all?"

"No, ma'am, not at all. By any chance would it be possible for me to get a copy of my school records? I realize I was only here for a year, but I thought there might be some information there that would help me figure out where to search next."

"Have you been to the police? Do they know that you're in town?"

"No, ma'am, but I plan to speak to them in the next day or so."

"You definitely should. They might even have some information about your mother, you know."

"Yes, ma'am, I know."

Convinced that she'd covered all her

bases, Mrs. Baronne turned to the task at hand. "Do you have some ID?"

Holly nodded, and fished out her driver's license.

"It's protocol when it comes to giving out records," the principal said, as she quickly made a copy and handed it back to Holly. "Where are you staying while you're in town?"

"At the Jameson, near the Arch."

The older woman made a note of the address. "I'll see what I can do," she said, and picked up the phone. After a brief conversation, she told Holly the older records were stored off-site.

"I've put in a request for a copy of your file to be couriered to you at the hotel. This is such a tragic story. I hope there's some information in it that helps."

"Thank you so much," Holly said.

"We also have group photos of our students that are taken every year. I'm not sure how far back they go, but there are a large number of them hanging in the lobby of the main hall. Let's go see if we can find your year."

"That would be great!"

Holly followed Mrs. Baronne back out to the lobby.

"They begin here," the principal said,

pointing to the far wall. She began scanning the pictures as they passed, counting back twenty years, and then stopped midway down the long hallway. "This would be the kindergarten class from twenty years ago."

Holly moved closer, scanning the tiny faces. Suddenly she gasped, then pointed. "That's me! I can't believe it! I have no memory of any of this, and yet there I am."

The principal eyed the photo, then Holly. "You're sure this is you?"

Holly nodded as she began digging through her purse. "A neighbor from back in the day just gave me some old photos of myself. I'll show you."

She pulled out a couple of the snapshots Ida Pacino had given her and handed them to the principal.

"That's certainly the same child," Mrs. Baronne said, and then handed them back to Holly. "Do you remember any of the other children?"

Holly hesitated briefly, then pointed to the little girl sitting to her left. "She looks familiar, but I can't remember her name."

Mrs. Baronne took down the picture, then popped the back off the frame and took out the photo. "We always write the names on the back. Let's see . . . Harriet Mackey, Harriet Mackey . . . ah! Here it is! You were right, that little girl is Harriet Mackey, and the girl next to her is Billie Jo Peoples."

"Billie Jo," Holly repeated, trying out the name on her tongue. She couldn't say she remembered, but it felt good to be putting some of the pieces of her past together.

Just as the principal was replacing the photo, her cell phone rang. She glanced at caller ID, then at Holly.

"I'm sorry. I'm going to have to take this call, then leave for my meeting. I hope I've been able to help you."

"You've been great," Holly said.

Holly shook the woman's hand, then left, buoyed up by the unexpected success.

Still reluctant to go to the police with nothing but her vague story, and without a specific place to go to next, she decided to go back to the hotel. At least there she could get warm, eat some lunch and wait for her school records to show up.

It was almost one o'clock and raining again by the time Holly got back to the hotel. Her stomach was growling, and her feet were wet and cold. Soup seemed like a good idea. She went back to the familiar hotel restaurant, and was thankful for the warmth and comfort as she was being seated.

After ordering, she tried to call Maria, but

it went to voice mail. Then she tried Savannah and got the same result. She felt the need to touch base with her sisters, to hear what was going on with them and find out if they were having difficulties, too, but it wasn't happening.

Disappointed, she dropped the phone back into her purse and picked at the bread the waiter left at her table. She thought about calling Bud. He would most certainly answer, but she hated to talk to him in this frame of mind. He would instantly know that she was feeling down, and she didn't want to have to explain herself. Not yet. Not until she had some answers.

It was late afternoon at the Triple S. The snow was beginning to melt, but not fast enough for Bud. He'd been counting cattle all afternoon, trying to ascertain if there were any more missing. They'd already lost two spring calves, along with a cow trying unsuccessfully to give birth, to the freezing temperatures since the snowfall. That was four head of Triple S cattle lost in less than two days. Damn weather. It had only added to his growing concerns. Earlier in the day he'd slipped on ice and caught himself with his bad hand. It was still throbbing inside his glove, but he'd refused to take the bandage off and check the damage. He didn't have time to baby himself. There were too many fires to put out at the Triple S.

Andrew's death had stirred up a mess from which the Slade family might never recover.

And then there was Holly . . . He'd always heard that absence made the heart grow fonder. He wondered if there was a saying for absence and unrequited love, because he ached for Holly like he never had before.

He glanced at his watch. It was nearly five. Sunset would be here before he was ready if he didn't get a move on. He still had to feed the livestock penned up in the corrals near the barn before he could call it a day. The thought of a roaring fire and a bowl of hot stew sounded good, so he put the truck in gear and headed for home.

It was nearing dinnertime, and still no papers had arrived from the school. Holly was just getting out of the bath when the hotel phone rang. She reached for a towel as she hurried to answer.

"Hello?"

"Miss Slade, this is the front desk. A courier just dropped off an envelope for you. May we send it up?"

"Yes, please!" Holly said. She hung up the receiver and quickly dried herself off, then grabbed some sweats.

The knock at the door sounded just as she was getting money out of her purse. She traded the bellman a tip for the envelope, then shut and locked the door. Her pulse was racing double-time as she carried the envelope to the bed and settled comfortably against the headboard before pulling out the contents.

The pages were few and the information sparse, which was not a surprise. There wasn't all that much information a five-year-old could accumulate in her first year of school. Still, it was more than a little shocking to see the photocopy of a school photo of the face she'd come to accept as hers beside the name Harriet Mackey. The address and home phone numbers listed were the same ones she had, but there was another name on the form she didn't recognize. It was the name and number of a person to contact in case of emergency if her parents couldn't be reached. Someone named Cynthia Peters.

She reached for the house phone and dialed the number on the form. After twenty years and numerous prefix changes, getting a not-in-service message didn't surprise her so she searched through the phone book. There were quite a few people with the last name Peters, but no Cynthia or C. Peters listed. Well aware that the woman could be long gone, or married or remarried, with another name entirely, she laid the phone book aside and went back to her school records.

What surprised her was learning where her parents had worked. Her mother had worked in a dry cleaners and her father for a company called Parks Wholesale. There was a copy of her immunization records, a mention that she'd won a coloring contest at Christmas and a notation of a trip to the emergency room after falling off a slide and injuring her leg. She pulled up the leg of her sweatpants and fingered the small white scar just below her knee. So that was where it had come from. It was beyond strange to put together her past this way.

She wasn't surprised there wasn't anything else useful in the file, but even so, it was something of a letdown. Out of curiosity she searched the yellow pages for dry cleaners, just to see if the place where her mother had worked was still there, and to her surprise, it was, complete with the same phone number. It was, however, past closing time, so calling the number now would be useless.

After making a quick note of the address and phone number for another day, she looked for a listing for Parks Wholesale, but found nothing. Satisfied that she'd checked all she could for now, she tossed the phone book aside and slipped the pages from her school file into the back of her journal for safekeeping.

The silence in the room was mocking — as empty as her knowledge of her past. Determined not to get maudlin, she slid down onto the bed with a dejected sigh and closed her eyes.

The rain was still hitting the windows. She wondered what Bud was doing. Had the snow melted? Was his hand healing? Did he miss her as much as she missed him?

She kept remembering her last day at the ranch, seeing the blood-soaked towel wrapped around his hand and the pain on his face. She couldn't get past the memory of his hard, flat belly when he'd stripped off his shirt, or the warm, musky scent of his body as she'd covered his bandaged hand with a plastic bag to keep it from getting wet. Startled by how it made her feel, she rolled over onto her belly in an attempt to stall the growing ache between her legs, and willed herself to cease and desist.

Just as she was about to conquer the longing, her cell phone rang. She rolled over to grab it from the bedside table, saw the caller ID and tried to ignore the fact that her heart was suddenly in her throat.

"Hey, I was just thinking about you."

Bud exhaled softly as he cradled an ice pack against his throbbing hand.

"That's the best news I've had all day," he said lightly, as he kicked back in the recliner and turned his boots toward the fire.

"Are you okay? How's your hand?" Holly asked.

Bud ignored the fact that the fall had popped a stitch, causing it to bleed.

"It's fine." It wasn't really a lie. It wasn't messed up enough to go back to the doctor. He'd had worse injuries and treated them with less care, and recovered just fine. It would happen again. Besides, the sound of her voice had put his world back on an even keel.

"So you were thinking about me and I was thinking about you. How's that for timing?"

Holly shifted nervously, thankful he couldn't see her face.

"Yes, quite a coincidence."

Bud smiled. "So tell me what you did today."

Holly began to relate the day's events,

while Bud listened to the rise and fall of her voice, and the intermittent sound of her breathing. It was the transfusion he needed to get through the coming night.

The storm front that had been hanging over St. Louis finally moved out of the area around 3:00 a.m., leaving the city streets a rain-washed clean.

Holly's restless sleep was evident in the tangle of bedclothes wrapped around her legs and the sweat-dampened curls at the back of her neck. She lay on her stomach, one arm hanging off the side of the bed, and both pillows on the floor. The only evidence of the nightmare holding her hostage was the twitching of her feet.

"You snooped. You knew better than to come down here, but you did it anyway, and now you'll pay."

"No, Daddy, no. I'm sorry. I won't tell. I swear I won't tell. Don't hurt me. Please don't hurt me."

"It's not you I'll hurt. You open your mouth and tell what you saw, and you'll never see your mama again."

Holly woke up with a gasp to discover that the sheet beneath her face was wet with tears. Desperate to get out of bed and away from the dream, she didn't realize her feet were tangled in the bedclothes until she fell trying to stand. By the time she stood up, she was sobbing.

"God, please help me get through this."

She stumbled to the bathroom and began sluicing her face with cold water. By the time she had her emotions under control, she was shivering. She dried quickly, then hurried back into the room, turned on the lamp and straightened the covers before getting back in bed.

The lamp cast a circle of light into the darkness and right into her eyes, but that was okay with her. She didn't want back in that dream. As her feet slowly warmed, her body began to relax, but her thoughts were still in turmoil. She feared these nightmares she'd been having were true memories of a resurrecting past.

She needed to go to the police, and soon. There were a couple more things she wanted to check out first: the cleaners where her mother had worked, and going through the many Peterses in the phone book to see if she could find Cynthia Peters or someone who knew her. Cynthia must have been a close friend, maybe even a relative, to have been named as an emergency number.

Finally she drifted back to sleep, comforted by the light beside her bed. When she woke again, it was morning.

FIVE

Holly had gone through all the Peterses listed in the St. Louis phone book by 10:00 a.m., but to no avail. No one knew the Cynthia Peters she was seeking, and she doubted the messages she'd left where no one was home would yield anything, either. There was nothing left to do but accept the fact that the woman was either dead or no longer in St. Louis, or had a different last name that made her impossible for Holly to find on her own.

Frustrated, she tossed the phone book aside and reached for her journal. The road to her truth was in there. All she had to do was decipher it. Now that she was having flashes of memory, there was a section she remembered reading that might finally make sense. She flipped through the pages until she found it, then leaned back against the pillows propped behind her head and began to read.

About six months after you came to live with me, an old trapper named Thorny Paulson came by the house just after daybreak. He'd had a flat and was looking for a better spare than the one he had to get him into Missoula. A couple of the ranch hands switched out the bald rubber he'd been running on and tossed an extra spare into the back, just in case the first one gave out on him, too.

It was obvious he'd been in the mountains for a good while. Sorely in need of a bath and a haircut, he looked every bit the wooly trapper that he was. You were leery of him from the beginning and stayed close by my side. No matter how much he tried to charm you into a smile, you weren't having it.

Finally it came time for him to leave, and we walked him out to say goodbye. Maria saw the stack of pelts he had in the back of his truck. Nothing would do but that she had to have a closer look. Happy that someone was interested, Thorny opened up the back and sat Maria up on the tailgate. She sat down on the stack and dug her little hands into the pelts, laughing and jabbering about how soft they were. Savannah was in the house asleep, and last time I'd looked, you'd stayed behind on the porch.

Then all of a sudden I felt you sidle up beside me. I laid my hand on your head and was shocked to feel your entire body trembling. When I looked down, you were staring blindly at the furs. I started to ask you if you wanted up in the vehicle with Maria when your eyes rolled back in your head. You fainted flat out in the dirt.

Maria scrambled out as Thorny took his leave. She followed me as I carried you into the house. I have to admit, I was scared. You were such a little thing, and so limp. Maria thought you'd fallen down. She kept talking to you, trying to get you to answer. I carried you into the bedroom you girls shared and laid you on the bed. Maria crawled up beside you and curled herself around you, then began patting your tummy, telling you it was okay to wake up now. I wondered if she was remembering her own mother lying on the floor, and if she was afraid you wouldn't wake up, either.

I can tell you for sure we were both relieved when you began to regain consciousness. You opened your eyes and muttered something about not telling Daddy's secret. I asked you what you meant. You looked horrified, as if you'd said something you shouldn't have, and then your expression went blank. Afterward you claimed not to know what I was talking about. To this day, I believe you knew something about what he'd done. It may have been why your mother wanted you gone. Yes, she intended to tell the police. I fully believe that. But I don't think she was as concerned about what the media might do to you if your father was arrested as she was about making sure you were out of his reach.

"Lord, Lord," Holly whispered. As awful as it was to consider, it actually backed up some of the things she was beginning to remember.

She closed the journal and then dropped it into her purse. Today she was going to find the cleaners where her mother used to work, and if she was lucky, she would also find someone who remembered her, but first, she needed to find her shoes.

It didn't appear to Holly as if Dalton's Quality Cleaners, In Business Since 1978, had updated their storefront since the day the place opened. It wasn't exactly seedy, but one could definitely say it lacked curb

95

appeal. She got out of her car and walked inside, curious to see the place where her mother had spent so much time.

The interior was about the same as the exterior, but the place was busy. Mechanical racks of bagged clothing filled a good two-thirds of the place. She stepped into line behind two other customers — one who was picking up, the other dropping off. The twentysomething woman at the register would certainly have been too young to have known her mother, but Holly was optimistic. Finally the other customers were gone and Holly stepped up to the counter.

"Name, please," the woman said.

"I'm not here to pick up," Holly said. "I have a question. Is there anyone who would have been working here twenty years ago?"

The young woman looked up. "I don't know. Why?"

"My mother worked here back then. I'm trying to find someone who would have known her."

"The owner is here. Give me a minute, and I'll go back and ask."

Holly's tension grew as she waited. Finally the clerk came back with a fiftysomething woman at her side. The older woman stopped at the counter, eyeing Holly curiously.

"I'm Lynn Gravitt. Bonnie said you wanted to talk to me."

Holly nodded. "Yes, ma'am. Is there someplace where we could talk for a few minutes?"

"What about?" Lynn asked. "You're not some process server, are you?"

"No, no! Nothing like that," Holly said. "My name is Holly Slade, and my mother used to work here twenty years ago. I was hoping to talk to someone who might have known her."

Lynn's demeanor shifted noticeably as she smiled. "Oh . . . well, Lord knows I've been here that long and then some. What was her name?"

"Twila Mackey. She —"

Lynn gasped. "Sweet Lord! Are you Twila's girl? No, wait . . . her name wasn't Holly, it was —"

"Harriet, but I go by Holly now."

Lynn's eyes widened. "Harriet! That's right." She waved at the clerk behind the counter. "I'm taking my break now," she said. "Back in a few." She took Holly by the arm and led her outside, and then around the side of the building to an old iron bench sitting up against the outer wall. "We can sit here."

Holly scooted onto the bench. There was

so much she wanted to ask, but Lynn spoke first.

"What happened to you two? One day you were here, and the next you were both gone. Your father filed a missing persons report. I heard he hired a private detective, too, but it came to nothing. Where is Twila these days?"

"That's part of why I'm here," Holly said. "I haven't seen my mother or father in twenty years. In fact, I don't remember much of anything about them or the first five years of my life."

Holly watched the color visibly fading from Lynn's face.

"You're not serious?"

"Yes, ma'am, I'm afraid I am. How well did you know my mother? Were you close friends? Did you know anything about my parents' relationship?"

Lynn swept a shaky hand across her forehead. "I knew plenty. I knew your father was an asshole. He was abusive and controlling, and Twila was afraid of him."

"Why did she stay with him?" Holly asked.

"I used to ask her the same thing. She would always shrug and say that she couldn't make enough money to take care of you by herself, so I'm guessing she stayed with him to make sure you had a roof over your head and food in your belly."

Holly felt sick. If she wanted to play with what-ifs, then the mere fact of that she'd been born could have gotten her mother killed — if, in fact, she was really dead. However, she wasn't ready to take herself down that road.

Lynn eyed Holly closer. "You say you haven't seen your mother? So what happened to you?"

"I was sent to live in Montana with a friend of hers, but it was only supposed to be for a little while. She was going to come get me so we could start over somewhere new as soon as she settled some stuff with my dad."

Lynn slapped a hand over her mouth. "Oh, my God! Are you saying she stayed behind to tell him she wanted a divorce?"

Holly wasn't going to get into the serial-killer aspect of the story, since it was obvious her mother hadn't mentioned any of that to Lynn.

"I'm not sure what she was planning to do. All I know is she never made it to Montana."

Lynn grabbed Holly by the wrist. "That means Harold lied about everything — about the both of you disappearing at the same time, I mean."

"Yes, I realize that," Holly said. "Unfortunately, I have no idea where he is, so —"

Lynn jumped up from the bench, her face flushed, her expression animated.

"I do! I know right where that lying bastard is at!"

Holly felt the ground shift beneath her feet. It took every ounce of courage she had to ask, "You do?"

"Hell yes! He still works for the same wholesale warehouse he used to, driving the same delivery truck he's driven for nearly thirty years. I see him now and then, but we don't speak. He doesn't like me any better than I ever liked him."

Holly's hands were shaking, but she had to keep pushing. All of this would matter when she went to the police.

"I thought they weren't in business anymore. I looked in a phone book, but —"

"Oh. Right. You wouldn't know. The old owner sold out to another company ten, maybe fifteen, years ago. It's Riverfront Wholesale now, which is stupid, because they're not on the riverfront, but whatever. They moved to a larger warehouse here in St. Louis but kept most of the employees who weren't ready to retire."

Holly felt sick. She had to leave — now. The skin was crawling on the back of her neck as she began digging in her purse for her car keys.

"I really appreciate you taking the time to talk to me, but I wonder if you'd do me a favor?"

"Sure, honey. What do you need?"

"Don't tell anyone I'm in town, especially my — Especially Harold, if you should happen to see him."

"Trust me. My lips are sealed," Lynn said.

"I'd better let you get back to work," Holly said, and stood. "Thank you again."

Lynn shrugged. "You're welcome. Really sorry about your mama."

Holly had no words for the fact that Lynn had immediately assumed that if Twila had gone missing, Harold was responsible.

She got in her car but was too stunned to trust herself to drive. She kept thinking about a mother she couldn't remember, sacrificing herself to make sure Holly stayed safe. The longer she sat, the more determined she became to see justice served.

She finally drove away, giving herself a stern reminder that she needed to think instead of react every time she got another piece of news she didn't like. She wasn't a crybaby, and she was disgusted that she'd been letting her emotions get the best of her.

Now she really needed to go to the police, but finding out that Harold Mackey was still alive and well and living in St. Louis had shocked her. The longer she drove, the angrier she became. How dare he go on with his life without a care in the world, presenting himself as the wronged and abandoned husband? Only a cold and calculating man could pull that off.

He hadn't eluded police for all these years by making mistakes, but she had one thing on her side. He had no idea who she was or that she was back in the city. It would give her the edge she needed. Before she went to the police, she was going to see him. Not to talk. Not so that he would know she was watching. But she wanted to see his face. All she had to do was be careful.

She drove into the parking lot at a strip mall and pulled up the phone-book app on her cell phone, got the number of Riverfront Wholesale and punched it in before she could change her mind.

The phone rang once, twice and then three times, while her nerves faltered and her good sense was telling her to hang the hell up and go straight to the police.

"Riverfront Wholesale. This is Sonya."

And then it was too late.

"Hi. I have a delivery that needs to be

signed for by one of your employees. What time do you close?"

"The drivers clock out once they've completed their routes, and the routes are all different. Who's the delivery for?"

Holly frowned. She hadn't intended to mention the name, but now she was caught between a rock and a hard place.

"Uh . . . Harold Mackey," she muttered.

"Okay, let me check the roster," Sonya said. There was a pause before she answered. "He should be back in around 6:00 p.m., or you could drop it off here. I'll sign and see that he gets it."

"Sorry, but it's something he needs to sign for himself," Holly said. "I'll make other arrangements. Thank you for your help." She hung up, aware that she'd already made her first mistake. She didn't know what might happen if the woman mentioned the phone call to Harold, but whatever it was, it wouldn't be good.

She glanced at her watch. It was nearly 3:00 p.m. Three more hours before Harold Mackey's quitting time. Andrew Slade had raised his girls to face their fears and enemies head-on. Turning her back on this one could be fatal.

Harold Mackey pulled up to the back door

of the Green Lantern Café and killed the engine. This was his last stop of the day, and none too soon. Thirty-plus years of getting in and out of this damn delivery truck had been hard on his joints. His left hip was killing him.

He grunted from the pain as his feet hit the ground, then paused a moment to give his body time to catch up with the job at hand. When he was sure he could walk without limping, he headed toward the back of the truck, lowered the lift, then hopped on and rode it back up.

The order was the last invoice on the clipboard, and he been doing this job for so long that he filled it without thinking. His life was simple these days, which was exactly the way he liked it. His mind was already on his easy chair, some take-out food and a couple of cold beers.

As soon as he had filled the cart with the restaurant's order, he rolled it onto the lift and rode down with it. When he got to the back door, he rang the bell and waited for the back door to open.

Harold eyed the thirtysomething redhead he knew as Lola. She was a first-degree bitch who got on his last nerve. She played on it just to piss him off. What she didn't know was that when she messed with him, she was playing with fire.

"Oh. It's you," she drawled, and ran her gaze up and down Harold Mackey's body as if big heavyset men with long gray ponytails and bushy brows got her hot. Mackey was one of the few men she knew who had never made a pass at her. It ate at her ego just enough that she felt obligated to bug him whenever she could. She stepped aside just enough for him to get by, but stayed close enough to be able to blow in his ear as he passed.

The hair crawled on the back of his neck as he moved into the kitchen. The urge to purge her from the face of the earth was so strong he could taste it, but he wasn't playing her games. If the time came that he wanted in on the action she was offering, he would be the one calling the shots. He would wipe that smirk off her face so fast she wouldn't know what hit her.

"Where's Danny?" Harold asked.

She pointed, then shouted, "Hey, Danny!"

The chef stuck his head out from behind the stove and started complaining.

"I needed some of this stuff at noon. Why are we always the last delivery on your route?"

"I don't make the rules. I just drive the truck," Harold said quietly, and handed

Danny the clipboard. "I unload. You check it off."

The chef muttered beneath his breath as he eyed the boxes being unloaded, then signed off on the invoice and handed the clipboard back to Harold.

Lola blew Harold a kiss as he pocketed his pen, but he ignored her.

"Have a nice day," he said, and walked out of the kitchen, pushing his empty cart.

Within minutes he was on the way back to the warehouse. He thought of the sleazy redhead he'd just left and smiled, which changed the dour expression on his face to a maniacal grimace. He liked knowing he held the power of life and death in his hands. It was like hunting. Harold believed in culling out the weak and useless, leaving only the strong to survive. It was a simple thing, really — just all in the way you looked at it.

It was ten minutes after six when he got back to the warehouse. He grabbed his clipboard, and headed into the office to turn it in and clock out.

Sonya, the dispatcher, was the boss's niece — a nice enough young woman, which meant she was off his radar. He nodded at her as he dropped off the invoices, then went to clock out.

"Oh. Hey, Harold, I almost forgot. You had a phone call today," she said.

He ran his card through the time clock, then put it back in the slot and turned around.

"Oh, yeah, who was it?" he asked.

"Some woman from a courier service had something for you. I guess you needed to sign for it personally, because she wouldn't leave it here." Then she grinned. "Sounded like one of those people who serve summonses and stuff. Are you in trouble?"

For a fraction of a second the blood roared so loud in his ears that he couldn't hear, and then the moment passed.

"No, I'm not in trouble. What else did she say?"

"Just that she couldn't get here at six, so she'd make other arrangements," Sonya said.

Harold frowned. "Yeah, sure."

He got his car keys out of his pocket as he headed out the door. The pain in his hip was forgotten in his desire to get to his vehicle. He scanned the parking lot as he walked, looking for anything or anyone that was out of place, but nothing he saw set off any alarms. He was about to unlock the door when he felt the hair rise on the back of his neck. Never a man to ignore his instincts, he lifted his head and then spun toward the street, scanning the far side, beyond the passing traffic. He couldn't explain it, but he knew he was being watched.

Why was this happening, and why now? Even more intriguing, who was this woman and who did she work for? He almost smiled. He wasn't used to being the one who was stalked. He could admire a worthy adversary, and it had been a while since he'd indulged his passion.

The urge to see if she showed herself was strong. Instead of getting in his car, he started walking toward the street. If he was right and someone was watching him, she would know she'd been made. And if he had become someone's prey, it was only fair that he see his enemy's face.

Holly had found a parking place over a block away and then walked down the street to the gas station across the street from the warehouse. She bought a bottle of pop and a bag of chips, and found a place to watch the street from inside the store. She'd been there less than fifteen minutes when a tall, heavyset man with a long gray ponytail came out of the building and headed toward the employee parking lot. There was something about the way he walked that made her stomach knot. She pulled the old photo of her father that Ida Pacino had given her out of her purse and compared it to the man across the street. From this distance, it was hard to tell for sure.

All of a sudden she saw him stop, then scan the area as if he were looking for someone. That was when she knew Sonya had told him about the call. When he started walking toward the street, she panicked. What if he was coming in here? What should she do? She felt cornered. She couldn't leave. He would see her. What if he recognized her? What the hell had she done? She stepped back away from the window, putting a floor display of fan belts between her and the street, then stared past the edge to see what he was doing.

He stopped at the entrance to the parking lot, looking up and down the street in a slow, methodical manner. His hands were curled into fists, his eyes narrowed against the glare of the setting sun . . . and in that moment she realized that the man across the street *was* the same man as the one in the photo, only older. Her heartbeat was pounding so loud against her eardrums that she didn't hear the clerk talking to her until he touched her arm.

She spun, her eyes wide with fright.

"What? What's wrong?"

The clerk frowned. "Nothing, miss. I just asked if you were okay."

Holly shoved a shaky hand through her hair as she nodded. "Yes, yes, I'm fine." She turned back toward the window.

The man — her father — was nowhere in sight.

"Oh, no, oh, my God," she mumbled, and dumped her snack into the trash can and headed for the ladies' room.

She flipped on the light as she closed and locked the door, then shuddered as a cockroach crawled out from behind the loose switch plate and headed up the wall. She leaned against the door and made herself calm down.

Footsteps came and went outside the door. The longer she was in there, the more anxious she became. She didn't know how much time had passed, but she knew she couldn't stay there forever.

Finally she gritted her teeth and walked out. She wouldn't look across the street as she started up the hill toward her car, but her heart was racing. When her cell phone rang, she answered quickly, hoping her voice wasn't shaking as much as her legs.

"Hello."

"Hey, Holly. I was taking a break and thought I'd check on you. How's it going?"

Bud. Just hearing his voice calmed her.

"Pretty good, actually." There was no need to tell him what she'd learned or where she was, at least not today. "What's been going on at home?" she asked with forced brightness. "How's your hand? Is it healing okay?"

Bud frowned. He knew Holly as well as he knew himself, and she was sounding far too animated for his peace of mind.

"My hand is fine. What the hell's going on?"

Holly frowned. He knew something was up. How did he do that?

"Nothing's going on." Her voice was sharp, her words abrupt. "I'm a little breathless because I'm walking uphill to where my car is parked, that's all."

"Oh. Well."

She snorted softly. "Well, indeed. For Pete's sake, I'm twenty-five years old, not five. I do not need a keeper."

"Look. I didn't call to insult you," Bud said. "I'm glad you're okay. I'll talk to you again when you're in a better frame of mind."

The click in her ear was startling. Irked with herself for letting her stupidity color her behavior, she got in the car and drove away.

Harold Mackey had taken a back route out — of the parking lot and circled the block, looking for vehicles that seemed out of place. The first thing he noticed was the rental car. It was parked up the hill from the warehouse, and with no residential houses nearby, he decided to wait and see who claimed it.

Almost thirty minutes passed before he noticed a young woman walking up the hill toward it. Like nearly everyone else he saw, she had a cell phone glued to her ear and was talking in an animated fashion. Something about her seemed familiar, although he was pretty sure he'd never seen her before.

To his surprise, she got in the rental car and drove away. The first thought that went through his mind was, if she had needed to stop at the gas station, then why the hell park a full block away? His curiosity piqued, he put his car in gear and eased back into traffic, taking care to keep some distance between them, and followed her all the way back to the Jameson Hotel.

He watched her stop at valet parking. Who the hell was she? The only living female who

112

could ever cause him trouble was his daughter. The irony of it was, he wouldn't know her if saw her. The only way to get the answer he needed now was to ask.

He thought for a minute, then pulled out his wallet and palmed a hundred-dollar bill. As soon as the woman went inside, he pulled up to the valet stand and jumped out. He was still in his work clothes, with his ID clipped to his shirt, and hoped that would give credence to the lie he was about to tell.

"Hey, you . . . that young woman who just valet parked her car . . . was her name Harriet Mackey?"

"We don't give out the names of guests," the man said, while eyeing the hundred-dollar bill that was now openly held in Harold's hand.

"Look, I'm an employee of Riverfront Wholesale — see?" Harold pointed to his ID. "A woman dropped a hundred-dollar bill at my last stop — the Buffalo Grill, over on Locust Street. The maitre d' told me her name, and I tried to catch her, but I couldn't. After I left work, I thought I saw her again and followed her here. But if she's not Harriet Mackey, then I had the wrong car and the wrong woman. Can't you at least check that much for me?"

Harold suspected that the thought of losing a hundred dollars, along with the fact that someone was honest enough to try to return it, was what sold his story.

"Hang on," the attendant said, eyeing the parking stub Holly had given him. "I need to check the computer. It won't take long."

"Thanks, man," Harold said, and followed him over so he could surreptitiously keep an eye on the screen. When he saw the man type in a room number and the name "Holly Slade" popped up, he looked away as the attendant stepped back.

"Sorry to tell you, but you must have followed the wrong car. No Harriet Mackey registered here."

"Damn," Harold said, and stuffed the bill back in his pocket. "Thanks for checking anyway," he said, and got back into his SUV and drove away.

He'd seen everything he needed to. He knew the woman's name now.

Holly Slade.

Although he'd never heard the name before, he needed to think about this. No need to pull some knee-jerk move that might get him in trouble. He hadn't gotten away with things and still stayed under the radar this long by being careless. It was probably nothing and he was just overreacting, but it never hurt to play it safe.

Six

Holly's evening was uneventful. Bothered about how her phone call with Bud had ended, and rather than face another meal alone in the hotel restaurant, she'd ordered room service. But when it finally came, all she'd done was shove her food around on the plate before putting the tray out into the hall.

She was missing an anchor, and the unknowns in her life were overwhelming. The sooner she could put this place behind her and return to the Triple S, the better off she would be. She was getting ready for bed when her cell phone began to ring. It was Bud, which meant he wasn't too mad or he wouldn't have called her again.

"Hi, Bud."

"Yeah . . . hey, Holly. I need you to hang on a minute."

She frowned. He sounded strained. He was definitely upset.

"What's —"

"Hang on," he muttered. "I'm connecting Savannah to this call."

Now she was in a panic. Something bad must have happened.

"What's happened? Are you okay?" He was no longer on the line. Had he put her on hold, or had she lost the call? "Bud! Bud! Hello!"

Then suddenly he was talking.

"Okay, I need you both to listen to me and try not to freak out. Maria is hurt. Someone put a bomb in her car. She wasn't in it when it went off, but she was close enough to be seriously injured. She's in the hospital under police protection. The hospital called me, then put me through to the detective in her room."

Savannah gasped.

Holly started to sob. "Is she going to be all right? Please, Bud, tell us she's going to be all right."

Bud's voice was shaking. "I don't know anything more than what the hospital and the cop told me. She's in ICU, has stitches in her head, arm and legs, a concussion, and bruised ribs. They're waiting for lab results for confirmation that nothing more is wrong. What you do need to know is that it looks like Maria has made a conquest.

117

Whoever this cop is, he's taken this attack on her very personally. I was getting ready to fly out there when he told me I could come if I wanted, but that I needed to know he wasn't leaving her side and wouldn't let anyone hurt her again."

"What should we do, Bud?" Holly asked. "Do you think we should all fly to Tulsa?"

"I don't know. I think I'm going to wait to make a decision until I hear from him again. I've got a mess on my hands here at the ranch, and I hate to leave right now."

"What's wrong?" Savannah asked.

"We had another snowstorm last night. It'll melt soon, but right now we're a little short on hay and trying to feed cattle in two feet of snow."

"Oh, my," Holly said. "I've been so focused on what's happening here that I haven't watched the weather once since I left." She felt even guiltier that she hadn't asked him more about what was going on back home when they talked.

"Me, either," Savannah said. "So you think we should wait until you call us again to make a decision?"

"Yes," Bud said.

"Okay," Holly said, then added, "Are you okay, Savannah?"

"I'm fine. How about you?"

"I'm good. Take care, okay?" Holly cautioned.

"Both of you be careful," Bud said. "I don't want to make another phone call like this. As soon as I hear an update, I'll call the both of you. And just so you don't forget, I miss you — both of you."

"We miss you, too," they said in unison. " 'Bye."

Holly dropped the phone and started praying. It was all she could do for a sister in danger too far away.

Harold pulled up to his house, grabbed the KFC takeout he'd picked up on the way home and went inside. The house smelled stale — a combination of cold coffee and cigarettes — and there was a thin layer of dust on all the surfaces. He cleaned now and then, but not often. He didn't mind a little clutter, and dust was a fact of life. He'd never understood the need women had to make everything shine.

He was still thinking about that woman calling his work. Even though nothing had come of it, he didn't believe the story she'd fed Sonya. As he dug into his meal, he turned his attention to the woman he'd trailed to the Jameson. There was no way he could pin her to the phone call, and trailing her like he had was probably overkill. This was most likely nothing to be concerned about, but he'd gotten away with pursuing his passion all these years because he'd been careful, and he wasn't about to stop now.

Later he wheeled his trash to the curb, and as he was walking back through the house, he glanced at a picture on the end table by the sofa. It was one he'd taken of Twila and Harriet on the front porch of their house. That had been a lifetime ago, and he rarely thought about either of them. The photo wasn't there for remembrance. Visitors were rare at his place, but it was a nice touch, just in case. It kept up his image as the abandoned family man, which had been his status for twenty years now, and he had no reason to drop it. He sat down to watch some TV.

The room bore evidence of Harold's passion for hunting. There were trophies of all kinds filling every open spot on the living room walls. He was a taxidermist's dream of the perfect customer: trophy fish, the rack from a twelve-point buck, even the stuffed head of a bighorn sheep.

He aimed the remote as he settled into his recliner. He kicked back and channel surfed until he found an episode of *Deadliest Catch*. Those men knew what it meant to fight the elements and succeed. If he were younger, he would have gone to sea, if for no other reason than to see how he fared against it.

Sitting amid these trophies gave him an itch to visit the ones he considered his prize possessions. He went down the hall and into the spare bedroom, which he used for storage. Except for a good thirty boxes as yet unpacked from his twenty-year-old move, the room was empty. He had no idea what was in boxes, nor any desire to search. It only took a few moments to shove a certain number of them aside and lift the door in the floor. It led to an old bomb shelter that had been installed during the early fifties and was the single reason he'd bought the house. He started down the steps, paused to pull the cord hanging from the cellar ceiling and switched on the light.

His pulse kicked. His skin got hot. The longer he stood looking at his collection, the harder he got. Each hunt had been special, but some more than others. He began to circle the room, running his fingers through each scalp he'd mounted and tagged. The names were as familiar to him as his own was. He'd chosen them not for the magnificence of the pelts of hair that he'd taken, but because of the meaninglessness of their existence. In one way or another, Harold Mackey had judged and found them lacking in any kind of ability to benefit the human race.

He paused, eyeing the first tag. Beverly Harlow. He palmed the hank of dark, brittle hair and closed his eyes, remembering the night he'd ended her worthless life.

A storm was approaching. Intermittent flashes of lightning ripped across the darkness, followed by low, distant rumbles of thunder. Harold liked hunting in this kind of weather. The noise from the storm hid the sounds of his approach.

He knew the back door to the restaurant would be unlocked, because he'd watched the skinny blonde carrying out garbage from the kitchen and knew she wasn't through. His pulse was racing, just like it always did when he was anticipating a kill. It was a heady thing, knowing he held the power of life and death in his own hands — just like God.

He'd already scoped out the parking lot. There were only two cars left. One belonged to the skinny blonde, the other to the night shift manager, Beverly Harlow. The blonde would leave first. Harlow last.

It began to rain a few minutes later, and as predicted, the blonde dashed out into the night holding a folded newspaper over her head. Harold waited in the shadows until her car had cleared the muddy parking lot, and then he moved to the door, standing off to the side so as not to be seen, waiting for Harlow to emerge.

He knew when she began going through the restaurant, turning off all but the night lights, because the place began to go dark. The anticipation of what was coming made him shiver. The endorphins shooting through his bloodstream shot him to a high so fast he nearly came. He rubbed the front of his pants, feeling the erection behind his zipper, and smiled. It was only going to get better.

Suddenly the door opened. Beverly Harlow was halfway out, carrying the bank deposit bag and to-go box with the leftovers of her half-eaten dinner, when Harold grabbed her by the throat.

In the half-light, he saw the fear, then the recognition, in her eyes. She dropped everything and began trying to tear his hands away from her neck.

"You're a worthless piece of shit," Harold said. "You bitch about your exes and the brats you whelped that the state has to raise." Before she could scream, he doubled up his fist and knocked her out cold. She dropped into the mud.

A quick glance across the parking lot confirmed that they were still alone. The door to the restaurant was ajar, the bank bag and her food were on the threshold where she'd dropped them, and the thunderstorm was gaining strength.

Harold didn't mind the rain. It washed away a multitude of sins — and evidence. He threw her unconscious body over his shoulder and retraced his steps into the alley where he'd parked, tossed her inside his van, then grabbed a piece of rope and tied her hands and feet. Within seconds, he was gone.

The rain was still falling, hitting the roof of the van like little bullets as he drove to a deserted place outside the city. He parked, then crawled between the seats and into the back, where Harlow's body was lying. She was semiconscious and moaning.

He knelt, eyeing the red smear of lipstick across her cheek and the imprint of his fingers already appearing on her neck, while he waited for her to come to. The moment she awakened she began to scream, begging him to let her go.

"The only place you're going tonight is straight to hell."

"Why? Why? Why?"

"You're flawed. You sleep with men who mean nothing to you. You give birth and then abandon your children as if they were nothing. You won't be having any more babies to dump on the foster system for someone else to raise, and you're gonna have to fuck the devil for your next piece of tail."

In her terror, Beverly's bladder gave way right where he was kneeling.

Harold smelled it and grinned. It didn't offend him. He knew how the body worked when faced with great fear. He'd seen animals do the same thing right before he ended their lives.

She started to plead in a thin, high-pitched voice. "Please, please, don't."

He opened the back door and shoved the upper half of her body out into the rain. When she saw him pull a knife from the inside of his boot and then grab a handful of her hair, her eyes widened in disbelief.

Before she could think, he had scalped her. Her screams of pain rose above the sound of the storm, then ended abruptly as he slit her throat.

Her trussed and lifeless body was still dangling halfway out of the van. The downpour was convenient, washing away the flow of blood. Harold dropped his trophy scalp into a plastic bag, then got out and dragged the body into the culvert at the side of the road. One more defective female competently removed from the population.

He eyed the crumpled heap of her butchered

body as he calmly cleaned his knife on the wet grass at the side of the road. Back in the van, he grabbed a roll of paper towels and wiped up the urine from the floor of the back, then tossed the towels into the rain before driving away.

It was the siren of a passing fire truck that pulled Harold back to reality. He moved past the Harlow plaque and continued around the room, reliving his conquests all the way to the last — the one that had caused him to quit hunting.

He eyed the thatch of long, dirty-blond hair without touching it. Pamela Ulster. Prostitute. The last thing she'd said before he cut her throat was that he'd just killed himself, too. It wasn't until her body was found a month later and the story came out in the papers that he learned what she'd meant. She had AIDS. The news horrified him. What if he had contracted it?

But after a year of periodic tests, he was still clean. He'd dodged the bullet, but enough was enough, and he called it quits on his harvest. The world was going to have to find another way to strengthen the gene pool without him.

He yawned. It was time to get to bed. He climbed up and out of his trophy cache, turning out the light as he went, then shut the trapdoor and pushed the boxes back in place. He slept a long and dreamless sleep, comfortable in the belief that his conscience was clear.

The next morning, he woke without need of an alarm, stretching leisurely before rolling over and swinging his legs off the side of the bed. It was his day off, and he planned to take a drive out of the city. Maybe stop by to visit with some people he knew who let him hunt on their land.

He pulled his hair back into a ponytail without bothering to brush it, dressed in old jeans and a sweatshirt with a picture of the Arch, and went into the kitchen to make coffee, only to find all his mugs were dirty. Eyeing the pile of dirty dishes in the sink, he opted for another look in the cabinets and began digging into the back of a higher shelf. When his hand curled around a mug, he pulled it out, then grunted with surprise.

It was a small white mug with a tiny ceramic frog in the bottom. He remembered Twila buying it for Harriet when she was still a toddler. It was meant to encourage a child to finish her milk so she could see the frog at the bottom. He hadn't seen it in years and hadn't even remembered that he'd brought it with him when he'd moved. The fact that he had a daughter rarely occurred to him, and he hadn't thought about her in ages until that strange call for him at work.

For a couple of years after she'd disappeared, he'd wondered where Twila had hidden her, but over time he'd forgotten all about her, never even noticing the photograph he kept as camouflage. The mug was a vivid reminder. Frowning, he put it back and dug a dirty mug out of the sink, then filled it with coffee. Seeing that tiny mug made him think of the woman who'd called his work. He wondered if the universe was trying to tell him something. Maybe he would take a second look at that woman from the hotel . . . just in case.

Sunrise was just moments away when Holly's cell phone rang again. She'd fallen asleep with it in her hand and was trying to answer it before her eyes were fully opened.

Please, God, let this be good news, she thought, then answered the call. "Hello? Bud?"

"Yes, it's me, honey. It's good news. Just let me get Savannah on the phone, too."

Holly sank back against the pillows and said a quiet prayer of thanksgiving as she waited for Bud. Seconds later, they were both on the phone.

"Talk to me," Holly begged.

"The cop called again. Maria woke up. He said she's going to be okay."

"Thank you, Jesus," Holly whispered, knowing last night's prayers had been answered.

"Amen," Savannah said, then added, "How bad is she hurt? Was she burned? I didn't think to ask last night."

"No. No burns. She was far enough away when it went off to escape the worst of that. She'll heal, and that's all that matters. And it was even clearer this morning Bodie Scott, that detective I told you about, has fallen for your sister."

"That's so great!" Savannah cried.

"I know," Bud said. "Can't say whether she feels the same or not, but here's hoping."

"That's amazing," Holly said. "I'm so happy for her. That's what we all want, right, Savannah?"

"Absolutely," her sister said.

Bud's heart dropped. He couldn't imagine the thought of Holly falling for someone and having to watch her live out her life with another man.

"So we still don't go see her?" Holly said.

"I can't tell you flat out not to, but I don't think it's a good idea," Bud said.

"We can call her, though, right?" Savannah asked.

"Sure, but not just yet. I don't think she would even remember it, let alone be able to talk. She's not even sitting up in bed. She woke up long enough to hear that she was going to recover, and then she was out again. I'd give it a couple of days, at least."

"Okay," Holly said. "But if you talk to her before we do, make sure she knows you told us and that we send our love."

"I will. Are you both being careful?"

"Yes," they promised in unison.

Holly didn't want to think about what she'd done. She'd already admitted to herself that it had been a stupid move. All she could do was hope it didn't come back to haunt her.

"Sleep well, ladies. I'll talk to you soon."

Holly set the phone aside, then got out of bed. This news had reinforced her decision. Today was the day she went to the police.

Harold was a hunter, but he freely admitted that he wasn't much of a detective. It had taken him a while to find out that Holly Slade's car was still in the underground garage. After that, he found a parking place close by and settled in to wait. A short while later, her car cruised past with a parking valet behind the wheel, so he quickly started his own car and drove out of the garage just in time to see her getting into hers. He waited until a couple of cars had followed her out, then fell in behind them. He wasn't thinking so much about where she was going as just hoping to get a chance to get a good view of her face when she got there.

When she finally turned into a parking lot, he was so focused on getting a look at her that he paid no attention to her destination. He followed a few moments behind her and wheeled into an empty space, but once again all he got was a glimpse of her profile before she walked up the sidewalk and into a building.

When he realized where he was — in the visitors' lot of the St. Louis Police Department — he started to sweat.

The day had started off warm and sunny. Holly was wishing she'd thought to bring her sunglasses as she made her way through the city traffic. The St. Louis Police Department was on Clark Avenue. She found it with little trouble, but once she'd parked, she suddenly felt hesitant about going inside. This was absolutely going to change her life, but after what had just happened to Maria, she had to be careful that it didn't also end it.

She checked to make sure she had her journal, as well as the photos Ida Pacino had given her, then got out and went inside. After asking to speak to a detective who handled cold cases, she was escorted to the desk of Detective Whit Carver.

Whitman Carver was a third-generation cop. He lived and breathed the job to such a degree that after his third wife had divorced him seven years earlier, he hadn't bothered trying to replace her. He was fifty-seven years old, about thirty pounds over-weight, with a full head of steel-gray hair and a smoking habit he was trying to quit. Today was his first day back at work after a three-day bout with the flu, and he was nursing his second cup of coffee as he shuffled through the paperwork that had piled up on his desk.

When he saw an officer come in with a young woman and head toward his desk, he guessed his day was about to get busier.

"Detective Carver, this lady has asked to speak to a cold-case detective."

"I qualify," Whit said and waved toward the chair beside his desk. "Detective Whit-man Carver, ma'am. How can I help you?"

Holly smiled nervously. "My name is

Holly Slade. I have an unusual situation and wasn't really sure who to talk to."

Whit frowned. "So what's your unusual situation?"

"It's about murder and a false missing persons report, and one is tied to the other, though maybe not entirely the way you'd expect."

Whit watched her pull some papers and photos out of her bag, then put them on his desk, and frowned.

This oughta be good. "So who went missing?"

"According to Harold Mackey, who filed the false report, that would be me and my mother."

Whit started taking notes. "Who's Harold Mackey?"

"He's my birth father . . . the man who raised me for the first five years of my life. I told you my name was Holly Slade, and up until last week, I thought that was the truth and that a man named Andrew Slade was my father. But at the reading of Andrew's will, I found out I wasn't really his child and my sisters weren't really my sisters. My real parents were Harold and Twila Mackey, from right here in St. Louis."

Whit shifted in his seat. "That sounds like a tough thing to hear, but what does it have to do with this murder you have yet to mention. Who died?"

"I'm getting to that," Holly said. "Twenty years ago, my mother left me in the care of a preacher from Montana by the name of Andrew Slade, with the intention of turning in her husband Harold, my father, to the police, then taking me back and starting over."

"So far this sounds like a plain old marital dispute. Is that why she was going to turn in your father to the police? Was he abusing her?"

Holly took a slow, calming breath. "She didn't say anything about being abused to Andrew Slade. She was going to report Harold Mackey to the police for an entirely different reason, only I know she never got a chance to make that report. Instead, my mother went missing and I think he had something to do with it. I think he filed that missing persons report to cover his own guilt."

Holly leaned forward. "Until Andrew died, I had no memory of any of this. After coming back to St. Louis, I've begun to remember bits and pieces, but I believe the reason I was sent away was because I saw something bad and my mother found out. She sent me away to protect me. And I think

134

my birth father, Harold Mackey, did something to her. That's why she never showed up."

Whit put down his pen and kicked back in his chair.

"Miss, that wouldn't be a cold case. Even if your mother went missing, as you put it and your father claimed, there's no proof that anything happened to her. Have you ever considered the possibility that after she dumped you off on the preacher, she went one way while you went the other, and that this Mackey fellow you claim is your birth father didn't know where either of you went, thus his reason for filing the missing persons report?"

"No. That scenario never crossed my mind."

"Why not? It's the most logical one I can think of."

"How long have you been on the police force?" Holly asked.

"A long damn time," Whit snapped. "Long enough to know my business. If you have nothing more to add, we're through here."

SEVEN

His sudden anger surprised her, then made her panic as she realized he'd misunderstood her question.

"Oh, no . . . I apologize. I wasn't disputing you, Detective Carver. I asked because I was wondering if you'd remember a particular cold case from twenty years ago."

"I've lived in St. Louis all my life, ma'am. If you would quit beating around the bush and just come right out and explain what you're getting at, we might save both of us some time."

"Sorry. Twenty years ago a lot of women were murdered here by a serial killer the media named the Hunter, right?"

The hair rose on the back of Whit's neck.

"Yes, but what's —"

"My mother believed my father was the Hunter. I don't know why, but that's what she told Andrew Slade. She told him that as soon as she went to the police and they arrested my father, she would come get me. But like I said before, she never came. And one other thing. I know for a fact that my father is still alive and living in St. Louis."

Whit couldn't believe what he was hearing. Even after twenty years, this case was a boil on the butt of the entire St. Louis Police Department. During the three years that the Hunter had been active, they'd never gotten a single lead that panned out. Now this young woman had walked into the department and basically handed them their first real lead on a platter? Was this too good to be true?

Holly kept waiting for him to comment, but all he did was stare at her.

"Well?" she finally asked.

He jerked. "I'm sorry. That's one hell of a story."

Holly frowned. "Story? You think that was just a story? It's not a story, it's a tragedy. I lost my mother and twenty years of my life because of something I can't remember, and you call it a story? I don't know why, but for some reason I expected a little more interest than that from the police."

Whit shook his head. "No, I'm sorry, Miss Slade. You misunderstand me. This is shock, not disbelief."

"Oh."

Whit nodded. "*Oh,* indeed. Sit tight. I need to make a couple of calls. There are some other people who need to hear what you have to say."

She watched as he began making calls. From what she could overhear, he called his lieutenant, his captain and someone he referred to as Chief. As soon as he hung up the phone, he stood.

"When they get here, they'll want to hear all of this, so I'm afraid you'll have to go through it again. Can I get you anything while you wait? Coffee? A cold drink?"

"Maybe some water."

"Yes, ma'am," he said, and darted off.

Holly began to get nervous. She'd wanted results and this was better than she'd hoped for, but it was also so . . . irrevocable.

Within half an hour three somber-faced men arrived. Holly was escorted into an interview room and introduced to Whit's superiors — Lieutenant Samuels, Captain Rouse and Chief Hollis. At Whit's urging, she repeated her story, watching the shock spread across their faces. When she was through, they all began to speak at once.

It was the chief who held up his hand for silence.

"Miss Slade, we'll need a copy of your journal and any papers that your mother

138

left with Andrew Slade, as well as copies of the photos you were given." He pointed to Whit. "See to that, and put in a request for all the files pertaining to the Hunter case." His gaze slid to the other two policemen. "Lieutenant, I want you to form a task force. See that Detective Carver has all the help he needs. Coordinate with Captain Rouse to make this happen. We don't have enough detectives working cold cases to go through the backlog of information on this. Assign as many detectives as you can spare from other departments. This killer is an animal. What he did to those women was barbaric, and he needs to be put down."

Holly felt sick as the shame of what he'd said began to sink in. This killer — the man they referred to as an animal — was her father. So what did that make her?

Hollis shifted his attention to Holly.

"We appreciate what it took for you to come forward, and we'll do what we can to put this information to good use. Given the twenty-year gap, it's not going to be easy finding old witnesses. But at least we should be able to discover your father's where-abouts pretty easily. Is there anything you can tell us on that score."

"I don't know where he's living now, but he works for Riverfront Wholesale, driving a

139

delivery truck."

Hollis's reaction was short and loud. "Holy sh—" He stopped in midsentence as a flush spread up his neck and face. "I'm sorry, Miss Slade. I apologize for my language."

Still rattled by how fast this was happening, Holly sank back into her chair. "So what do you need me to do?"

"You've done enough," Hollis said. "I'm correct in understanding that he doesn't know you're in the city, right?"

She hesitated, then nodded, omitting the fact that she *had* spied on him, since he hadn't known she was there.

"Good. We don't want you to go anywhere near him, much less talk to him. If your claims are correct, the mere sight of you might spook him."

"I don't think he'd recognize me. We haven't seen each other in twenty years. However, I have no desire to be around him, and if what I suspect is true, he not only murdered all those women, he also murdered my mother. I want justice for all of them."

"We understand. And if you remember anything else in the meantime, don't hesitate to call Detective Carver."

"Yes, of course," Holly said.

Hollis eyed the men in the room and spoke, his voice sharp, his words pointed. "I don't want to open a newspaper and see that the media has picked up on the fact that the Hunter case has been reopened, or anything else that might give Mackey a reason to run, especially if he *is* our man."

Captain Rouse spoke up, "Serial killers are a unique breed. A lot of them have a God complex. They think they're smarter and wilier than the police, and that they can't be caught. Part of the high of what they do is eluding authority. And very few of them ever stop unless they get too old, get sent to jail for something else, or die. To our knowledge, there hasn't been another murder connected to this case in almost twenty years, which is very unusual if your father is the killer and has been walking around free that whole time. And if he finds out that the case has been reopened, then he might assume there's new evidence, which could lead him to leave the area before we have enough evidence for an arrest. Or, even worse, amp up and kill again."

Holly shuddered. "Rest assured I won't be talking about this to anyone. And if I do remember something more that might be helpful, I'll certainly call Detective Carver."

"Thank you," Hollis said. "We'll be going.

Carver, keep me abreast of all that's happening."

"Yes, sir," Whit said.

The other men left the interrogation room, leaving Whit and Holly alone.

Whit picked up the journal and photos.

"I'm going to take this stuff and run copies," he said. When he saw the strain in her eyes, he touched her shoulder briefly. "It won't take long."

Holly stifled a sigh. Moments later she was alone. After all the drama, she felt emotionally drained and had a strong urge to cry. When she glanced at her watch, she was surprised to see it was almost 2:00 p.m. No wonder she felt shaky. She hadn't eaten since early that morning. She needed some food and a nap, but what she wanted was Bud. He would be the voice of reason she needed to hear. Swallowing back tears, she stared down at the floor, willing herself not to come undone.

Carver returned a few minutes later and handed her the originals of what he'd copied.

"Here you go. I just want to thank you for getting up the courage to come in. I know it couldn't have been easy. We'll start going through our old files to see if we can find a link."

"My . . . father, Andrew, used to say that life wasn't meant to be easy, but it was meant to be lived to the fullest. After finding out about all this, I realized I had to settle the past before I could look to the future. I know you're focused on finding a serial killer, but don't forget my mother. If she became one of his victims, I want to know."

"I promise we won't forget about her. I think we're done, and I'm sure you must be ready to get out of here. How about I walk you out?"

Holly nodded. She was ready to go.

As they neared the exit, Whit reiterated the chief's earlier warning, "I can't say this often enough. Stay away from Harold Mackey and let us do our job."

"Yes, sir, I will."

Whit walked her out, shook her hand and went back inside.

Holly's legs were shaking as she headed for her car. She felt light-headed and a little sick to her stomach as she waited for a police cruiser to pass before she reached her car.

Harold glanced at his watch again. The woman had been inside for hours. He couldn't imagine what the hell she was doing and was on the verge of believing he'd made a mountain out of a molehill. What if she were in there applying for a job? She was driving a rental and staying in a hotel, which meant she was probably new to the area. He was cursing himself as a nervous dumb-ass when she suddenly exited the building.

He grabbed the binoculars he always kept in the glove compartment and trained them on her face. Again, he felt a faint sense of familiarity but no real recognition. Despite his conviction that there was nothing to be concerned about, he still decided to keep an eye on her — just in case. But for now, he had plans that would take him outside the city.

Holly pulled out of the parking lot and drove away. Her focus for the moment was on finding food. She passed plenty of fast-food places, but the thought of anything deep-fried turned her stomach. A restaurant advertising Italian food caught her eye, and she quickly moved into the right lane and took the turn into the parking lot. Less than a half-dozen cars were there, which made sense, considering the time. It was too late to be eating lunch and far too early to consider calling it dinner, but she was too hungry to care.

After spending almost an hour and a half enjoying a big plate of spaghetti and meatballs, her next destination was back to the hotel. She was tired, but her hunger had been sated and she planned on making it an early night.

Back at the hotel, she stopped in the snack shop and bought a cold bottle of pop, as well as a local newspaper, then headed for her room. Once inside, she kicked off her shoes, stripped out of her clothes and into some sweats, then crawled up on the bed with her pop and her journal.

Christmas 1993

This was the year I bought all three of you dolls for Christmas. It seemed like a safe bet, right? Three little girls, ages 8, 7 and 5. Girls are supposed to like dolls, but to my dismay, I found out that for you, there were exceptions. Oh, you'd had dolls before, but I hadn't paid attention to what you all played with so much as the fact that you were happily playing. Anyway, I stayed with all of you so Hannah could Christmas shop. That night after she came home, she showed me the dolls that she'd bought. They were, to my eye, dandies. All three dolls had long wavy hair and fancy little dresses, and shoes you could take on and off. They even came with a little comb and hairbrush apiece. We wrapped them up, and come Christmas morning, all three of you came flying down the hall squealing and laughing. Hannah and I got up and followed you into the living room to the tree. She handed out the presents, while I started a fire in the fireplace. Bud came in the back door just in the middle of the melee, grabbed the camera off the mantel and began to take pictures for us.

Maria's doll had dark wavy hair just like hers, Savannah's doll was a blonde for the same reason and Hannah had managed to find a doll with auburn hair like yours. The first thing Savannah did was take off all her doll's clothes, which made us laugh, because she then carried that naked baby around the entire morning without dressing her again. Maria went straight for the hairbrush and began brushing the hair on her dolly. You followed suit by getting the hairbrush for your doll, but then the brush got stuck. I watched you frown as you tried to untangle the hair, and then you pulled, and a few strands of hair came off in your hand.

You flinched, as if someone had just slapped you, and then you dropped the doll and began frantically trying to get the hair off your hand. It had wound itself between two of your fingers and wouldn't shake off. By the time I realized the hair was really upsetting you, you were hyperventilating. It was Bud who yanked the hair off your hand and picked you up. He kept telling you it was okay, that the dolly still had a lot of hair, but you wouldn't be consoled. We thought you were going to pass out, which greatly upset your sisters. I didn't understand why you reacted the way you did, but I guessed it had something to do with your life before you came to live with me. I took you out of Bud's arms and walked out of the room, leaving Hannah to smooth everything out with your little sisters.

You kept shivering and gasping, and your eyes wouldn't focus. It was as if you were looking at something that the rest of us couldn't see. I wrapped you up in an afghan, then sat down with you in that rocking chair that used to sit by your bed. I began to rock as I talked, telling you in a calm, quiet voice that you were not in danger, that you were safe here in Montana. I reminded you that Hannah and I loved you, Bud loved you, both your sisters loved you and no one could hurt you here.

Finally you grew calmer and relaxed, lying quietly against my chest as I rocked. You got so quiet that I thought you'd fallen asleep when, out of the blue, in this soft little voice, you said, "I wasn't supposed to touch the hair."

I couldn't imagine what that meant, but I wasn't going to push the issue by getting you upset again. It was Christmas after all. I wanted the day to be joyous for you, not a reminder of some hell you'd remembered. Then you added, "He puts them on the wall, like his fish."

I had no idea what that meant, but I knew you did, and that, whatever it was, it was too horrible for you to remember. All I could do was repeat that you were safe, and that no one could hurt you.

Then you looked up at me, your eyes brimming with unshed tears. You asked, "You're my daddy forever, aren't you?"

With a lump in my throat, I agreed. It seemed to satisfy you enough that you wanted to go back and play. But while you did carry your doll around a little that day, I think you did it just to please Hannah and me, because I never saw you play with it again.

So whatever you know, whatever the secret is that you've been keeping, I think it's time you got brave enough to face it. Oh. And for what it's worth, I'm still your daddy forever, even if only in spirit.

Holly was in tears by the time she laid the journal aside. As an adult, and knowing from reading about the crimes online that the Hunter had scalped his victims, she had to face the fact that she must have seen the gruesome trophies. The biggest questions still remained. Did Harold Mackey know she'd seen them? And had she told her mother? Was that really why Twila Mackey had so desperately wanted her daughter out of St. Louis?

Holly realized it would be impossible for a child as young as she had been not to tell her father what she'd seen — maybe even ask him about it. Had Harold threatened her life if she told? Or had that nightmare been correct? Had he known that the most effective avenue was to threaten her mother? God, she wanted to remember. She needed to remember. As Chief Hollis had said, the man was an animal who needed to be put down.

Overwhelmed by everything that had happened and the growing horror of what the rest of her life would likely be like, Holly rolled over onto her side and started to cry. If Harold Mackey truly turned out to be the Hunter, eventually everyone would find out that she was the daughter of a serial killer. Her life would be ruined.

Bud kicked the snow off his boots on the back porch before entering the house. He was tired to the bone, and as worried and lonely as he'd ever been.

He'd gotten a call from Savannah's boyfriend, Judd Holyfield, that he was going to Miami tomorrow to join her. The lawyer she'd hired there was about to file papers on her behalf, claiming her share of her birth father's estate, and Judd knew it could get nasty. After what had happened to Maria, they were all on edge. Bud kept thinking about Holly having to face the police alone, telling her story to a bunch of strangers and opening herself up to everything that came with that. He needed to be there. But he didn't have the right or the reason that Judd had, and he couldn't just walk away from the Triple S for an undetermined amount of time. The sisters expected him to take care of the Triple S, and for now that was the best thing he could do for them.

When he entered the kitchen, the empty feeling only escalated. He was used to walking into a house filled with the aroma of something cooking on the stove, and the sounds of laughter and people talking. The day was nearly over, the house was dark and all he could smell was the scent of cold coffee from this morning. The only positive thing was that it was warmer in here than where he'd been.

He hung his coat up on a hook by the door and headed for his bedroom, turning on lights as he went. He was hungry, but not for food. He wanted Holly. She and her sisters were all in a hell of a mess, and as much as he loved his old friend, they had Andrew to thank for it.

After a quick shower and a change into some warm sweats, he went back to the kitchen. Food was fuel, and he had to keep his body in motion. Too damn many people and animals depended on him. He switched on the television as he heated up a can of soup and then made himself a sandwich. The weatherman was in the middle of his report, which turned out to be the only good thing that had happened today. The storm front that had been stalled over the state was finally moving out.

No more snow.

He ate without thought, filling his belly and then finishing off the meal with a handful of store-bought cookies. With the weather behind him, he had no more stomach for television and switched it off as he walked out of the room.

An hour in the office catching up on daily invoices and cursing through the payroll that Savannah usually did put him in a worse mood. He didn't know what the future had in store for the Triple S, but he was part owner now, and letting it go to hell wasn't on his short list.

The clock in the hall was striking seven when he finally logged off the computer and left the office. It was seven here, which meant it would be eight in Missouri — not too late to call Holly. He wanted to hear her voice.

Holly had cried until her eyes were swollen and her nose was stopped up. She'd gotten past her hysterics, and was down to the occasional sniff and a good case of hiccups. Her cell phone began to ring as she was reaching for another tissue. When she saw it was Bud, she blew her nose, then cleared her throat, before answering. No need letting him know she was falling apart.

"Hello," she said, and then winced when her voice came out as a harsh croak.

The expectant smile on Bud's face disappeared. "What's wrong with you?"

"Nothing's wrong with me. I just . . . I'd been sleeping. I haven't talked to anyone since early afternoon. You know how it is . . . your voice just gets raspy."

He frowned. It wasn't like her to lie, but she was lying now. He just wasn't sure why.

"Sorry. I didn't mean to snap. I guess I'm a little antsy since Maria was attacked."

Holly sighed. "It's okay. We're all upset about her. How is she? I didn't get a chance to call all day."

"She's good," Bud said. "So it sounds like your day was productive, right?"

"I finally went to the police."

"How did it go?"

"Good . . . really good. They were very receptive to everything I had to tell them. Excited, even."

"I can imagine. A chance to close a twenty-year-old cold case is a big deal."

"Yes," Holly said, and closed her eyes, willing herself not to cry again. "So . . . is the snow melting?"

"Yes, and the storm front is moving out of state."

"That's great. How's your hand?"

"Healing."

"That's good."

The silence lengthened as they both ran out of chitchat and couldn't think of a safe subject to address.

Finally Bud's patience snapped and he asked, "Are you mad at me?"

Holly inhaled sharply. "No. God, no. Why would I be mad at you?"

"I don't know. I'm a man. We're supposed to be oblivious to stuff like that."

Holly tried to laugh, but it sounded more like a sob, and they both knew it.

"Damn it, Holly, don't play games with me. Something is wrong. Are you hurt? Are you in danger? Has something happened that you're not telling me?"

She started to sob. "No . . . everything's fine! Why wouldn't it be? I spent the day telling the police that my mother was convinced my father was a serial killer. You know what the chief of police said? He said the Hunter was an animal . . . an animal that needed to be put down!"

Suddenly Bud got it. "Oh, honey . . . I'm sorry. I know this has been hard on you, but after they make their case, they'll put out a warrant for his arrest. It might take a long time to find him, if he's still alive. But you will have done everything —"

Holly cut him off. "He still lives here in St. Louis. They know where he is. They're going through all the old files to see if they can find a link between him and the victims. But that's just it," she sobbed. "When they arrest him, everyone will find out about his past, his background, the whole thing. And the fact that he was turned in by his daughter will make me fresh fodder for the media. To be able to do what he's done makes him a freak, which makes me a freak, too."

"Damn it, Holly, you're not a freak! That's just not true!"

"Yes! It is true! Once I'm marked as the Hunter's daughter, what man will ever love me? I won't dare have children for fear they might turn out like him. No one will want me — ever!"

"That's not true!" Bud yelled. "I want you! I've always wanted you."

Holly choked, then clapped a hand over her mouth. Her pulse was roaring in her ears. Had she really heard that, or was it just her imagination?

Bud groaned. Now he'd done it, but by God, he wasn't taking any of it back. When she didn't answer, he knew she was shocked.

"Are you going to cry all night?"

"No," Holly said, then winced. She sounded like a damn mouse, squeaking in the dark.

"Good. So keep your sweet ass in one piece and come home as soon as you can. Do you hear me?"

"Yes."

"Good. Talk to you later."

Holly shivered. "Later."

The dial tone was suddenly buzzing in her ear. She dropped her phone and then covered her mouth with both hands, muffling her words.

"Oh, my God, oh, my God, he did not just say that."

She bolted out of bed, dashed into the bathroom and flipped on the light. What she saw in the mirror made her wince. She looked like hell, with her hair all over the place, her eyes red and puffy, and her lips all swollen.

"Bud Tate loves me," she whispered. It was her best dream come true.

She bent down and began splashing her face with cold water. After she'd dried herself off, she looked back at herself again. Still the same woman, with the same screwed-up life — except for one thing. Bud Tate loved her — and she loved him.

She shook her head and flipped off the light. Even after she'd crawled into bed and turned off all the lights, she still hadn't come up with an answer to the million-dollar question.

Bud loved her, but in the cold light of day, would it be enough to get past who she was?

EIGHT

Holly went to bed thinking about Bud, reliving the moment of his revelation. There was no doubt in her mind that she loved him. They all loved him. But she loved him more.

She began thinking back to all the times in the past couple of years when she'd turned to him instead of her father for comfort or advice, how she'd planned certain meals around his comings and goings, knowing that she was making his favorite foods. It should have been obvious to a fool, but he'd never said a thing. The sound of his footsteps on the back porch had always made her heart skip a beat. Had he said what he had just to make her feel better? Surely not.

The longer she thought, the more she wanted to tell him right away how she felt. The panic she'd felt when she'd seen him bleeding, the lurch of longing she'd had when she'd seen him strip off his shirt, the fear that something would happen to him while she was gone. Her love for him was there. It had been there for years. She knew Bud well enough to know that the next step would have to come from her. He'd said what was in his heart, but he wouldn't cross a line. They were always going to be family, regardless of what came next. She had to find the courage to face him despite this blight on her soul. She had to look into his eyes to see the truth.

The one thing that hadn't changed was her horror of the situation she was in. She couldn't wrap her head around being related to a man who could commit murder . . . repeatedly. Bringing children into the world who would be blood kin of a serial killer seemed like an irrational thing to do. Her emotions were in chaos by the time she finally turned off the lights and closed her eyes.

Someone was hammering. It was loud enough that it woke Harriet up from her nap. Confused, she crawled out of her bed and went down the hall, calling for her mother, but she didn't answer. She went into the kitchen, because that was where Mother always was, but the room was empty. When she looked out the window, she saw that the family car was gone.

The hammering stopped. Harriet called out for her daddy, and when he didn't answer, she went to the basement door and opened it. The basement light wasn't on, but she could see a faint light beyond the stairs. The stairs always scared her. They were steep and, even with the light on, appeared to disappear into a black void. The repetitious sound of hammering began again. It was scary being up there alone. The need to see a familiar face overcame her fear of the dark.

"Daddy?"

Still no answer, just another round of hammering.

Taking a deep breath, she started down the steps, holding on to the wall for balance. The light from the kitchen behind her illuminated enough of the steps for her to navigate safely. When she reached the floor, she made a beeline for the faint glow of light escaping from around a closed door, then grabbed the doorknob and turned it quickly, anxious to find her daddy.

The light inside momentarily blinded her. She stumbled and reached out toward the wall to keep from falling. Something brushed across the back of her hand, something that felt like spiderwebs. She shrieked and yanked her hand back, but some of the strands had become entangled around her fingers.

"Daddy!"

His face was angry. So angry. She'd never seen him this angry before.

"You're not supposed to be in here!" he yelled, then grabbed her by the arm and began dragging her back through the basement and up the stairs.

"I'm sorry, Daddy. I'm sorry!" she screamed, as she kept trying to get the spiderweb off her hand.

He saw what she was doing and grabbed her hand. He began ripping away the strands, then slammed her against the wall.

"You tell anybody what you saw in there and I'll make you sorry. Do you understand me?"

"Yes! Yes!" she repeated. "I'm sorry. I'm sorry. I won't tell. I promise."

"If you tell, you'll never see your mama again."

She gasped. It was the worst threat possible. Everything around her seemed to stop. She could see her father's lips still moving, but she couldn't hear what he was saying. Her heart was pounding so fast it was hard to catch her breath. Then her daddy raised his hand as if he were about to hit her. Everything began to look fuzzy, and then it all went black.

Holly woke up with a start, grabbing at her fingers. It took a few moments for her to realize she'd been dreaming and that there was nothing on them. What was startling to her was that she'd just dreamed the answer to what she'd read in the journal the night before. Obviously having the hairs from the doll's head wrapped around her fingers had become confused in her mind with that day and triggered the memory of the incident with her father. She could only wonder what else lay below the surface of her memory, and if she would remember it in time to help the St. Louis P.D. All she had now were bits and pieces of what might or might not be truthful memories.

"Oh, Lord," Holly whispered, as she threw back the covers.

She wanted out of that bed and could tell from the light coming through the drapes that it was daylight. A quick glance at the clock verified the time — after 9:00 a.m. She hadn't slept that late in ages. She started toward the bathroom to grab a quick shower before dressing, then realized she had nowhere to go. After her trip to the police department yesterday and the order to stay away from Harold Mackey, her investigative days were over.

What to do? Should she go back to Missoula? It wasn't as if there was anything more she could do here. She plopped down on the side of the bed. The longer she sat, the more convinced she became that leaving now would be like running away. It wasn't time. Not yet. Not until she saw him arrested.

She put out the Do Not Disturb sign, then locked herself in and stripped off her clothes as she headed for the shower.

As she closed the bathroom door, she caught sight of herself in the full-length mirror on the back of the door. She'd never thought all that much about her body. Hard work had kept her fit, and she'd worn the same size for years. But how would Bud view her body? Where Maria was tall and lanky, she had curves, and breasts that hung like ripe, heavy fruit. She turned sideways, eyeing her flat belly and firm limbs. It might not be perfect, but she was comfortable in her own skin.

She ran her palms down her belly, then closed her eyes, pretending it was Bud who was touching of her. Just the thought made her ache. There was a sharp thud in the hall outside her room, then the sounds of someone laughing. Startled, she yanked her hands away and quickly got into the shower, but in her mind, she knew one day soon she and Bud would make love.

The new task force was hard at work. Files

163

containing every detail of the Hunter's victims were scattered all over the tables as a half-dozen detectives went through the info. Whit had sent another detective down to the evidence locker to find out what, if any, physical evidence was still in existence.

A lot of things happen that deter solving cold cases. The most common ones were witnesses dying, physical evidence deteriorating, even disappearing . . . and no new leads.

But in this case, they'd been given a name. And if it turned out to be the right name, Harold Lee Mackey was going to go down in the history of serial killers as one of the worst ones . . . if they could make their case.

Carver hadn't wasted any time. The task force had commandeered one of the interrogation rooms and turned it into their headquarters. The beginning of a murder board was already in place and growing, with photos of the known victims tacked up on the board. Beneath each photo was a list consisting of age, place of employment, church affiliation, what kind of car she drove, where she got her hair done — everything that the detectives could find out in hopes of uncovering a pattern somewhere within the lists.

So far, nothing was jumping out at them,

which was the same consensus the detectives had come to twenty years earlier. There wasn't even a pattern as to where the killer had dumped the bodies, other than that they were all obscure locations. The only things the victims had in common were that they were all female, and they'd all been murdered after dark and scalped while they were alive — *before* their throats were cut.

They had a map of the city up on one end of the board, with color-coded pushpins denoting where the victims had worked and lived, and where the bodies had been found. Some victims had disappeared from a place of business. Others had been just outside their homes. But none had been kidnapped from inside a building, which the detectives noted was smart on the Hunter's part. If he kept all the crime scenes outdoors, there was less chance of leaving behind physical evidence that would survive the elements.

Small flags designated Harold Mackey's old house, as well as the location where he worked. There didn't seem to be any more relation between those locations and the sites of the killings as there seemed to be between the killings themselves. They were going to need something that indisputably tied him to the crimes before they could get a search warrant.

Whit was holding out hope that Holly Slade might remember something that would give them an edge, but it wasn't a sure thing. They needed cold hard facts. He stared at the murder board for a few moments more, then picked up another victim's file and sat down at his desk. The answer had to be in there somewhere.

Bud hadn't been able to sleep. After he'd gone to bed, he'd lain there thinking about what he'd said to Holly and praying that it wouldn't ruin the bond between them. In an odd way, he was relieved that his feelings were out in the open. Either she would reciprocate them or she wouldn't. He wouldn't let himself think of a total rejection. Even if she didn't love him that way, they had too much in common for her to cut him out of her life. With them being co-owners of the Triple S, she had to get past what he'd said so that life could go on. He loved all three women. But Holly was in his blood.

He got up before daylight and went to the kitchen to make coffee, padding through the silent house in his sock feet as he turned up the heat. When he glanced at the kitchen clock, it dawned on him that Judd Holyfield was already boarding a plane to Miami.

Before the day was over, he would be with Savannah, the woman he loved. At that moment, he almost hated Judd for having something he didn't.

As the day progressed and he didn't hear from Holly, his mood grew darker. He was convinced that he'd ruined everything that had been good between them. If it hadn't been for the stitches still in his hand, he would have run his fist through a wall. At least then he would have a real pain to focus on and not this awful emptiness that kept spreading inside him.

Harold's day off had proved fruitful. The landowners he'd visited had been welcoming, which meant he would be good to go come the various hunting seasons he enjoyed, and welcome to use the farm pond where he usually fished.

That strange woman and his trek to the police department were the last things on his mind when he pulled into the warehouse parking lot the next morning. He grabbed his cap and headed for the office. It was time to clock in and load up. The route he made every week rarely changed, and that was why he liked it.

Bill Riley had been an undercover cop for

six years. He was a small, wiry man with deep-set eyes and ordinary features. He'd come straight out of the academy with a sterling record and an uncanny ability to blend in that had not gone unnoticed by the St. Louis Police Department.

This morning was the beginning of a new assignment but, in an unusual twist, one pertaining to an old case. He was too young to remember the Hunter murders, but as of this morning he'd been fully briefed. Compared to some of his assignments, this was a simple task. Follow a suspect named Harold Mackey. Map out his work route and get a handle on his after-hours routine. And don't get made.

Satisfied that he was good to go, he pulled the wig he was wearing down a little tighter on his head and scratched at a spot on his chin through the days-old growth of whiskers he maintained. He had an assortment of caps and wigs that he would change during the day, in case he felt Mackey was getting antsy.

He'd taken an abandoned vehicle from police impound — an ordinary white van. He'd put a temporary logo on it mimicking the one of Case Uniform Services, a well-known business in the city. It wouldn't take long to get Mackey's route down. As for tailing him at night if he was on the move, Riley had other transportation choices in mind.

Harold was loaded up and on his route before 7:00 a.m., eating his usual breakfast as he drove. He had a fondness for McDonald's breakfasts and chose a different one each morning. Today was Monday, which meant two sausage-and-egg biscuits plus a large to-go coffee — black.

His first stop was at a supermarket. He pulled into the alley behind the store and honked once. Within a few moments the back door opened and a couple of the employees emerged. He grabbed his clipboard as he exited the truck and rolled up the back door. Thirty minutes later he was on to the next stop.

As he pulled up at a four-way stop, he glanced in the side-view mirror to check the traffic behind him. It had become habit after being rear-ended years earlier. He saw a sports car and a Case Uniform van — nothing out of place, nothing out of the ordinary — then drove through the intersection.

When he began to get hungry around noon, he got the mini-cooler with the lunch he'd packed from home, so he could eat as he drove. He was allowed a lunch break, but he liked to get through with the route on his own time. He unwrapped his sandwich and took a big bite, making a mental note to leave off the pickles next time he had corned beef. The bread was a little soggy.

He caught a red light at the next intersection, which gave him time to get a can of pop from the cooler and take a quick drink. As he waited, another Case Uniform van drove through the intersection in front of him. He eyed it absently, thinking to himself that there was a business he should have gotten into years ago. It was the second one he'd seen this morning, which proved people were always getting dirty. The light turned green, and he drove on through, eating as he went.

Riley knew Mackey had seen him at least twice, although he'd spent the entire morning on his tail. It was time to change up. While Mackey was making a restaurant delivery, Riley parked the van in an alley and called the P.D. to tow it in. It was time for plan B.

It was nearing 4:00 p.m., and Harold was two stops away from being done for the day. He was thinking about picking up some barbecued ribs and fries for dinner when he pulled into the parking lot of Tom's Quick Stop. A young guy on a big motorcycle wheeled into the parking lot and pulled up to the gas pumps as Harold opened up the back of the truck. He eyed the bike, then the rider, and thought it was a hell of a way to travel. The rider would be exposed to the elements and vulnerable to all kinds of vehicles, especially the big rigs and delivery trucks like the one he drove. And with only that small storage compartment on the back, you couldn't carry much of anything, either.

He dismissed the ride as useless, climbed up in the truck and began loading up the items to be delivered.

But the rider had not dismissed him.

Riley gassed up the bike, then drove off behind the station long enough to switch jackets, change his silver helmet for a black one he pulled from the bike's storage compartment and put a stick-on emblem of skulls and crossbones on both sides of the bike to change it up. He sent himself an email marking the address on the route, just as he'd done at every stop Mackey made, and waited for the truck to pull out. When it left, Riley waited a few moments, then rolled into traffic a few cars behind and continued to follow.

At the end of the day, Mackey went home with his ribs and fries, and a cop on his tail.

Holly had gone to ground. She'd holed up in her room all day, refusing maid service and ordering room service. She'd tried to call Maria but instead got a nurse who said she was out of her room for tests. She tried to call Savannah, but the calls kept going to voice mail. She wanted to call Bud, but she didn't know how to say what was in her heart. She needed to be looking at his face when those words came out of her mouth, and that wasn't going to happen just yet. She wanted to know what was happening with the police but guessed it was too early for revelations. Her only solace came from rereading her journal. It was like hearing Andrew talk, and she missed him so much.

When you were ten, you began following Hannah around the kitchen like a little shadow, abandoning the games you'd been playing with your sisters for the chance to get to measure or stir, or your favorite task — cracking eggs for her baking. Hannah began calling you her right arm. You quickly became adept at anything to do with cooking. On your eleventh birthday you baked your own cake. It was quite a sight. Instead of the sheet pan that Hannah suggested you use, you insisted on making a layer cake. You got the layers out in one piece and the icing in between them, but one side leaned a considerable amount to the south. You didn't care. You'd accomplished what you meant to do.

That's one of the things I've always admired about you, honey. There's no bullshit with you. You're not only straightforward, but you're tenacious. You don't know the meaning of quit. That's not something I taught you. You came that way. I suspect you have a good deal of your mother in you. She was just as determined to do the right thing, even though it meant putting herself in danger. Remember always that she thought of you and your safety first.

This gave Holly the boost of confidence she needed. She flipped through a few pages more, searching for the story about Bud going after a boy who'd tried to force her to have sex. She remembered it vividly, but she'd never known Bud's side of it until she'd read the journal. Now that Bud had revealed his feelings for her, she wanted to read it again.

Remember the year you turned sixteen, and that date you had with Tommy Wolford? You hadn't wanted much to do with boys. I think part of it was because you began looking like a woman long before you became one, and the boys — of all ages — began treating you differently. Hannah took you shopping for a bra before you were ten. Between the teasing you endured and the older boys all wanting to date you, you'd had enough of silly boys even before you were twelve. By the time you turned sixteen you were a fine figure of a woman, and you were slowly learning how to cope with unwanted attention.

The Fourth of July rolled around. Missoula was having their annual parade and fireworks display, and Tommy asked you on a date. I think you'd had a crush on him for a while, because your excitement when he asked was pretty high. Your sisters spent hours helping you pick out what you were going to wear and doing your hair — the whole girly thing. When he came to pick you up, you were pink-cheeked and as happy as I'd ever seen you. You waved goodbye at all of us and climbed in his pickup truck as if it were a stretch limo.

I had no reason to worry. We knew the Wolfords well, and you and Tommy were in the same class. It should have been a fun time for you. But it turned out to be something of a nightmare.

Our phone rang just after dark. I answered. You were crying, and all you kept saying was "Come get me, come get me." After you calmed down enough to tell us where you were, I got in the car and took off to Missoula, leaving Bud in the house with your sisters. It was, without a doubt, the longest drive I ever made.

When I drove up to the gas station at the edge of town and saw you through the window, I know I breathed a little easier. At least you were still in one piece and standing. You saw me pull up and came running out. Your hair was in tangles. Your pretty new sundress had a tear on the shoulder, and your lower lip had been bleeding.

You threw your arms around me and just hugged me. I felt your desperation but was too tongue-tied to ask what I was thinking. I got you in the car, then began looking around for Tommy, but he was nowhere to be found. I remember when I asked you where he was, all you would say was that you'd told him to leave you alone and never talk to you again.

I wanted to pursue the issue, and fully intended to the next day by paying a visit to their ranch and confronting the boy myself. But Bud beat me to it. When we walked in the house, he took one look at the shock on your face and the tear on your dress, and froze. When he saw your bloody lip, he pretty much lost it.

He looked straight at you and asked what the hell had happened. You spoke out, still in shock and embarrassment, and said that it was over. To let it be.

Bud, being Bud, asked what I'd been afraid to ask. "Did he rape you?"

Your face got red, but you said no. I breathed a sigh of huge relief. I wanted the boy's head on a platter, but I wasn't ready to castrate him. I think Bud was of a different mind. When he asked you why your lip was bleeding, you told him that he got mad when you told him no. That was when Bud started getting hot. "He hit you? Tell me he did not hit you!" he yelled, and you said, "Not with his fist." That got my dander up, just thinking about some stupid boy putting his hands on my girl and scaring her so bad, but I was supposed to be the adult. Bud wasn't operating under the same restraints.

If you'll remember, Maria and Savannah came in then, and the three of you took off to your room. I got on the phone to call Tommy's dad and read him the riot act about what his son had done to my baby girl, and when I turned around, Bud was gone. I heard his truck start up and went to the window in time to see his taillights disappearing up the drive.

You came in later to tell me you were sorry. You seemed afraid, as if I might blame you for what had happened. When I told you not to apologize, that you were the one who was wronged, you hugged me and then went to bed. Later, I found all three of you piled up on one bed, with you in the middle. One thing was always certain in this family, when things got tough, you three banded together.

What you never knew was that Bud found Tommy Wolford in town, popped him in the mouth, then dragged his sorry ass into his truck and drove him back home to his family. Course they already knew what he'd done, but Bud punctuated my story with a threat of his own. He told Mr. Wolford that if Tommy wasn't over at the Triple S in the morning with a personal apology, he was going to beat the hell out of him, regardless of the difference in their weight and ages, and whether his daddy liked it or not.

That's why Tommy and his daddy were on our porch bright and early the next morning. Not so much because he was ashamed of his actions, but because he was scared of what Bud was going to do to him. I tell you this now so that you'll know, if you're ever going through something bad that you can't handle, call Bud. He'll always have your back.

Holly closed the journal, then clasped it against her breasts and rolled over on her side. Even then, he'd been her hero.

NINE

Bud was in a mood he couldn't shake. It was just after 10:00 p.m., and Holly still hadn't called. He couldn't sit still, and had been pacing between the living room and the kitchen, refilling his coffee cup, then letting it sit and go cold. He couldn't concentrate on the television — it might as well have been in a foreign language. He couldn't think about anything but what he'd said to Holly. When the phone suddenly rang, he grabbed it before the second ring, hoping it was her.

"Hello."

"Hey, Bud, it's me."

Bud's hopes sank, but he tried to hide it. "Judd! You're there, I take it. I'll bet Savannah was glad to see you. How's she doing?"

"We've got problems," Judd said.

Bud tensed. "What happened?"

"I'll preface this by saying she's okay now, but to make a long ugly story short, there

179

was an attempt on her life today. Someone rigged the accelerator in her car and then, while it was out of control, forced her onto the MacArthur Causeway, which is basically a long-ass bridge over a whole lot of water. She hit the bridge, then went over the railing into the bay."

Bud's knees buckled. Grabbing the nearest chair, he sat down. It had happened to Savannah, too! What had Andrew been thinking when he gave them all that information without a solution to the problem?

"Shit! How bad was she hurt?"

It took all of Judd's control to say the words without crying.

"She hit the steering wheel with her chest. She has a concussion, some cuts, and some of the worst bruises I've ever seen in my life. But the miracle is that she managed to get herself out of the car after it sank. She wasn't breathing when she was rescued by the harbor patrol, but she seems to be okay now. They're keeping her in the hospital for a couple of days to make sure she doesn't suffer any aftereffects to her lungs."

Bud felt sick. "I shouldn't have let them go. I thought it was a bad idea from the start. I don't know what the hell Andrew was thinking when he told them all that."

"I'm beginning to agree," Judd said.

"Anyway, I'll keep you updated on her progress and where we go once she's released. However, I have one piece of advice for you. If you're as much in love with Holly as I think you are, pack your damn bags and go get her while she's still in one piece."

Bud was so shocked that for a moment he couldn't think. Finally he had to ask, "How did you . . . I didn't think anyone . . . Damn it! Does everyone know?"

"No. At least, I don't think so. I just recognized the signs. I've felt the same way about Savannah for as long as I can remember. And as soon as those damn papers she's been talking about are filed, I'm bringing her home."

Bud's hands were shaking. "Yeah, okay . . . thanks for calling."

"Listen, I've got to go. I don't want to leave Savannah alone for too long."

The dial tone was all the punctuation Bud needed. He didn't have a lot of time to prepare, but this was the last straw. He grabbed the Missoula phone book, found his uncle Delbert's number and punched in the number. It rang four times before the call was answered, but the old man's familiar voice was music to his ears.

"Who's callin'?"

"Hey, Uncle Delbert, it's me, Bud."

181

Delbert Walker's wife had been a sister to Robert Tate's unmarried mother, and both women had died young, leaving young Robert to bounce from one family to another until he was grown.

"How you doin', boy? Takin' good care of yourself?" Delbert asked.

Bud smiled. He was thirty-nine, and his uncle still called him "boy."

"I'm fine, Uncle Delbert, but I have a favor to ask."

"Sure, if I can. What do you need?"

"I need a temporary foreman. All three of Andrew's daughters are gone, and one of them, Holly, is in serious need of my help. I need to fly to St. Louis. Not sure how long I'll be gone."

Delbert resisted the urge to show his delight, considering the serious reason he'd been asked to help out. It had been a while since someone really needed him, and moving to a retirement home hadn't been a choice but a necessity.

"I'm sorry to hear Holly's got problems, but I sure don't mind coming out to the Triple S. I reckon I can handle whatever needs to be done until you get back."

"Basically it's just a matter of issuing orders, Uncle Delbert. The ranch hands are a good, hardworking group, but I'd feel a lot better if there was someone with your experience calling the shots."

"Truthfully, it'll be good to get back on the land," Delbert said. "Moving into Missoula after I sold the ranch was probably good for me, but I sure do miss the outdoors. When do you need me?"

"I'll get the men started in the morning and let them know you're coming, but if you could be here by noon, I would appreciate it. I'll leave a house key for you on the kitchen counter, and the back door will be unlocked. There's plenty of food. You'll have to dig around to find out where everything is, and you can sleep in my bedroom. It's the last room on the left, down the long hall."

"You can count on me," Delbert said.

"I thank you," Bud said.

"You're welcome, boy. You be careful and take good care of Holly."

"I will do that for sure," Bud said, and hung up, then headed for the office.

Within fifteen minutes he'd booked a 6:00 a.m. flight to St. Louis, getting him into the city before 2:00 p.m. He glanced at the clock. It was a hell of a time to wake someone up and with bad news, but he had to let Holly know about Savannah. He didn't know how high profile the wreck had become, but the last thing he wanted was for Holly to hear the news on TV or see some clip online. Maria was still in intensive care. For the time being, she didn't need to be bothered with anything more than concentrating on getting well.

He dialed Holly's number, then took a deep breath, willing himself to a calm he didn't feel.

Holly had fallen asleep on top of the covers, and when her cell phone began to ring, she sat up with a jerk, fumbling for the lamp. When she saw who was calling, her hands began to shake. It was all she could do to answer.

"Hello?"

"Honey . . . it's me, Bud. I'm sorry to be calling so late."

"It's okay, it's okay," she said. "I was hoping you would call."

Bud frowned. "I'm not sure you're going to think that when you find out why I called."

"What's wrong? Is it Maria? Did she take a turn for the worse?"

"No, it's not Maria. It's Savannah. I'm telling you first that she's okay, but someone tried to kill her today. They rigged her car, and she went over a bridge called the Mac-

Arthur Causeway into the Atlantic."

Holly moaned in disbelief. "Noooo. Oh, my God, Bud . . . Oh, my God."

"Judd said nothing is broken, but she has a concussion, some cuts and bruises. They're keeping her in the hospital for a couple of days."

"I'm scared."

"So am I — for you," Bud said. "I need you to do something for me."

Holly couldn't quit shaking. She wanted to pack up everything she owned and get on the first plane back to Montana.

"What?" she mumbled.

"Don't leave your room again until I get there."

Holly's heart leaped; then her eyes filled with tears. "You're coming here?"

"My plane leaves Missoula at six o'clock tomorrow morning. I'll be in St. Louis around 2:00 p.m. if there are no delays."

"Thank you, Bud, thank you so much."

"I don't need thanks."

Holly shivered. The gruff, raspy tone in his voice rattled her. Even as she asked the question, she knew what he was going to say.

"What *do* you need?"

"Just you, baby."

"That scares me, too," she whispered.

Bud pinched the bridge of his nose to quell a surge of panic. Was this where she told him that she didn't feel the same way he did? He had to make it right. He couldn't bear it if she suddenly became afraid or uneasy around him.

"It's okay. I shouldn't have ever said anything to —"

"No, you misunderstand me," Holly said softly. "I'm not scared of you. I've loved you for years."

Bud could have wept with relief. "Then it's all good," he said softly. "I just need you to stay safe until I can get to you. Can you promise to do that for me?"

"I didn't leave the room all day," Holly said. "I won't budge until you get here, I promise."

"Thank you, honey," he said. "It's going to be okay. We'll get through this thing you're dealing with, but we'll do it together, so you won't be in any danger, okay?"

"Okay."

"I love you, Holly."

The breath caught in Holly's throat. "I love you, too."

"Thank you, God," Bud said, and hung up.

Holly dropped the phone, then covered her face. First Maria, now Savannah. What had they gotten themselves into?

Bill Riley had gone from a van and a motor-cycle to a stakeout of Mackey's residence. He'd set up shop in an empty house across the street, with a telescope on a tripod, a hookup for his laptop, a large everything-pizza from Pizza Hut and a liter of Moun-tain Dew. Even if Mackey was the man they were looking for, Riley had a feeling the killer in him had hung up those shoes years ago. With no new bodies showing up and a man who didn't even have a speeding ticket to his name, whatever had triggered his kill-ing spree had either resolved itself or Mac-key was the slickest SOB he'd ever met when it came to covering his tracks.

He watched the lights going on and off in different parts of Mackey's house until they all went off for good a little before 11:00 p.m., then went back to his laptop to finish typing up the route Mackey had taken today. Once he'd completed his notes, he emailed them to Detective Carver, then moved from email to some police-friendly search engines and began looking up every-thing he could find on Harold Mackey. It wasn't part of his assignment, but Riley was an overachiever. And it helped pass the time.

Mackey knew the house across the street was empty. It had been for sale for months. So what the hell was that faint glow coming through the curtains? The possibility that someone had broken in and was vandalizing the place was the most logical answer, but Harold wasn't the kind of man to get himself involved. He stayed in his recliner, watched his usual shows and, when it was bedtime, went through the house turning off lights. Then he stood in the dark, staring out the window at that strangely stationary glimmer of light.

It bugged him. Harold liked routine, and this was out of place. Again he thought about calling the police, then changed his mind, took off his slippers and put on his sneakers, and went out the back door, took the alley behind his house all the way down to the end of the block, crossed the street under cover of a broken streetlight, then made his way up the back alley leading behind the empty house.

He stopped, listening as he would if he'd been in the woods, aware of the sounds of his neighborhood. There were no dogs, which was helpful. He heard a door slam a few houses down and guessed it was the new father carrying out another garbage bag full of dirty diapers. He heard sirens, but that meant nothing. Cities were full of sirens. He heard the sounds of televisions and could tell from the two nearest houses what shows they were watching. But there was no sound coming from the empty house.

Once he'd committed himself, there was no stopping. He walked into the backyard, the sounds of his footsteps muffled by the growth of new grass that had yet to be mowed. The night air was chilly, with a brisk breeze that blew his ponytail across his left shoulder, but he paid it no mind. His focus was on getting around to the side of the house without being detected. Between the shades on the windows and his years in the woods, he had no problem accomplishing the feat.

He reached the side of the house and the living room windows. The venetian blinds hadn't been pulled all the way down. When Harold peered in, he could see nearly everything.

He had expected to see someone, but he hadn't expected the telescope on a tripod, or the man kicked back in a folding chair with a laptop on his knees. The glow of the screen was even brighter from where he was standing, but he was too far away to see anything but a blur.

What surprised him was that the man didn't appear to be some homeless guy looking for a place to crash or a thief looking for something to steal. And there was that telescope. The son of a bitch had it aimed straight at his house.

The hair rose on the back of his neck as he backed away from the window and retraced his steps. By the time he got back to his house, he was shaking. What the hell did this mean? If it had been twenty years ago, he would have known, but now . . . ?

He locked the door behind him and walked through the house in the dark, his mind racing. He got into bed without turning on the lights, but he couldn't sleep. He needed to think.

What about his life was different now than it had been? Had he done anything different? He began thinking back over the past few days, trying to remember what, if anything, stood out. There was the phone call to his work, and then the young woman he'd tailed. What was her name? Oh, yeah, Holly Slade. He'd also followed her to the police department. He'd written that off as nothing concerning him, but it seemed now that he might have been wrong about that. The big freaking question was what the hell was going down?

Holly was sick with worry. She tried to call Savannah, but it went to voice mail over and over. Then she realized that Savannah's phone was most likely at the bottom of the ocean with the car she'd been driving. She had to trust that her sister would call when she could. Until then, she had to wait.

When daylight finally came, she was exhausted. She hadn't done more than doze. Her head was throbbing, and there was a knot in her stomach. They'd all been so happy before Andrew died, and now everything kept going from bad to worse.

She needed to get a grip on her emotions, but her thoughts just keep moving in the same hopeless loop. No matter how many times she tried to deny it, the truth was, she and her sisters were in serious danger because of their pasts.

When the maid knocked on the door asking to clean the room, Savannah let her in, then curled up in a chair to watch her work, thinking she used to do the very same tasks back at the ranch and take pleasure in a job well done. Within twenty minutes the sheets had been changed, the bathroom cleaned and the floor vacuumed.

"Is there anything else that you need?" the maid asked.

"No, thank you," Holly said.

Once she was alone again, there was little to do but watch TV and the clock, counting down the minutes until that knock on her door. It was almost eleven before she realized she hadn't eaten since last night. She ordered extra sandwiches and chips, knowing that Bud would most likely be hungry when he arrived, but when the meal came, she couldn't eat much for the knot in her stomach.

Finally she covered up the food, crawled up on the bed and, as always, reached for the journal. She was asleep before she read past the first page.

Bud had never been to St. Louis, but he recognized the Arch as the plane was circling to land. His anxiety was at an all-time high. All he could think about was seeing Holly's face, holding her in his arms, as he prayed that this nightmare would soon be over.

After he picked up his luggage he opted for a cab instead of a shuttle, wanting to get to the hotel as soon as possible, but they kept running into traffic snarls. It seemed as if the universe was plotting to keep them apart.

When he finally reached the hotel, he was a bundle of nerves. He grabbed his bag and strode into the hotel lobby, paused for a moment to orient himself, then headed for the elevators. He knew she was in Room 663. All he needed now was to get to the sixth floor.

He got on the elevator, unaware of the attention he was drawing as a tall, good-looking cowboy wearing a leather jacket, a Stetson and his best pair of Justin boots.

When he reached the sixth floor, he hefted his suitcase and once again paused just long enough to determine his direction, then headed down the hall. The closer he got to Holly's room, the longer his stride became.

Room 663 brought him to a halt. He knocked, knowing when this door opened it would mark the beginning of the rest of his life.

The rapid knocks were loud and sharp, waking Holly instantly. She leaped off the bed and ran toward the door, pausing only long enough to look through the security peephole, then swung the door inward.

"You're here!"

Bud slid his suitcase inside the room,

swung her up into his arms and kicked the door shut behind him.

"I have missed you so much," he said softly, and buried his face in the curve of her neck.

Holly couldn't quit smiling. Why had it taken them so long to get to this moment?

Bud fully intended to take this slow. But when he pulled back and looked down into her face, he was lost.

"Hey, honey," he said softly.

"Hey," Holly echoed, then pulled off his hat and tossed it onto the bed.

Bud grinned. He'd feared this moment might never come.

"My life is a serious mess," she said. "Now's your chance to take back everything you said. I won't hold it against you."

Bud shook his head as he cupped her face. "Never. For me, it's always been you . . . only you."

Holly shivered as Bud's lips lightly brushed the surface of her mouth. Then they centered, claiming ground with a gentle coaxing push.

She slid her arms around his neck, lost in the magic of that first kiss. She could smell the leather of his coat, feel the steady thump of his heartbeat, and she knew that spending the rest of her life with him would be the best thing she would ever do.

Bud was shaking. He wanted her in every way a man could want a woman, but that would come later. He broke the kiss with a muffled groan, then ran his thumb across the dampness of her lower lip.

"One kiss at a time, honey. One kiss at a time."

Holly felt as if she were flying. At that moment she could almost believe the hell that her life had turned into might turn out okay.

"I ordered some extra food a couple of hours ago. Are you hungry?" she asked.

He grinned as he took off his coat. "You've known me too long to ask that question. Are you hungry?"

"I am now," she said and, just like that, slipped into the mode that made her happiest: taking care of the people she loved.

She began uncovering the food, filling the glasses from the ice bucket, then adding Pepsi. It was his favorite. By the time Bud came out of the bathroom, the food was waiting.

"Oh, man," he said, eyeing the small feast. He kissed her quick and hard before picking up half a sandwich and settling into a chair. "That's for always being you."

Holly blushed, but she was smiling. She took the other half of the sandwich, crawled up onto the bed and began to eat.

The room was quiet for a couple of minutes as they ate, but it wasn't long before Bud began talking.

"What's the status on your situation?"

She shrugged as she tossed away the remnants of her food. "I'm assuming the newly-opened case is progressing. I haven't been out of this room in two days. However, I don't expect them to keep me updated. Unless I have more information for them, they don't really need me."

"The more you stay out of the public eye, the better off you'll be," Bud said, and then popped a chip in his mouth.

Holly nodded, then looked away.

Bud frowned. "I've seen that look on your face far too many times not to know what it means."

"What look?" Holly asked.

"The one that tells me you're keeping secrets."

She sighed. How did he always know this stuff?

"Holly?"

"I might have failed to mention one thing to the police."

"Like what?" Bud asked.

"Like the fact that before I talked to them, I went by the place where my father . . .

where Mackey works."

Bud nearly choked on his food. "What the hell did you do that for? Did he see you?"

Holly frowned. "What do you think? I wanted to see him, and no, he didn't see me. I wanted to know if I'd recognize him. I was hoping that if I saw him it would trigger more memories for me."

Bud laid down the sandwich. " 'More' as in you have other memories?"

"Some."

He frowned. "Like what?"

"Without going into the gory details, I'm pretty sure that, as a child, I stumbled onto my father's trophy stash."

Bud's frown deepened. "Trophy stash? What kind of trophy stash?"

"I've been having a lot of dreams since I read the journal. The other night I was dreaming that I heard hammering. In the dream, the sounds led me to a small room off the basement. He was inside, at a worktable. There was stuff hanging on the walls."

"What kind of stuff?" Bud asked.

"I think it was the scalps he'd been taking."

Bud felt sick. "Is that all you remembered?"

"No. There was something else. He told me if I told anyone what I'd seen, he would make me sorry. He said I would never see my mother again."

Ten

Bud shuddered. There were so many emotions going through him right then that he had to struggle to find words. What he did know was how strong she must have been, keeping twenty years of ugly, evil secrets. He set his food aside, and pulled her off the bed and into his arms.

"Not that I'm complaining, but what's this for?" Holly asked.

"I'm giving that scared little girl the hugs she needed and didn't get."

Tears welled. Her heart was so full, but she refused to cry. She laid her head against his chest, savoring the strength of his embrace and the steady heartbeat against her ear. Bud had always been her anchor. That he loved her like this was a gift she hadn't expected. She wanted to be with him — to know this man in a way only his woman could know him.

She stepped back. "Maria has always said

she was holding out for her hero. In the middle of all this mess, she seems to have found him. Judd loves Savannah beyond reason, and she knows it, but she's always kept him at arm's length. Maybe what's happening to her will change the way she feels. And then there's me. The oddest thing about all this is that the older I got, the more I cared for you. I think this took so long to happen because you were already there, just waiting for me to wake up. So, Robert Tate, you've kissed me and hugged me, but there's something missing, and we both know what it is."

Bud's heart began to hammer against his chest.

"There's no need to rush this, honey. You've got a hell of a mess on your hands. I don't want you to feel pressured to take this further until you're ready. It's enough for me that I can finally claim you. You are my heart. You're the reason I draw breath. If you hurt, I bleed. Understand?"

"I understand," Holly said. "But if there's one thing this situation my sisters and I are in has taught me, it's that waiting for the perfect moment can be a mistake. Maria nearly got killed waiting for her hero. What if Savannah had died before she and Judd could make a life together? You're here. I'm here. I don't want candlelight and roses. I want you."

The curtains were already drawn. Bud kicked off his boots, then turned around and, one by one, turned off the lamps, leaving the room bathed in dusky shadows.

Instead of panic or uneasiness, peace settled within Holly so quickly that she knew this was right. Without a hint of embarrassment, she started to pull off her sweatshirt, but Bud stopped her with a touch.

"Let me."

He feathered a kiss across her lips, then slid his hands beneath the edges of her waistband and onto her skin.

Holly shivered as she braced herself, holding on to his shoulders as he pulled her sweatpants and panties down in one swoop. She stepped sideways, leaving them where they'd fallen, and reached for Bud's shirt. The snaps popped as they opened one by one. She put the palms of her hands against his belly and pushed them upward. Then she looked down at his hand. The rawness of the healing cut was evident, and yet he never complained.

Bud shucked the shirt within seconds, leaving himself bare-chested and aching for what came next.

Holly reached for his belt buckle, running a forefinger between his belly and the denim of his jeans, but Bud wasn't a man for games. He came out of the jeans almost as fast as he'd taken off the shirt, leaving him naked to the world with an erection that made Holly weak at the knees.

Seconds later he had her sweatshirt over her head and tossed her bra over the back of the chair.

"Ah . . . so beautiful," he whispered, and cupped her breasts, then rolled the nipples between his fingers just hard enough to awaken a surge of longing deep within Holly's core.

She groaned from the urgency of the lust that swept through her.

When he pulled her hard against him, his erection slid right between her thighs.

A perfect fit, Holly thought.

He sat her back on the bed, then took a step forward, cupping her hips. Holly locked her legs around his waist, her eyes closing in ecstasy as he slowly slid inside her. For a few seconds he stayed motionless, wanting to remember every nuance of this moment, every facet of her expression.

His woman. Before he was through, she would have no doubt of that fact. She would be loved without boundaries, sated sexually to the point of exhaustion.

"Look at me, Holly."

She opened her eyes, saw her reflection on the dark surface of his pupils, and then inhaled swiftly when he started to move, rocking steadily within her in long, steady strokes. His penis was thick and hard, delving deep into the heat of her womb, taking her higher, getting her hotter and hotter.

A minute passed, then another, and when a third had come and gone, Bud felt like he was going to explode. The muscles in his legs were starting to burn, and the ache in his belly was next to unbearable. He needed to climax. He wanted to let go so bad that he hurt.

Then salvation came. He felt the tiny quivers of her body beginning to contract around him, and he knew. Gritting his teeth, he slid his hands beneath her hips, pulling her hard against his pelvis as he increased the power of his thrusts.

Lust had coiled itself so tightly in Holly's belly that when Bud slammed into her, moving harder and faster, there was nothing left for lust to do but explode. And she did, her body bucking uncontrollably as the climax burst within her.

As he came, Bud grabbed her hips to keep from falling, spilling his seed into her with a deep, guttural groan. When there was nothing left of him, he collapsed on top of her, then crawled onto the bed and took her into his arms.

"Oh, my God," Holly whispered, as she buried her face against his chest.

"Who loves you?"

"You do," Holly said.

He tightened his grip. "Who do you belong to?"

"You."

"Yes, me," Bud said. "And I belong to you and no other. I will cherish you, and honor you and our children, for the rest of our lives, and nothing — and no man — can change that. Understand?"

Holly sighed. She knew he was talking about the taint of being her father's daughter.

"Yes."

"Then close your eyes, sweet baby, and rest. No one's ever going to hurt you again."

He pulled the covers over them as Holly closed her eyes. She'd awakened this morning as alone in the world as she'd ever been, but from this moment on, she had the love of a good man at her back. A woman couldn't ask for more.

The task force was still sorting through the

evidence. More and more facts were added to the murder board with each passing hour. At the end of the second day, they'd accumulated quite a spread of information, and yet not one thing they had could physically connect Harold Mackey to any of the victims.

Whit Carver had received Riley's notes on Mackey's route, but with only two days' worth of info from twenty years after the murders, there wasn't anything there to latch on to, either. His current route didn't coincide with any of the victims' places of employment, and it was going to take time to find out what route he'd driven all those years ago — if that were even possible. They were at a loss. Carver had even let himself toy with the fact that Holly Slade's mother could have been wrong. He didn't want to think that he'd jumped the gun by assuming her accusation was true. But the possibility existed that her mother — and she — had been mistaken. Still, his instincts told him that wasn't the case. He felt certain Mackey was their man. He just needed to prove it.

As was his habit, Harold did his job without fraternizing with the other drivers, clocked in and out with his usual gruff demeanor, and picked up his dinner on the way home that night.

But when he settled down in front of the television, instead of watching the screen, he was watching the house across the street, looking for that faint glow of light between the parted curtains. To his relief, he saw nothing. He began to consider the possibility that the man might not have been watching him after all. He knew for a fact that the kid three doors down was selling dope to his friends. The steady stream of cars full of teenagers coming and going from that house weren't because of some party. Maybe the guy was a vice cop and had been watching that house, not his. Just because the telescope had been aimed at his house, that didn't mean it had started or stayed that way.

He was relieved enough that by ten o'clock, when he should have been thinking about going to bed, he got up and got himself a beer from the kitchen instead. He popped the top on his way back into the living room and took his first sip just after he'd settled into his chair.

He felt the burp coming up his throat at the same time he saw the light, and he frowned. Okay. So someone was still over there watching, but Harold was no longer convinced he was the target. He downed the beer as he watched the late-night news and weather, mentally cursing the fact that if the weatherman was right, he would be making deliveries in the rain tomorrow. When 11:00 p.m. rolled around, he got up and began going through the house, turning off the lights. If the guy across the street was watching him, he wasn't giving him anything to see.

After a few moments he walked back through the house into the kitchen, then out the back door and, just like the night before, up the block through the alley, crossing the street under the broken streetlight, then back to that house through the alley on the opposite side of the street.

Again he paused at the back of the yard, then glanced up at the sky. It was overcast from the impending front moving into the area, which he took as an omen that he was being protected from being seen. Tonight the air was cool but still. This time he noticed a motorcycle parked in the shadows against the house. Wanting a closer look, he crossed the lawn without issue, then checked out the bike. Something about it seemed familiar. He flashed on the biker he'd seen at one of his delivery stops yesterday, then grunted. Except for the decals.

He checked closer and realized they were peel-off decals. It was the same fucking bike.

Son of a bitch! How long had the cops — because who else could it be? — been tailing him?

He flattened himself against the side of the house and moved silently toward the living room windows.

When he looked in, he saw the same man as last night, this time standing at the telescope. Harold's eyes narrowed. The man was wearing a shoulder holster, and the telescope wasn't aimed at the teenager's house. It was aimed straight at his.

The laptop was on the floor beside the same folding chair. The screen was bright enough that, even at this distance, he could see the image on the screen was of a newspaper. Harold wasn't a techie, but he wasn't that behind the times, either. He knew lots of people read newspapers online. Then his gaze caught a word in the headline, and he shifted his position enough that he could see it more clearly.

Even at this distance he could read the words THE HUNTER STRIKES in bold black caps. He stepped back in shock.

That wasn't news. That was history.

He swiped a hand across his face, then looked again. The man was no longer at the window — he was no longer in the room at all. Afraid he'd been made, Harold bolted from the yard and didn't stop until he was in the alley, behind the cover of a hedge. He looked back to see if the man was in pursuit, but the back door didn't open. No one was coming around from the front of the house with a flashlight and a gun. Troubled by what he'd seen, he retraced his steps back to his own place. Even though he was safe inside, he felt the walls of his house drawing in on him. Not once in the years he'd been active had anything this dire occurred. So what the hell could they have found twenty years later that would prompt them to consider him a target?

There was only one person who'd known anything that could tie him to the killings: Harriet. But he had no idea where she was, or if she were even still alive.

Holly Slade was the one unknown, but he hadn't recognized her. She didn't look like what he thought Harriet would have grown up to be. She sure didn't look anything like him — and she hadn't looked like Twila, either. Still, a woman had called the company office, talking about a package that had never appeared. And that same evening he'd seen the woman who turned out to be Holly Slade come out of the gas station, then walk a block and a half up the hill to a parked car, as if she hadn't wanted anyone to connect her to where she'd been. And it was that same woman he'd followed to the police station — and now he was the subject of a stakeout.

It was all a fucking mystery, but there was one thing that wasn't a mystery to him. He had to make sure that if the cops did come into his house with a search warrant, the only things they would find would be his clutter and dust. He felt his way through the house without turning on the lights, and then into the spare bedroom, where he began moving boxes. He knew the way so well that he navigated it in the dark without turning on the cellar lights until he'd closed off the stairs from above.

He wanted one last tour around the room, and then he would seal it off for good. It was the only sensible thing to do. As was his habit, he went from plaque to plaque, touching the hair, reading the engraved nameplates, noting names and dates as if this were a display in a hall of fame. He took pride in the fact that he'd ended what he viewed as weakness in the gene pool. These women would not be bearing more children that would continue to diminish humanity. His heart raced faster as he moved from wall to wall, getting high on the memories, until by the time he reached the last trophy, he threw back his head and jacked off in front of the name. She'd ended his streak, but he'd ended her disease-ridden life. He considered it a fair trade.

Calmed by the sexual release, he wiped himself clean, then dug through his workbench for a hammer, some finishing nails and a large bottle of wood glue. With a rueful glance, he turned his back on his past, turned out the light, then climbed up the stairs. Once inside the bedroom, he ran a huge line of wood glue all along the three edges of the opening where the cellar door came to rest, then closed the door on the glue. He walked the edges repeatedly, utilizing his two hundred and sixty-five pounds to set the seal. Then he got the hammer and the thin nails and began driving them into the seam along the crack, taking care to counter-sink the nails into the wood.

When he was finished, he unscrewed the handle from the door, then went back into the kitchen to his junk drawer. He pulled out his flashlight, turned it on long enough to find a small pencil-shaped stick of wood putty and headed back into the bedroom.

Once again he closed the door behind him, making sure that the window shades

211

were down before he turned on the flashlight, and got down on his hands and knees. Spotlighting his work, he began rubbing putty over the heads of the tiny nails to hide their presence. Then he moved to the place where he'd removed the handle and rubbed putty into the holes where the screws had been. It would all be dry by morning, and he would come in and inspect it in full daylight, touch up what needed to be fixed and then drag the boxes back over the opening. The only way that bomb shelter would ever come to light again was if the house burned down around it. Once he finished, he stepped back to examine his work. The tongue and groove flooring looked seamless.

He stripped off his clothes and got back in the shower, even though he'd showered before. It was after 1:00 a.m. by the time he got in bed, but it didn't matter. He already had a plan, and the longer he thought about it, the more excited he became. It had been a long time since he'd been on this kind of a hunt.

Bud woke up with Holly in his arms. Even before he looked down at her tousled head and the thick dark lashes shading her cheeks, he smiled. He'd dreamed of this moment since her eighteenth birthday. His feelings had startled him to the point that he'd pulled himself away from the family unit for the better part of that year until he'd come to terms with his own emotions. After that, he'd taken great care never to overstep the bounds of friendship. But here they were, and he didn't know if he would be able to wipe the smile off his face.

Holly shifted slowly, waking, as Bud had, to the fact that she was not alone in her bed. She remembered last night before she opened her eyes, which explained the smile on her face when she looked up and saw him watching her.

"Hi."

Bud laughed. "That's my girl . . . ever the master of understatement. Hi yourself. Are you okay?"

"I feel good, if that's what you're getting at. In fact, I feel amazing — able to leap tall buildings and stuff."

Bud's laughter rolled through her in waves, filling her with such joy that she had to look away to keep from crying.

" 'Scuse me, I have pressing business elsewhere," she said, and got out of bed and headed for the bathroom.

Bud propped himself up on one elbow to watch the curvy shape of her bare backside as she crossed the room.

"Lord have mercy," he muttered, then turned on the television to catch the morning news as he got out of bed and pulled on his jeans. By the time she came out wrapped in a bath towel, he'd found his shaving kit.

He tugged at the corner of the towel, as if he were going to unwrap her like a piece of candy, and grinned when her cheeks turned pink.

"Just teasing, honey. However, you do look good enough to eat. And speaking of food, as soon as I get shaved, I'll take you to breakfast, how's that?"

"Fabulous," Holly said, and then, just to watch him freak, dropped her towel before she went to get clean clothes.

"Oh. You did not just do that," Bud growled, and yanked her off her feet, then tumbled back onto the bed with her in his arms.

Holly was laughing so hard she couldn't talk as he planted kisses all over her face and neck, then rubbed his stiff, scratchy beard over the tips of her nipples, before moving down her belly with his kisses.

But when he parted her legs and slid a finger into her depths, he wiped the laugh right off her face. He found the nub of her clit with his thumb, and before she could

214

take her next breath, he took her to a place she'd never been. The climax that hit her came so hard and so fast that she screamed. Bud rocked back on his heels, satisfied that he'd started her day off in a proper fashion, and considered it a smart move that he'd turned on the television earlier. That had been one hell of a scream, but then again, he reminded himself, she was one hell of a woman.

It was almost ten-thirty before Harold spotted the tail. It was the same man he'd seen in the empty house. He recognized him by his small stature and the same bike that had been parked behind it.

"You're not as good at your job as you think," Harold muttered, and turned right at the intersection, on his way to his next stop. He had plans for the little bastard that he wasn't going to like.

Whit Carver was on his way back into headquarters when his cell phone rang. He answered it absently, then focused quickly when Holly Slade identified herself.

"Good morning, Miss Slade. How are you doing?"

"I'm okay," Holly said. "If you're free this morning, I have to talk to you."

Whit glanced at his watch. "Yeah, sure, where are you now?"

"About five minutes away."

"I'll meet you down at the entrance. That way you won't have to wait for an escort up."

"Thank you. See you soon," Holly said.

"So it's a go?" Bud asked, as Holly braked for a red light.

She nodded. "We're almost there. I want you to meet Detective Carver, and I promise I'll be up front with him about seeing my . . . about seeing Mackey before I went to the police."

Bud had been adamant and wasn't settling for anything less. They couldn't afford slipups with this much at stake.

A few minutes later they were walking up the sidewalk toward the police station. Bud saw a middle-aged man with a full head of gray hair exit the building, then stop.

"Is that him?" Bud asked.

Holly looked up. "Yes," she said, then started smiling as she reached the door. "Detective Carver, this is my . . . uh, this is my —"

Bud grinned and extended his hand. "Robert Tate, but I go by Bud. The relationship part is new, and she doesn't yet know what to do with me."

Carver laughed. He liked the big cowboy on sight, and the humor only added to the man's charm. "Detective Carver, and you can call me Whit. Follow me. We'll talk in the office."

A few minutes later Whit had them settled at his desk, offered them coffee, which they politely refused, then sat down, kicked back in his chair and eyed Holly closely.

"So, what do you want to talk to me about, Miss Slade?"

"Call me Holly, please, and I've come to give you a little bit more information, as well as confess to something."

Whit frowned. "The info is good. Confessions at a police station rarely are, so how about we get the bad over with first, okay?"

"You remember when you told me to stay away from the warehouse where Harold Mackey works?"

Whit sat up with a jerk. "Tell me you did not go there."

"Not after you told me not to. The thing is . . . I'd already done it before I saw you. He didn't know it. I just wanted to look at him. I couldn't remember what he even looked like. I thought maybe if I saw him, I might remember something important — something that might help your case against him."

There wasn't anything to be done about it now. "You're sure there's no way he would recognize you, no reason why he'd be suspicious of you in any way?"

"I doubt he'd recognize me if we passed on the street. I didn't recognize him at first. I just waited until he went back to the warehouse."

Whit frowned. "So how did you find out where he worked and when he would be getting off work?"

"There was a woman named Lynn Gravitt who worked with my mother. I talked to her. She's the one who told me about Harold Mackey still being in St. Louis, and where he worked."

"She knew his work schedule?" Whit asked.

Holly hesitated.

Bud frowned. There it was again, that expression that made him nervous. What else didn't he know about what she'd done?

"Dang it, Holly, this isn't the time for secrets, remember?"

"I might have called the warehouse and asked what time he got off work."

Bud groaned.

Whit Carver's frown deepened.

"And you didn't think that would make him suspicious?" he asked.

218

"I pretended to be a courier with a package that needed to be signed for."

Bud groaned again.

"I'm assuming you never showed up with anything to be signed for, right?" Whit asked.

"Right," Holly said.

"So a man with secrets to hide finds out about a phone call from a courier asking about his work hours, then never gets the promised delivery. What do you think he's going to do?"

Holly suddenly felt faint. She looked at Bud for help, but he wasn't talking.

"I didn't think," she whispered. "I just needed to see him."

Bud put his arm around her for moral support, while wondering how fast he could get them on the first plane back to Montana.

Carver was already playing catch-up in his head. "I need to let my undercover guy know that Mackey might be watching for something to happen. Are there any other surprises you have for me?"

Holly was near tears. "I'm sorry."

Bud gave her a quick hug. "Tell him about the dreams you've been having."

Whit reached for his notepad.

"I'm pretty sure that when I was little, I actually saw him with his stash of trophies from the murders. I think that's why my mother got me away from St. Louis so fast."

"Stash of trophies? Are you talking about —"

"The scalps."

Whit looked up. "You saw those?"

"What I saw were a whole lot of wooden plaques with pieces of hair on them that were hanging on a wall in a little room off our basement. There were little gold nameplates underneath each hunk of hair, like the way his trophies that hung on the walls in the den were mounted."

"Holy shit," Whit mumbled. "Hell of a thing for a kid to see."

"I don't think I knew what I was seeing back then. But in dreaming about all this now, I realize what they must have been. It explains how freaked out he got when he saw me, too. He grabbed me and slammed me up against the wall, told me not to tell what I'd seen or I'd be sorry. He said if I told anyone, I'd never see my mother again."

Whit's gut knotted. Yet another bit of info to add to Holly Slade's theory that Mackey had killed her mother.

"And that's all," Holly added.

Whit sighed. "That's enough."

ELEVEN

The moment Holly and Bud were gone, Whit got on the phone. He was pulling Riley off the case ASAP. If Mackey was already suspicious, there was a good chance he might spot a tail, which could jeopardize the case even more. They didn't need Mackey to disappear before they got a chance to make an arrest. Just when he thought his call was going to voice mail, he heard Riley's voice.

"Yeah, this is Riley. What's up?"

"This is Carver. What are you doing?"

"Watching Mackey disappear," he said, as the delivery truck disappeared over a hill.

"Let him go," Whit said.

Riley frowned. "Okay, but why?"

"We have reason to suspect Mackey knows something's up. It's a long story, but suffice it to say, you're done."

Riley shrugged. "Except for mapping the rest of his route, I was done anyway. You could set your watch by this guy. He's in bed by eleven every night."

"I assume you didn't leave anything at the surveillance site?"

"A folding chair."

"Consider it a donation to the real estate agent. Don't go back to the neighborhood for anything."

"Then consider me gone," Riley said, and disconnected.

Holly was noticeably silent as she and Bud got back in her car. Even after they'd buckled in, she sat quietly, without turning the key in the ignition.

"Do you think I've messed up the entire investigation?"

Bud reached for her hand. "No, baby. I'm sure it's okay."

She nodded, but still didn't start the car.

"There's not more, is there?" he asked.

"No, no, of course not."

"Then what is it?"

"I feel like something bad is going to happen," she said.

Even though he wasn't completely sold on his answer, Bud gave her hand a quick squeeze and said, "It's understandable why you would feel that way, but I think we're okay. You know what he looks like, right?"

She nodded. "A great big man with a long gray ponytail."

"So have you seen him following us any-where?"

"No, and I have been looking."

"I guessed as much. Andrew didn't raise any fools. Although you did call the ware-house about him, there's no way to pin you personally to the call, right?"

Holly thought back to the sequence of events leading up to her trip to the police station and finally agreed.

"You're right. Even if they told him about the call, no one saw or overheard me make it, and there's no reason to assume I'd be the first person he thought of. After all he's done, there have to be other people he's crossed who don't like him. And I don't see how he could recognize me. I was a little girl when he saw me last, and honestly, I don't think I look like either one of them now."

"Then there you go, home free," he said. "What do you think about going home now? You did what you came to do."

Holly couldn't shake her anxiety, but there was nothing that she could do to change that. "No. I can't leave until I know what happened to my mother."

Bud sighed. He'd been afraid she might

say something like that. But at least he was here with her now.

Holly threaded her fingers through Bud's and gave his hand a squeeze.

"So what do you want to do now? There are some great places to see here in St. Louis. Would you like a mini-tour of the city? I could show you where I used to live."

Bud frowned. "I think we need to stay away from anything to do with your past. Why don't we go back to the hotel, then walk down to the Arch? I think I've got enough guts to go up in that monstrosity, even if I don't much like heights."

"Oh, good, I haven't done that yet. We can do it together."

It was midafternoon before Harold realized he was no longer being tailed — at least by the man on the bike. The knowledge made him nervous, and he began watching all the cars and people around him even more closely. What if they'd pulled a switch? Now he wouldn't know who to look for. He tried to spot a new tail but couldn't pinpoint anyone who looked suspicious.

At quitting time he followed his usual routine and picked up dinner on the way home, this time from a local Italian restaurant. Spaghetti and meatballs were good, and easy to heat up in the microwave. But the whole time, he couldn't stop worrying. He didn't believe that someone would go to all that trouble and then just quit. It didn't make sense, but he couldn't see anyone who seemed remotely interested in where he was going. Even so, he wasn't naive enough to think this was over.

At home, he ate his meal in the living room in front of the television. Once he'd finished, he decided he had enough daylight left to mow the lawn. The new grass was getting tall enough that he would be getting looks from his neighbors if he didn't get it cut down, and Harold's determination to stay under the radar meant never calling attention to himself.

It was almost dark by the time Bud and Holly left the Arch and started back to the Jameson. Bud felt uneasy about staying out so late and being on foot. Except for the vague description Holly had given him, he didn't know what Mackey looked like. He took her by the hand, then slid his arm around her shoulders and pulled her close.

"Are you cold, baby?"

"No, just tired."

As they waited for the light to change, she looked up into his face. The strong cut of his jaw was so familiar to her, and yet, as her lover, this man was nearly an unknown. She'd had no idea of the depth of his passion, and the thought of the years they had ahead of them made her shiver with joy and longing.

Bud felt her gaze and looked down, then winked.

Holly grinned. There he was — the Bud she knew.

"Want to get something to eat in the hotel?" he asked.

"Yes. There's a steak house I haven't tried, and then another place called Annie's Kitchen that I *have* tried."

"I'm thinking steak," Bud said.

She smiled. "I would have bet money on that."

"Light's changing," Bud said, and eased her off the curb. "Let's hurry. I'm starved."

He had her laughing as they jogged across the intersection, and completely unaware that his haste had been a need to get her inside into a safer location, rather than a need to feed his hunger.

The steak house proved to be a good choice, and by the time they were back in the room, they were both groaning.

"I ate too much," Holly said.

"I know a way to work it off," Bud said.

Holly felt a flush spread up her neck and face, but she wasn't going to argue the point. Before she could answer, her cell phone began to ring.

She glanced at the caller ID but didn't recognize the number.

"Hang on," she muttered, as she answered the call. "Hello?"

"Hey, sugar, it's me."

Holly spun toward Bud, her eyes dancing. "Savannah!"

Bud took off his Stetson, hung his jacket across the back of a chair and smiled as headed for the bathroom.

"Tell her I said hi," he said.

Savannah frowned. "Is that Bud? Is Bud there with you?"

"Yes. Your jump into the ocean freaked him out. He's taking his guard duties very seriously," she said, not yet ready to talk about the recent change in their relationship. "Are you okay?"

"Yes, I'm fine," Savannah said. "Judd's here with me, which is part of why I'm calling."

"So what's up?" Holly asked.

"We're engaged!"

Holly squealed. "Finally! I can't believe it. Congratulations, honey. I'm so happy for the both of you."

"It's just awful that it took nearly dying for me to get my act together."

"Don't remind me," Holly said. "First Maria, then you. Bud's a basket case thinking I'm next, but he won't admit it."

Bud came out of the bathroom in time to hear Holly's words. "I am not a basket case," he said. "So what's going on?"

"Savannah and Judd are engaged."

"Congratulations to the both of you," Bud said loudly.

"Tell him we said thank you," Savannah said. "Hey, Holly, Judd's here, and it looks like something just came up. I've got to go, but I'll talk to you later. Take care of yourself."

"You, too."

Holly hung up the phone, and then turned around and gave Bud a big hug.

"I'm so happy for them. This has been a long time coming."

"And so has this," Bud said, as he took the phone out of her hand and laid it on the bedside table, then began kissing her as he backed her toward the bed.

Holly was already taking off her clothes as he turned off the light.

The sun was going down by the time Harold finished mowing. He wiped sweat from his

228

forehead before rolling the mower back into the shed, then stood in the backyard for a few moments, inhaling the sweet smell of fresh-cut grass before he made his way into the house.

After a quick shower, he changed into comfortable clothes, dug his hunting knife out of the closet, pocketed his car keys and settled in for a little TV. As he kicked back in his recliner, his gaze slid to the mounted elk head on his wall. Something about it looked off. He got up for a closer look and then frowned. An industrious spider had spun an interstate of webbing from one side of the elk's antlers to the other. Yet another clue as to how badly his house needed cleaning. As a rule, he didn't like people in his house, but he liked cleaning even less, and there was a limit as to how much even he could tolerate. He made a mental note to himself to call that Happy Helpers cleaning service he occasionally used, then settled back in his chair, aimed the remote and focused on his show.

Every so often he would glance over to the house across the street, expecting to see that glow of light from the snoop's laptop. Once he knew the man was back at the house, he intended to get rid of him . . . permanently.

But it never happened. At his regular bedtime he turned out the lights, then moved to the window. The empty house was still shrouded in darkness.

Harold frowned. He didn't like loose ends and wasn't going to sleep until he knew for sure that the man was gone. He palmed the hunting knife just in case, and for the third time in as many days, exited his house through the back door, jogged up the alley, across the street, then back down the opposite alley to the empty house. The motorcycle that had been there last night was gone. The backyard was empty. He strode through the grass to the side window and peered in. The room was dark and empty of everything but that folding chair.

It wasn't what he'd expected to see, and the fact that he would not be disposing of this snoop as he'd planned made him uneasy. He didn't like it when plans changed without his say-so.

Frustrated, and even more confused than before, he went back to his house. Once inside, he stood within the silence, listening . . . thinking.

The kitchen faucet had a drip he needed to fix, and he could hear the faint sounds of scratching, which meant there was a mouse in the house. He could live with dust, but he cursed at the thought of sharing his home with a rodent. He turned on the kitchen light long enough to find a mouse trap, baited it, then set it beside the refrigerator, near the back door. Satisfied, he turned off the light as he left, stowed his hunting knife back in the closet, then headed for his bedroom.

He finally got to bed, but he lay awake, rethinking his options. With the snoop gone, the only other person on his radar was Holly Slade. He needed to find out what he could about her. If she were part of what was happening, he would make sure her participation met with a swift end. Satisfied with his plan, he rolled over on his side, punched his pillow a couple of times until it felt just right and then closed his eyes.

The next day Harold worked his route on autopilot. His mind was racing through every stop as he tried to recall the bits and pieces of his life before.

He'd actually cared for Twila. He'd chosen her specifically because she came from good people, had a good work ethic, and took good care of him and their house. When their baby, Harriet, came along, he felt no parental bond and simply eyed the baby as an inevitable aspect of his life with

Twila. It was his job as the male and head of the house to procreate. He didn't want anything bad to happen to her, but he never stayed awake at night worrying about her, either.

His life as a married man had revolved — around the convenience of having a sexual partner at his disposal, and always having a clean house and good food. It never occurred to Harold that there was something lacking in him. He viewed himself as a perfect male — strong, resourceful — and lived by a credo that amounted to "survival of the fittest."

When he got to the Green Lantern Café where that skanky bitch Lola worked, again, he was so distracted about what was going on in his life that he completely ignored her digs and sexual innuendoes. As he left, he even missed the curious look she gave him, though ordinarily he wouldn't have missed a thing and would have been bothered to know he was giving off vibes that something was wrong.

He ate lunch in the truck on the way to his next stop, then delivered the order without anything more than a "Sign here" when he was done. He showed up at Riverfront Wholesale, turned in the signed work orders and clocked out without even telling

Sonya, the dispatcher, goodbye.

— Harold got into his car and drove out of the parking lot, circled the block rapidly to see if he could spot anyone suspicious in the vicinity, then whipped through an alley and came out four blocks over before turning in the opposite direction from home. He sped through the streets, taking back roads and shortcuts to get to the Jameson. Now that he knew the woman always valet parked, he knew where to look for her car. It took him a few minutes to find it once he entered the garage. The fact that it was there meant that either she was in the hotel or sight-seeing on foot. He drove out of the garage and around to the front of the hotel, found himself a parking spot where he could see the front entrance and settled down to wait. The longer he sat, the more amped he became. He was doing what he did best: waiting for game. The Hunter was back on track.

— First thing that morning, Bud called home to check on his uncle and see how things were going at the Triple S. Delbert Walker didn't carry a cell phone, so Bud knew he had to call early enough to catch him in the house in the morning, or wait until night. His main concern was to make sure he hadn't given the old man too much to handle.

He was counting the rings while admiring the way Holly's jeans fit the curve of her backside when Delbert answered the phone.

"Start talkin'," Delbert yelled.

Bud grinned. Why waste a hello? "Hey, Uncle Delbert, it's me, Bud."

"Hey, Buddy. You got things under control out there?"

"Yes, things are under control," Bud said.

Holly heard what he said and turned to face him with a "How dare you?" look on her face.

Bud winked. "Are you having any problems? I watched the weather. Looks like a clear forecast for at least a week."

"Yeah, the weather's just fine," Delbert said. "You got yourself a good crew out here. They pretty much know what they're doin' and just let me pretend I'm givin' orders."

Relieved to know there were no fires to put out, Bud visited for a few minutes more, then hung up. By that time Holly had finished getting ready. She came out of the bathroom patting her hair into place, then caught Bud's gaze and stopped.

"What?"

He shook his head. "Nothing, honey. I'm

just admiring the view."

"So am I," she said, eyeing the tailored Western-cut shirt and the Wranglers hugging his butt. In her opinion, nothing fit better on a good-looking man than a pair of jeans.

"I hope you have a plan," Bud said. "Because if you don't, I do."

"I have plans," Holly said. "We can save yours for later."

He closed the space between them with two long strides and then slid his hands around her back to cup her hips, leaving her in no doubt as to the fact that he meant what he said. Then he lowered his head and nestled his face in the curve of her neck.

"Lord, but you smell good."

"I wish Daddy was still alive to know this was happening."

"He knew how I felt. You were the unknown in the equation."

"He did? You told him?"

Bud sighed. "I didn't have to. He saw it in my face every time I looked at you. The only thing he ever told me was, 'Don't hurt her.' That went without saying."

"I can't believe I didn't know."

"I'm fourteen years older than you are, honey. You were all busy growing up."

"Well, I'm all grown up now," Holly said,

and then kissed him.

Bud groaned as want surged through him; they had to stop before they wound up back in bed again.

"You ready to go eat breakfast?"

She nodded.

After a late breakfast, instead of driving, they walked back down to the riverfront. They'd seen the riverboats the night before, and Holly wanted to take the one-hour cruise. When they got off, they had their next destination in mind.

A tour of the nearby Anheuser-Busch factory lasted into the early hours of the afternoon. By the time the tour reached the paddock and stables to see the famous Clydesdales, Holly was tired. Then she took one look at the magnificent animals and was excited all over again.

"Oh, my gosh, would you look at the size of them!"

Bud eyed them with the skill of a man who knew horses, admiring not only their size, but also their conformation. "The smallest one of these guys would probably scare the hell out of Andrew's old Jim Beam. They're huge."

"Not to mention the hassle of trying to get up on one," she said, which made Bud laugh. Everyone at the Triple S knew Holly could ride, but she wasn't an avid outdoors-woman. Her heart revolved around her home and the people she loved.

By late afternoon their steps were dragging. They'd just left Union Station, an old-time railroad station that had been renovated years ago into an enormous two-story shopping mall.

They were heading back to the hotel when Bud spied a horse-drawn carriage parked on a street corner. The old-world charm of the carriage and driver, plus the perfectly matched horses, made a package too good to pass up. He pointed.

"Hey, honey, how about a ride back to the hotel in one of those?" he asked.

"I'll take a ride back to the hotel in anything. My feet are killing me."

A few minutes later they were on their way, their sacks of souvenirs on the seat beside them. The gentle motion of the carriage and the repetitive clip-clop of the horses' feet lulled Holly to relax. She leaned her head against Bud's shoulder. He took her hand, then lifted it up to his lips and kissed it.

"Thank you, Bud," she said, and kissed him full on the lips. "This has been the most marvelous day."

It was one of those moments in life when,

for the space of that instant, everything was perfect. Bud couldn't speak for the emotion he was feeling. Instead of talking, he just hugged her.

The sun beamed down on them as they rode, but there was always that cooling breeze off the Mississippi River to take away the heat. Once back at the hotel, the driver got down to help them out.

Bud stepped out first, carrying the sacks, then turned to help Holly down. She clasped his hand to steady herself, and just before she reached the last step he grabbed her around the waist with both hands and swung her down onto her feet.

She threw back her head, laughing from sheer delight. They walked back into the hotel, arm in arm.

Harold saw the carriage coming long before he was able to see the people in it. When they got close enough, he recognized Holly.

But it wasn't her arrival that shifted his world off its axis. The moment she stepped down from the carriage and tossed her head back as she laughed, his heart stopped. He'd seen Twila do that a thousand times. Just like that.

His gut began to rumble. Either he was about to pass gas or shit his pants. Everything was beginning to make sense. That had to be Harriet, and if it was, his days as a free man were numbered. She'd seen his utmost secret, and he'd let her live. Twila had surprised him by sending her away and had died without telling him where she'd gone. Now here she was, grown up and back to talk about what she'd seen. He had no one to blame but himself. If he'd needed to keep his trophies, he shouldn't have stayed in St. Louis. And even though he'd blocked off access to where they were hidden, he was no longer going to bet his life on them staying undiscovered. But there was a problem. Now that he knew the cops were on to him, he didn't dare try to get his collection off the property.

The only option he had was to get rid of her and make it look like an accident or a robbery gone bad.

He frowned as he watched the big man walking her into the hotel. The guy was at least as tall as he was himself, and a good twenty years younger. Harold didn't like the fact that he'd let this slide until she had protection. It would have been a lot easier to get her while she'd still been alone. But it was just one man. Harold had faced more difficult situations and lived to tell.

■ ■ ■ ■

The dream started in the wee hours of the morning, long after Bud and Holly had fallen asleep in a tangle of arms and legs.

She could hear her mother's footsteps coming toward her room as the sound of her daddy's truck disappeared down the street. Good. At least he was gone for a while. Maybe if she kept her head down and kept coloring, Mama wouldn't be able to tell she'd been crying. She discarded the yellow crayon for a pink one and began coloring in the Easter Bunny's hat as if her life depended on it.

"There you are, honey," Mama said. "I'm back from getting groceries. Do you want to come help me put them up?"

She shook her head no and kept coloring, hoping that her refusal to do something she always liked to do hadn't set off warning bells in her mother's head.

When her mother's footsteps came into the room instead of receding back down the hall, Holly flinched, then gripped the crayon so hard it suddenly snapped in two.

Relieved to have an excuse, she began crying again as her mother knelt beside her.

"Don't cry, honey. It's just a crayon. Look. Now you have two pieces instead of one."

240

Mama peeled back a little bit of the paper so the crayon would work from either end, but it didn't help. The fact that Harriet had an honest reason to cry was alleviating the sheer terror that was in her heart.

"Honey . . . can you tell Mama why you're so sad?"

"No," Harriet said. "I can't tell. Ever."

"Who said you couldn't tell?" Mama asked.

"Daddy. He said he'd make me sorry."

Mama started to shake. She grabbed Harriet by her shoulders and then pulled her fiercely against her chest.

"No, baby, he won't do anything to you. Mama won't let him. Now tell me, what happened to make you cry?"

"I saw in Daddy's secret room, and I wasn't supposed to," she said, and then started sobbing all over again.

Mama frowned. "What did you see in Daddy's room?"

"Hair like on Daddy's trophies, lots of hair. All kinds of colors of hair. It got tangled in my fingers. I tried to put it back, but he got mad."

She couldn't see her mother's reaction, but she felt her body suddenly shudder.

"Hair? You mean fur, like on animal skins?" Twila asked.

"No. People hair. Stuck to his wooden trophy boards."

"Oh, dear God."

All of a sudden her mother sat her down on the bed and jumped up. "I'll be right back."

Harriet jumped up and ran after her mother, crying all the way. "No, Mama, no. You can't look. He'll know I told. He'll know I told!"

TWELVE

Holly sat up in bed, choking on tears, a scream caught at the back of her throat.

Bud was awake within seconds, reaching for her and pulling her into his arms.

"What's wrong, honey? What's wrong? Were you having a bad dream?"

Holly turned and buried her face against his chest as she started to sob.

"I told. Oh, my God, he told me not to, but I told her anyway."

"Look at me, Holly." When she wouldn't look up, he grabbed her by the shoulders and forced her. "Look at me."

She lifted her head as tears streamed down her face.

"Talk to me. Tell me what you remembered."

"Mama came home and found me crying as Daddy was driving away. She began asking me what happened, and I told her, even though he'd told me not to."

Bud was still confused. "Exactly what did you tell her?"

"That Daddy had trophies in his secret room, that there were pieces of hair on trophy boards, and that he told me I'd be sorry if I said anything."

"Oh, hell," Bud said. He got out of bed to get her some tissues, returned with the box, then crawled back in bed.

"What did she do?" Bud asked.

"I'm not sure. I woke up from the dream as she was heading for the cellar, but I'm sure she found them. That's got to be the reason she sent me away with Andrew. She was afraid of what my father would do to me. I think I blocked it all out because when she sent me away, I believed it was because I was the one who'd done something bad. I'd told when I wasn't supposed to. I didn't understand that it was for my protection, and not because of what she was afraid my father might do."

Bud ached for the torment he could see in her eyes. Poor little girl. No wonder she'd blocked it all out.

"I'm sorry, honey, so sorry." He scooted her into his lap and rocked her where they sat. "As an adult, you can see how much she loved you, and what a sacrifice she made

244

to get you safe before she went to the police."

Holly nodded as she continued to cry. "And that's part of the reason I feel like I have to stay. I need to find my mother. I need to know what he did to her. I know now she must be dead, but I have to find her body. She deserved a long and happy life. At least I can find her and make sure she's buried properly in holy ground. That would matter to her. It would matter a lot."

"Then we'll stay awhile longer," Bud said. "Surely they'll connect the dots soon and he'll be arrested."

Holly nodded as she pulled a fresh handful of tissues from the box.

"Thank you, Bud. I don't know what I'd do without you."

"You're welcome, darlin'. And the feeling is mutual." He glanced at the clock. "It's too early to get up. It doesn't matter if you can't go back to sleep, but we can stay here and cuddle, okay?"

"Okay."

Holly slid beneath the covers as Bud spooned himself against her. She tried to sleep, but the devil was still too fresh from the dream. Every time she closed her eyes, she saw the rage on her father's face, then heard the sound of her mother's footsteps disappearing down the cellar steps.

Holly was in the shower when she heard the bathroom door open. The shower curtain slid back, and before she knew it, Bud was in the tub behind her.

She laughed. "What do you think you're doing?"

"Multitasking," he said, and took the washcloth out of her hand. "You missed a spot."

He ran the washcloth across her breasts, then beneath them, gently cupping the ivory globes before giving the dusky pink nipples a brief tweak.

A surge of heat hit her core so fast her legs went weak.

"Oh, Lord."

Bud put a finger to her lips, turned her to face him and slid the washcloth around her waist, down her buttocks, then around to her belly.

"Hold on to me."

Holly grabbed hold of his shoulders, then locked her hands around his neck as he moved the washcloth down between her legs. The nubby texture of the warm, soapy cloth quickly aroused her. Bud dropped the washcloth, pulled her out from under the spray and pinned her against the wall.

She saw his eyes darken and his nostrils flare, as he parted her legs and slid inside. His erection was full, his penis hard and swollen, and the feel of him slowly filling her was an excruciating moment of completion.

"You like that, baby?"

She nodded.

He gave a quick thrust, filling her completely.

She moaned.

He braced himself, planting his hands on the shower wall on either side of her head. "You want more?" Their gazes locked. His eyes were so dark they looked black. She saw heaven waiting for her. All she had to do was say yes.

"All of you, Buddy. I want it all."

A muscle jerked at the side of his mouth, and then he swooped. His lips caught hers in a hard, hungry move, capturing and parting them before the onslaught of his tongue. He began to move within her in a steady rhythmic motion — all the way in to his hilt, all the way back out to the swollen head, then back again . . . over and over, slowly increasing the tempo, pushing deeper, taking her higher.

Holly met him thrust for thrust as the steam from the hot water began to build, filling the shower and then the bathroom, until they were lost in a fog of lust. One moment she was still with him, and then she shattered. The gut-deep groan came up her throat just as the climax burst within her, turning the blood flowing through her body into a heat-seeking missile. It slammed into her groin with such force that she forgot to breathe.

Bud pulled her hard against his chest with one hand while he held on to the shower rod with the other, and then, thrust after shuddering thrust, emptied himself into her womb.

Whit Carver strode into headquarters, then straight to his office, carrying a handful of files and a box of doughnuts. He dumped the files on his desk, then carried the doughnuts through to the headquarters of the task force.

Two detectives were still going through old files, and another was moving pushpins on the map.

"Anything I should know about?" Carver asked.

The detective turned around. "We had the addresses wrong on a couple of the first victims — just correcting them."

Whit walked up to the map and gave it a

new look, then frowned. It didn't change anything obvious. He snagged a doughnut and went back to his desk.

It was a little over an hour later when one of the detectives came looking for him.

"Hey, Whit, did you know that Riverfront Wholesale wasn't always Riverfront Wholesale, and that it used to be at a different address?"

Carver stood up. "Why are we just now becoming aware of this?"

"We started out going through the old victim files with the task of matching those victims to Mackey and his place of work, which is Riverfront Wholesale. We were told he'd always worked for them. It was only when we started looking for info on his old routes that we found out the company had changed hands and its name, and moved."

Whit's interest surged.

"Get the address of the old company, and if he's still alive, I want to talk to the original owner."

Whit went back to his paperwork but couldn't concentrate. He rejoined the task force on the pretext of getting himself another doughnut and a refill on his coffee. In truth, with this new information, he wanted a fresh look at the map.

■ ■ ■ ■

Bud was at the concierge desk, while Holly was trying to call Maria. She'd gotten through to her sister's room, only to find out she wasn't there because she was in the process of being released. That was good news, but Maria wasn't answering her cell phone. Then it occurred to Holly that it might not have survived the explosion, so she would have to count on Maria to call her when she got a chance. She dropped her cell back into her purse as Bud came up behind her and slid his hand along her waist.

"Come on, sugar. Let's get the car. We have some where to go."

Holly turned. She was still reveling in the fact that the man she loved was freaking amazing in bed — and in showers, and standing up, as well as lying down. She shivered with longing. He was a habit she didn't want to break.

"Where are we going?"

"You'll see." He took her by the hand and headed for the exit.

When the valet brought the car, Bud surprised her by putting her in the passenger seat.

"I have the directions, so I'm driving.

Buckle up," he said, and winked to soften the order as he slid behind the wheel.

Holly reached for her seat belt as Bud started the car.

The secrecy of the moment was a rush, as she was sure Bud had known it would be.

Watching her reliving the devastation of her past without being able to help or fix it was torture for him. He wanted her happy, not in this constant stage of torment and fear. And right now Holly's eyes were dancing.

Holly kept up a constant run of questions. Every time they passed a tourist attraction, she asked, "Is this it? Is this where we're going?"

"Nope, that's not it," he would say, his delight increasing, and keep driving.

After the third failed guess, Holly threw up her hands.

"I give up. Surprise me."

"That's what I've been trying to do ever since we got in the car, and I think we're almost there. I see the turn coming up."

Bud took the turn onto South Brentwood Boulevard. When he turned into the parking lot of the St. Louis Galleria, she leaned forward.

"We're going shopping?"

"In a manner of speaking. Just let me get

parked here, woman."

Holly was excited about spending the day with Bud again and had no complaints about the choice of location. But then they parked and didn't get out.

Bud leaned across the seat and cupped her face.

"In all the years I've loved you and imagined what this moment might be like, not once did I ever think it would take place in the parking lot of a shopping center in St. Louis, Missouri."

"What moment?"

"The moment where I tell you how much I love you and that I want to spend the rest of my life with you. Granted, in one respect this is sort of sudden. But from my point of view, it's been a long time coming. I already know you like making love with me, but would you like to spend the rest of your life with me, too?"

A huge smile spread across Holly's face as she clasped her hands against her breasts in sheer delight.

"I would like that very much."

Bud began laughing as she came out of her seat and crawled onto his lap. He cradled her there, cupping the back of her head and pulling her close. The kiss began as a gentle, seal-the-deal moment, but the longer he held her, the harder and more passionate it became, until they broke apart a little flushed and a lot breathless.

Bud pushed a tumbled curl from the corner of her eye and stroked her lower lip in a slow, sensuous caress.

"Come inside with me, darlin'. According to the concierge, there's a great jewelry store in here. We're about to pick out your engagement ring."

Holly was teary-eyed but laughing. "Kiss me one more time for good luck, and then let's do it."

Bud happily obliged.

Hours later, Holly still couldn't quit looking at her ring — a white-gold band with a one-carat princess-cut solitaire setting. It was perfect, and the smile on her face was proof of her joy.

With a recommendation from the jeweler, they were on their way to a special celebration dinner at a place called Tony's Restaurant, which happened to be on Market Street near their hotel. That it was a St. Louis icon as well as a four-star restaurant was just an added bonus.

The host who seated them caught on to the fact that they were celebrating, and when Holly flashed her ring, the reason for the celebration became obvious.

He passed the news to the waiter, who spread the news inside the kitchen. Tony himself came out to greet them personally, carrying a complimentary bottle of champagne.

The day couldn't have ended better if Bud had planned it. The horror of the past few days was forgotten in the old-world glamour of the place and the expectation of an exquisite meal.

Bud couldn't stop touching her. He took every chance he got to reach toward her, brushing a tendril of hair away from her face, touching her arm before he spoke. A part of him felt as if he were in a waking dream.

Holly was in a slight state of disbelief herself. Bud took her breath away. He was so open with his feelings now, yet she kept thinking of how skilled he'd been at hiding them. All of this should have been startling, even shocking, because it was happening so fast, but they'd known each other far too long to stand on ceremony.

And after what had happened to Maria and Savannah, she'd learned the hard way how fleeting life and happiness could be. She didn't intend to miss her chance.

When their food came, Holly focused

intently on the quiet elegance of the uniformed waiters and the deliciousness of the meal. She began imagining owning her own catering business or even a restaurant one day. Cooking food to perfection was a skill she'd learned years ago at Hannah's knee, and learning new techniques was a source of delight.

Once the entrées were in front of them, the waiters stepped quietly away. Finally they were alone. Bud dug into his filet mignon with Chianti sauce as passionately as he'd made love, groaning in happy ecstasy as he chewed.

"This is one of the best pieces of beef I've ever tasted . . . with the exception of your steak with mushroom sauce."

Holly rolled her eyes. "Please, I'm competent. This is heaven."

"Taste this," Bud said, as he fed her a bite.

"Yum," Holly said, savoring flavors as she chewed. "That is amazing . . . and so tender it just melts in your mouth."

"Sure beats those steaks I burn on the grill back home."

She laughed. "They aren't that bad. We eat them, don't we? Now you have to try my linguine with lobster and shrimp."

She stabbed some pasta, then spun it into the bowl of her spoon before popping it into

Bud's mouth.

"What do you think?" she asked, absently wiping a tiny droplet of sauce from the corner of his lips with her thumb.

Bud caught her hand before she could take it away.

"Hey, I was saving that for later." He licked the droplet from her thumb without taking his eyes from her face.

It was instant lust. Holly stifled a soft moan as his tongue slid across the surface of her skin. To save her sanity, she quickly pulled her hand away.

"You are so bad," she whispered.

Bud arched an eyebrow, then leaned over and whispered against her ear, "Then I'll have to practice some more tonight to improve my skills."

Holly shivered, but she wasn't going to let him get the best of her. Before he knew it, she'd turned her head and kissed him full on the mouth.

Despite the food they'd been eating, all he could taste was Holly. She was in his heart and his blood, and there was nothing to be done but enjoy it.

"I love you, Robert Tate."

She gutted him. "Love you more," he whispered.

Nearly two hours later, they were on their

way out with a to-go box of ricotta cheese-cake with raspberry sauce and two little plastic forks tucked inside for their convenience.

The moment they walked out of the restaurant Bud shifted into protection mode, scanning the area as they waited for the valet to return with their car. Even after they were back inside the hotel, he didn't operate under the assumption that they were safe. He paid close attention to anyone who came close to them as they made their way up to the room. It wasn't until they were behind a locked door that he let himself relax.

"At ease," Holly said, as she tossed her purse onto the table and kicked off her shoes.

"What?"

"I saw you scoping everyone out."

He put his arm around her waist and then planted a swift kiss beside her earlobe.

"I didn't come here for my health. I came for yours."

And just like that, reality returned. Holly had two sisters in hospitals in two different cities, because people had tried to kill them.

She cupped his cheeks. "You made today so special, I almost forgot why I'm here."

"You make every day special for me."

"Thank you, Bud, for waiting around for me to grow up."

"I would have waited forever."

He tilted her chin just enough, then kissed her — softly at first, and then with increasing fervor.

"No more waiting for either of us," she said, then gave her ring yet another look. "And this is so special. You have amazing taste."

Bud slid his fingers through her hair, then touched his forehead to hers.

"Yes, actually I do. That's why I fell in love with you."

A group of people passed outside their doorway, talking loudly. It was enough to break the mood and the moment.

"How about we change into comfortable clothes and watch some television?" Holly said. "I need to let my meal settle a bit before we tackle that dessert."

"Definitely," Bud said, and reached for the remote as Holly began digging in the dresser for her sweats.

Bud tweaked her nose in a quick teasing manner as he headed for the bathroom. Holly smiled, knowing there was more than teasing behind that look in his eyes. Just thinking about making love with him again made her shiver.

She took off her good clothes and put on the sweats, then crawled up in the middle of the bed and began flipping through the channels.

All of a sudden she saw the name *Savannah Slade* flash across the bottom of the screen in a crawl and fumbled at the remote to turn up the volume as she began screaming, "Bud! Bud! Come here quick!"

He bolted out of the bathroom on the run, ready to fight, and found her on her knees in a panic, pointing at the television. She was crying and talking all at once, and he couldn't understand what she was saying.

"What, honey? What?"

She leaped off the bed, still pointing at the screen, just as Savannah's name scrolled past again.

"Look! Look, there's Savannah's name. They're saying Savannah died in an explosion. They're referring to her as Gerald Stoss's love child. That means she'd finally filed the papers with the court. Oh, my God, look what happened. They got to her again, and this time they killed her. I can't believe this is happening. Please, God, please, this can't be real."

She was sobbing hysterically when Bud took her in his arms. The joy of their day had just been shattered. It was his worst nightmare come to life. He couldn't think beyond the wave of grief that swept through him as he pulled her close against him.

All of a sudden Holly's cell phone began to ring.

She threw herself on the bed, too distraught to talk, so Bud picked it up.

"Hello?"

"Bud? It's me, Judd. You need to know that despite anything you might hear, Savannah's okay. You didn't already see anything, did you?"

Bud stood and reached for the back of a chair to steady himself.

"Thank the Lord. . . . And unfortunately we did, which explains Holly's sobbing in the background. Hang on. Holly! Sweetheart, Savannah's okay."

Holly rolled off the bed and bounded toward him, wiping the tears as she went. Bud pulled her close and gave her a quick hug. "Holly's here," he said into the phone. "She needs to hear her sister's voice."

"Hang on a minute."

Bud could hear Judd calling to Savannah, and he handed the phone to Holly.

"Here, darlin', Savannah's coming to the phone."

Holly waited anxiously. There were other voices in the background, as well as the

260

sound of a television, and all of a sudden she felt light-headed and leaned over onto the desk.

"I need to sit."

Bud grabbed a chair and pushed it behind her.

"Thank you. Going from absolute grief to pure joy in less than a minute is a little difficult to handle."

He kissed her cheek, then started to walk away, but Holly stopped him. "I put the phone on speaker so you can hear, too."

Then Savannah was on the phone, the pitch of her voice high with anxiety.

"Holly? Holly? Are you there?"

Relief flooded through Holly. "Yes, I'm here. Oh, my God, you nearly scared me to death! What's going on? They said you were dead. It's all over the news."

"I didn't know about the report until just a few minutes ago. It's a long ugly story, but the bottom line is, my lawyer and the police have released this fake story to make the Stoss family think they've finally accomplished what they've been trying to do since I got here."

"Are you sorry you started all this?" Holly asked.

"No." Now Savannah's voice was full of anger. "They're responsible for murder, as well as for trying to kill me. They even killed my grandmother, who I just met, because they were afraid I'd told her something. I want them to pay. Are you okay? You haven't raised any red flags about your past?"

"None that I know of," Holly said, and then her voice softened. "I'm so sorry about your grandmother. That's awful."

"You're lucky you're not on anyone's radar. Try and keep it that way. Let the police do their job, and you get yourself home."

"I'll go, but not until I find out what happened to my mother. I've been having terrible dreams. I'm pretty sure that as a child I found out that my father was killing people. I think I told my mother, and I believe that's why she wanted me out of St. Louis so fast. She was afraid of what he would do to me. Sending me away got her killed. I'm sure of it."

"Oh, honey . . . I'm so sorry," Savannah said. "Is Bud still there with you?"

"Yes, I'm here," Bud spoke up.

"I'm so glad you're there, Bud. After all that's unraveling, it's not safe doing this alone."

"I'm pretty glad he's here, too," Holly said, absently rubbing the underside of her engagement ring with her thumb. "There are lots of things happening that we didn't plan, but not all of them are bad."

"Like what?" Savannah said. "What's going on?"

"Oh . . . I'll tell you all about it when we all get home."

"Okay, just be careful. I love you," Savannah said.

"I love you, too," Holly echoed, then disconnected.

"You didn't tell her," Bud said, pointing at the ring.

Holly shook her head, and then put her arms around his neck.

"I'm feeling a little selfish about you and the engagement. Once everyone knows, they'll be all in our business, asking questions, wanting answers as to when we're going to get married, all that stuff. I want you to myself, at least for a little while longer."

"Then that's how it will be," he said.

THIRTEEN

Whit Carver's day started off on a positive note when he came to work and found a note on his desk. Someone on the task force had found the name of the past owner of the wholesale company, along with an address and phone number. According to Whit's information, the old man was in an assisted living center in Little Rock, Arkansas, near one of his children.

Whit headed for the command post in case he needed quick access to additional information, then made the call.

"Whispering Pines Retirement Center. How can I help you?"

"I need to speak to Kenneth Parks."

"One moment, please. I'll put you through to his room."

"Thanks," Whit said, as he was put on hold. He was just getting past the fact that the music in his ear was Elvis Presley's "All Shook Up" when it stopped.

A gruff but shaky voice said, "Kenneth Parks speaking."

"Mr. Parks, my name is Whitman Carver. I'm a detective with the St. Louis Police Department. I understand you're the past owner of Parks Wholesale House, and I was hoping you could help me with a case we're working on."

There was a brief moment of silence, then a faint cough.

"Did you say you were a detective?"

Whit frowned. This might turn out to be a long conversation.

"Yes, sir. I work cold cases. You know . . . cases that were never solved."

"I watch television. I know what cold cases are," the old man muttered.

Whit's frown shifted to a smile of amusement. Point taken. "All right, then. So, the questions I have for you are in regards to Parks Wholesale, the business you used to own here in St. Louis."

"I may be old, but I'm not senile. I remember I owned it, too, sonny. What about it?"

Whit stifled a chuckle. He'd found himself quite a character. "Yes, sir, sorry, sir, I didn't mean to offend you. I'm trying to map out a specific route that one of your old employees used to make. It pertains to a series of murders that happened nearly twenty years ago and —"

"You wouldn't be meaning that serial killer, the Hunter? Is that the case you're working? It's about time you people got that solved."

"Yes, sir, that is the case, and we're definitely trying."

"That was awful. My wife, God rest her soul, used to play cards with the mother of one of those victims. I'll do anything I can to help. Which employee of mine are you talking about?"

"The employee's name is Harold Mackey. Do you remember him?"

"I remember Mackey. Odd duck."

"How so?"

"Kept to himself. Didn't socialize with anyone. Did his job just fine, but people oughta be friendly once in a while, don't you think?"

"Yes, sir. Now, about Mackey's route, would you by chance remember any of his delivery stops or know someone who would?"

"I'll do you one better. You got a map of the city there close?"

"Yes, sir, I do," Whit said, and moved over to the murder board, focusing on the record they'd made of Mackey's truck route.

"I owned that business for forty-seven years. I remember everything about where my trucks went and who was driving them. So find the eleven-hundred block of Market Street on your map, and we'll go from there."

"Eleven-hundred Market Street," Whit repeated, and motioned for one of the detectives to start marking.

"Yes. Eleven-oh-seven was his first stop on Mondays."

Whit began repeating each address that Kenneth gave him, and one of the other cops made sure they went on the map. One by one, the old man went down a mental list of every stop on Harold Mackey's route for the entire week, until he was through.

"And that's the last one," Kenneth Parks said.

"You're sure that's everything? I'm not questioning your memory. I just need to make very sure this is the entire route."

"I'm a hundred percent sure," Parks said. "And if this means what I think it means and you suspect Mackey of being the Hunter, it damn sure fits his personality."

"Why do you say that?" Whit asked.

"As far as I know, he never missed a hunting season. He saved up all his vacation days so he could take off and go hunting or fish-ing or some such endeavor. I told you he didn't talk much, but the only thing I ever heard him brag about was that he liked collecting trophies. I was never in his house, but I heard him mention more than once that he had the big kills mounted and hanging on his walls."

"Really?"

"Yes, sir. And if he turns out to be that killer, I'm gonna be real upset that I paid the bastard even a dime of my money. Anything else you wanna know?"

"Not right now, sir, but thank you. Thank you very much. You have an amazing memory."

Whit heard a brief snort, then a chuckle. "That's about the only thing that still works. Have a nice day."

The line went dead in Whit's ear. He turned to look at the map.

"Where does this put us?"

Two of the detectives were already comparing the victims' places of employment against Mackey's route, while another was checking their places of residence.

There was excitement in the first detective's voice when he spoke. "Hot damn! We're getting matches! Already have two, no . . . three of the victims working at places where he stopped, and I'm still checking."

Whit shivered. After all these years, were they finally going to be able to close the case?

Harold called in sick.

It was so unusual that Sonya didn't have a backup driver. The scramble it took to find a sub so the deliveries would go out was so hectic that by the time she had a driver on the road, she was ticked. She complained to her boss about the lack of planning for such contingencies, and then went into the bathroom and cried from frustration.

Harold couldn't have cared less. He had made himself a plan and needed the better part of the day to carry it out. By late afternoon he had everything he needed to make it happen: a duffel bag with a change of clothes, a fake ID he'd bought from Party Favors and Gifts, his toolbox — including a pipe wrench and his hunting knife — and a fifty-dollar arrangement from a flower shop.

He'd gone over the plan in his head many times — just like he used to do when he was taking down the scourges — and was ready for a trip to the hotel. He'd already shown up once as himself, so this time he had to come up with another approach. He didn't know how long they kept security tapes, but he was covering all his bases.

He couldn't remember the last time he'd worn his khakis and was a little surprised to find he could barely button them. He added a blue knit shirt and tucked his ponytail up beneath a red baseball cap, then headed for the Jameson Hotel in his SUV.

He parked alongside the front curb, got the arrangement he'd purchased and carried it into the hotel, straight to the concierge.

"Got a delivery for a Holly Slade," he said, putting down the arrangement, then began fumbling in his shirt pocket. "Dang, I lost the invoice with her room number. Sorry, man. You'll have to look it up."

The concierge typed the name in the hotel computer, then took the card from the flower arrangement and wrote down a number. Harold was watching every move the concierge made, and even though he was reading it upside down, it was easy to decipher the number — Room 663.

"Thanks again, man," Harold said, and strode out of the hotel without looking back.

Now he knew her room number, too.

The deciding factor in whether he ran or made an attempt to eliminate his witness had to do in part with his reluctance to let a woman best him.

He would have bet his life that after what

Harriet had seen, and how he'd scared her, she would never tell. But she had told, and then Twila had made it worse. She hid Harriet before he could rethink his earlier decision to let her live. Running now would have meant admitting defeat, and Harold wasn't a quitter.

It was nearly sundown as Harold exited the hotel, then drove away. But he didn't leave the premises for long. Instead, he circled the hotel to the delivery entrance and parked on the far side of a semi. Shielded from the view of passersby, he jumped out of the SUV and pulled an old pair of coveralls from his duffel bag. He put them on over the clothing he was wearing, traded his red baseball cap for a black hard hat, clipped the fake ID he'd made onto the pocket of his coveralls and then changed the shoes he was wearing for old work boots.

He pocketed his car keys, grabbed his toolbox and then headed for the delivery entrance with his head down. As he neared the door, it suddenly swung open, and two of the hotel's employees came out.

"How's it going?" Harold muttered, catching the door before it went shut and striding inside.

He was in! He began searching for the freight elevator. As soon as he located it, he went straight up to the sixth floor. Once off the elevator, he began looking for a house phone and found one near the guest elevators. After a quick glance to make sure he was alone, he made a call to Room 663.

Holly was just getting out of the tub when the house phone rang.

"I'll get it, honey!" Bud yelled, giving her the space to finish dressing. They had a seven o'clock reservation at the hotel steak house, and he didn't want to show up late.

"This is the front desk. There's a package here for Miss Holly Slade."

"Can you send it up?" Bud asked.

"I'm sorry," Mackey said. "The courier is waiting. It has to be signed for."

"By her personally?" Bud asked.

"Just a minute and I'll check," the man said.

Mackey held his hand over the phone for a minute, smiling to himself at how easily this was going down, then got back on the phone.

"Her representative can sign for it, but a hotel employee cannot."

"I'll be right down," Bud said, and then hung up the phone.

"Hey, honey, that was the front desk. You have a package that needs to be signed for.

The courier is waiting. I'll go get it for you and be right back, okay?"

Holly came out of the bathroom wearing a bath-towel sarong and holding her hair dryer.

"Okay. I wonder who it's from?"

"We'll find out soon," Bud said.

Holly nodded. "I promise I'll be ready by the time you get back."

Bud eyed the towel and that mass of wet hair, and shook his head. "Don't make promises you can't keep, woman. You're at least forty-five minutes from ready or I'll eat my hat."

"You . . . you man, you," Holly said, laughing. She ripped the towel from around her body and threw it at him from across the room, then stepped back into the bathroom and closed the door.

The sight of that gorgeous curvy body put a smile on Bud's face that he wore all the way down to the lobby.

For Harold, the moment he heard the disconnect, he made a beeline for the hallway that led to Room 663, then ducked into the stairwell and stood behind the door, watching through the small window for the man to emerge.

When the cowboy came out of her room,

273

Harold ducked and waited for the footsteps to pass. Then he counted to ten and strode out into the hall with the toolbox in his hand. Even if the man should happen to turn and look back, he would think nothing of a workman in coveralls and carrying his tools.

All the way to the room, he kept going over the fact that he was about to kill his own seed. Yes, he'd killed Twila, but she had been a mate — someone he'd chosen.

That wasn't the case with Harriet. She was his only link to immortality — the lineage that would continue his bloodline even after he was gone. He wasn't feeling remorse for his decision so much as for the fact that with her gone, once he was dead, it would be end of his contribution to the gene pool.

However, necessity was the mother of his decision, and by the time he reached the door, purpose was firmly fixed in his head.

He removed the pipe wrench from his toolbox, slipped his hunting knife into a pocket on the side of his coveralls and then knocked on the door, using the head of the pipe to increase the sound.

Holly was determined to make Bud Tate eat his words about her being slow. She quickly stepped into her brown slacks, then pulled the lightweight beige sweater over her head. Still barefoot, she went back to the bathroom to put on some makeup. Just as she picked up her mascara, there was a knock at the door.

"No way," Holly muttered and dropped the mascara and hurried across the room to answer. She was laughing as she swung the door inward. "What did you forget?"

But it wasn't Bud.

It was Mackey.

For a fraction of a second they stood frozen in place.

It went through Harold's mind that she was a fine specimen of a woman.

Holly's thoughts had gone in a completely different direction.

The devil was at her door.

Harold lunged.

That was the impetus that broke Holly's spell. She reacted with an ear-piercing scream as she swung the door in his face, then threw all her weight against it in an attempt to slam it shut.

Harold was unprepared for her to fight back rather than retreat and didn't protect himself. The door hit him square in the face, crushing his nose and staggering him with pain.

Holly panicked. She couldn't close the door.

She was still screaming when he burst into the room, blood running from his nose and down his chin. She was halfway across the floor when he dropped the pipe wrench and went for the knife. He needed to shut her up fast.

She had no thought of trying to fight him as she bolted for the bathroom. He was far too big for her to handle, and the bathroom had a lock. Even though she knew he would eventually kick the door open, she was betting her life that it would give her the time she needed, because the bathroom had a house phone.

With only feet to spare, she slammed the door between them and locked it, then grabbed the phone and called the front desk.

"Good evening, Miss Slade, how can I —"

The moment Holly heard the voice, she started screaming, "There's a man in my room! He's going to kill me! Help me! Help me!"

She dropped the phone, leaving it dangling toward the floor as the first kick sounded. The door rattled on its hinges, and Holly began shrieking in a mixture of fear and rage.

"You're a monster, Harold Mackey! The

police already know everything about you! Killing me won't stop them from coming after you! They know you're the Hunter! You're dead! Dead! Just like those women you killed!"

He kicked again, and Holly saw the hinges beginning to give way. In a rage, she threw herself against the door.

Harold knew it was about to give way. He lifted his foot for what would be his third kick, then landed the blow with a hard thud. The door actually rattled.

He grinned.

She was fighting back, throwing her weight against the door and screaming at him, telling him that he was going to die, and in that moment, he lost focus. The fact that he'd sired a woman of such great physical and mental strength gave him a moment of pride. She wasn't cowering behind the door and begging for mercy. She was fighting him.

Bud reached the front desk and waited a few seconds for a clerk to look up.

"May I help you?"

"Someone just called about a courier waiting for a package to be signed. The package was for Holly Slade in Room 663."

The clerk frowned. "I'm sorry, sir, but you

must be mistaken. I've been on duty since four, and there haven't been any couriers. But let me check to see if someone left a package."

"No, hang on," Bud said. "The man said a courier was waiting. He said the hotel couldn't sign for it, that it had to be —"

Then it hit him. Someone wanted him out of Holly's room. Suddenly it felt as if everything began happening in slow motion.

A phone rang behind the desk. Another desk clerk answered. Even from where Bud was standing, he could hear the woman's screams.

Holly! That was Holly!

The desk clerk's reaction was as frantic as Bud's. "Call security! A woman is being attacked in Room 663!"

Bud was already running toward the stairwell. He hit the door with the flat of his hand and took the stairs up to the first landing in four leaps, then up, and up again, with his heart in his throat and a prayer on his lips that he wouldn't be too late.

He kept thinking about how easily they'd been tricked, knowing that her life was in danger. The killer hadn't used elaborate techniques to separate them. It had been the mundane that had deceived them.

He was coming up to the sixth floor when he realized he could hear her screaming, which meant she was still alive.

He came out of the stairwell on the run, then raced down the hall with the room key in his hand. Doors were opening. Guests were curious. Some looked frightened.

"Call 911!" Bud shouted, as he ran past.

His hands were shaking as he ran the key card through the slot. Waiting for that little light to turn green felt like a lifetime, and then blessedly it clicked, and he burst into the room. He didn't even hear the door slam shut automatically behind him.

He saw a giant of a man with a long gray ponytail at their bathroom door. The imprint of his boot was on the surface, and he was about to kick again.

Bud attacked with a roar of rage.

Shocked, Mackey turned as Bud scooped the pipe wrench from the floor. With less than a second to think, he palmed his knife and braced himself for impact.

Harold swung the knife upward, then grunted from the impact as the man hit him chest high. They went down with a gut-wrenching thud against the bathroom door, sending Harold's hard hat flying.

Bud had one hand around Mackey's throat as he swung the pipe wrench straight at his head.

Harold managed to turn away at the last moment. The wrench hit the floor less than inch from his left ear. With a roar of rage, he shoved the hunting knife into the cowboy's shoulder. He felt it go in, then glance off a bone.

Pain shot through Bud's body so fast he lost his breath. The pipe wrench fell from his hand as his body went momentarily limp.

Harold grunted as he shoved the man off his belly, then rolled over onto his hands and knees to get up. His back was to the bathroom door when he heard it open. He heard a scream, caught a glimpse of the woman reaching for the wrench, and before he could get up, pain exploded at the back of his head.

Holly was hysterical. She hadn't even known Bud was in the room until it was too late. Mackey had killed Bud while she'd been hiding. Sobbing uncontrollably, she started to hit Mackey again when she heard shouts out in the hallway, and then someone yelling and beating on the door.

The blood was spilling out from beneath Bud's body, but she saw his fingers curl, as if trying to make a fist.

He was alive!

She leaped over Harold's leg in a frantic rush toward the door. She was halfway there with the pipe wrench still in her hand when the door flew inward.

Hotel security rushed into the room, their weapons drawn.

She pointed at the men on the floor. "The man in coveralls broke into my room. My fiancé has been stabbed!"

Security moved aside as a team of paramedics were the next to come inside. The medics began assessing the wounds of the two victims as a man with a badge confronted Holly.

"What happened here?"

"The man in coveralls knocked on the door. I thought it was my fiancé wanting back in the room. When I opened the door, he pushed his way inside and tried to kill me. I locked myself in the bathroom and used the house phone to call the front desk, and then my fiancé came back and saved me." She moved past the man to the medics tending Bud. "Is he going to be okay? Please tell me he's going to live."

"The other man has a severe head injury," a paramedic said.

Angry that they were even tending to Mackey's wound, she snapped.

"That's because I hit him with the pipe

281

wrench," Holly said. "And if he's still alive, it was unintentional."

The security officer frowned. "That sounded personal. Do you know your attacker?"

"Yes. His name is Harold Mackey, and he's connected to a case the police department is working. You need to contact Detective Whit Carver and tell him what happened." Then she dropped down at Bud's feet and grabbed the toe of his boot. "Help is here, Bud. You did it, darling. You saved my life. Now you have to stay strong. You have to come back to me. Damn it, Robert Tate. You better be hearing me. Don't you die! Don't you dare die on me!"

Someone touched her shoulder, then physically picked her up and moved her away. "Miss, you need to get back so we can get him on a stretcher."

Holly grabbed the paramedic's arm. "Can I go with him? I need to go with him."

"I'm sorry, miss. You can't ride in the ambulance."

Holly panicked. "You can't leave me behind. I need to be with him. Where are you taking him?"

Before he could answer, the room was suddenly filled with St. Louis police. Holly kept getting pushed farther and farther from where Bud was lying.

She saw when they rolled him onto the stretcher and started out the door, and she pushed forward, clutching his hand in a frantic grasp.

"I love you, Bud. I love you forever!"

She thought she saw his eyelids flutter, and then he was gone. She staggered to a nearby chair, still in shock and too drained to cry another tear. This day had become a nightmare. This must have been how Maria and Savannah had felt — scared out of their minds.

A few moments later another set of paramedics came into the room carrying a second stretcher. It had to be for Mackey.

She got up from her chair, then pushed through the throng of hotel security and policemen to where he was lying. His head wound was still seeping blood, but his nose had almost stopped bleeding. Even though he was lying on his side, she could tell his nose was broken.

The knife he'd stuck in Bud's shoulder was still on the floor. She knew it would be taken as evidence. A sudden chill ran through her body. She'd seen it before — that white bone handle and the initial *M* carved in the hasp. He'd never been without it.

She thought of all his victims who'd fallen prey to that knife, and how he, in complete disregard for their existence, had added to their horror by scalping them before they died. And at the same time he'd been humiliating them. A woman viewed her hair as part of her beauty, and he'd taken it, even before he'd taken their lives.

She stared at his face, so different in unconsciousness, and then her gaze slid to his hair and that long gray ponytail. After all these years he still wore it long, like Samson, as proof of his superiority and strength. Rage burned in her gut as she bent down and picked up the knife.

In a roomful of cops, no one was paying attention until it was too late. A cop spotted her from across the room and screamed, *"No!"*

Another officer turned, then lurched toward her, but not in time to keep her from grabbing the ponytail. She pulled it out straight and, with one swift slice, deftly removed it from his head and dropped it on his chest.

"It's no more than you deserved," she said, then handed the knife to the first policeman to reach her. "Yes, it'll have my prints on it. But you'd be advised to keep it just the same. That man is the serial killer called the Hunter, and he used that knife to scalp his victims before he cut their throats."

The room was in an immediate uproar, with the cops all shouting over each other.

"How do you know?"

"Who told you? Did he tell you?"

"How did you know that?"

"Call Detective Whit Carver" was all she would say.

More questions came at her from every direction, but she wouldn't talk. She watched them carry Harold out on a stretcher, flanked by a half-dozen of St. Louis's finest, with that hank of his hair, still bound by a single rubber band, lying across his chest.

FOURTEEN

Carver got the news about the attack as he was sitting down to dinner. He took one look at his microwave meat loaf and spuds, covered it with a piece of foil and stuck it in the refrigerator.

He was out the door before the scent left his nose and halfway to the hotel before he heard the first sirens. He didn't know anything except that Holly Slade had told them to call him and two people were down, but not which two. The knot in his gut kept getting bigger as the hotel finally came in sight.

He pulled in behind an ambulance and got out on the run, moving through the lobby and flashing his badge, then up the elevator. He wouldn't panic. Not yet.

But all the way up, he kept thinking they'd been too late. The task force had finally pinned down every victim to Harold Mackey's old route. They had filed the papers

286

for a search warrant for Mackey's house as he was leaving the office. If he'd been expecting a phone call, it would have been from the task force informing him that they had their warrant and were about to go in. Not a call like the one he'd gotten.

He got out on the sixth floor and started counting down doors. When he turned the corner and saw the crowd of cops and bystanders, he knew he was almost there.

As he approached, the crowd suddenly parted and a team of paramedics came out with a man on a stretcher. He stepped aside to let them pass, then saw the man's face.

It was Mackey.

Inside, the room was chaos. Hotel security and uniformed P.D. officers were all talking at the same time. He paused in the doorway to get his bearings, then saw her sitting alone on a small chair. She was alive! But she looked like she'd seen a ghost, which, as he thought about it, was probably right on target for how she must be feeling.

He looked around the room for her boy-friend and didn't see him. That wasn't good.

He entered the room and started toward her just as she looked up.

Their gazes met.

He saw a flicker of recognition, and then she stood up then started toward him.

He grabbed her arm.

"Miss Slade."

She didn't blink. She was in shock.

"Bud saved my life," Holly said, and then swayed on her feet.

Whit grabbed her to keep her from falling.

"What happened here?"

"I already told the police. Mackey tricked us. He separated us and tried to kill me." Then she leaned so close that her mouth was only inches away from his ear. "What kind of man kills his own child?"

"A crazy man. A mean man. A sick man," Whit said.

Holly swayed on her feet, her whisper softer still. "That blood runs in my veins, so what does that make me?"

Whit groaned inwardly. As usual, he'd said the wrong thing to a woman. He never had been able to get that right.

"Where's Bud, Holly?"

Her chin quivered. "I don't know. They took him away and wouldn't let me go with him."

"Wait here. I'll find out where they took him, and then I'll take you there myself."

She watched as he made his way across the room to a detective on the other side. She saw them talk, saw the detective turn and look at her. She didn't care what they were saying as long as she got to see Bud.

Whit was back with a grim expression on his face. "Get your purse and whatever you need. We're leaving."

Holly shoved her way through the crowd and found her purse on the floor beside the desk. She clutched it to her chest as she made her way back to him.

"I'm ready."

Whit took her by the elbow and steadied her all the way to the elevator. By the time he got her out of the hotel and into his car, she was shaking. The adrenaline rush was gone, and she was crashing.

"If you need to cry, feel free," he said, then reached across the seat and buckled her in.

She nodded, but her eyes stayed dry and fixed on the windshield, as if she were seeing something else besides the night lights of St. Louis.

He ran hot all the way to the hospital, with lights flashing and siren blaring.

Bud woke up in a place he didn't recognize. Some woman kept telling him to open his eyes and asking if he was cold. His thoughts were in a jumble, and he kept trying to pick them out and sort them into an order that would make sense. Pain rolled through him in waves, coaxing him to fall back into the void where pain didn't exist. But he didn't go. He kept thinking there was something he needed to remember.

"Robert. We need you to open your eyes."

Who was talking?

"Robert, you need to wake up."

He didn't recognize that voice. She didn't sound like anyone he knew, and he was sick and tired of hearing her say the same damn thing. So he opened his eyes just to shut her up.

"There you are!" she said brightly. "Can you tell me your name?"

His tongue felt thick, and the words were at the edge of his consciousness.

"Can you tell me your name?" she repeated.

"Bud."

"Oh. You go by Bud, do you? All right then, Bud it is."

He opened his eyes a little more, and saw bright, blinding light and green walls.

"Where . . ."

"You were injured, and the doctors operated on your shoulder. You're in recovery."

Shoulder? Shoulder. The fight. The knife. Oh, shit. Holly! Everything came flooding back.

"Holly," he mumbled.

290

"Holly? Is she your wife?"

Bud exhaled softly then slowly shook his head.

"Heart . . ."

The recovery nurse paused. She was a hardened veteran of misery and pain, but his answer took her by surprise.

"Holly is your heart? Are you saying she's your heart?"

"My heart." His thoughts slid out of sight. Too drugged to fight, he went with them.

The nurse paused, and for the first time since they'd wheeled him into recovery, she looked past the injury to the man who'd suffered it.

He was tall and well built, with a hard, chiseled face. His nose was strong and straight, his cheekbones high, angling to a nearly square chin. He looked like a man who could hold his own in the world. And somewhere there was a woman named Holly who was his heart.

Holly was waiting a short while later when they moved him to Intensive Care. She was waiting for him at the recovery room door, and she'd been given special dispensation to walk beside him as they wheeled him into ICU.

She didn't even care that he was unconscious again. It was enough that his heart was still beating. He had eight internal stitches in his shoulder, and ten external, but they'd told her that, barring unexpected complications, he would be fine.

It was all that mattered.

She never asked about Mackey's condition, but Whit knew he was two floors down, with cops guarding the door and his hands cuffed to the bed. He had a broken nose and a serious concussion. No one was sitting by his side. No one cared if his eyes ever opened again.

Six hours later Harold came to, saw the handcuffs on his wrists and knew it was over. There was no getting away from what he'd tried to do. But there was a measure of satisfaction in knowing they would probably never be able to pin the other stuff on him. It was still his word against the word of a five-year-old child who'd simply gotten in trouble for being where she shouldn't have been. It could be argued that over the years she'd become confused about what she'd seen. One thing was for sure, Twila wasn't going to show up and dispute his word.

Bud woke up to the feel of lips on his cheek and a gentle hand on his brow.

"There you are," Holly said.

He opened his eyes.

Holly reached for his hand.

"Are you in pain?"

"Not much," he mumbled, then felt himself drifting away again. He wanted to stay, but the drugs in his system were stronger than his will.

"Bud . . ."

He inhaled slowly. That was Holly — his Holly.

"My Holly."

Her vision blurred. "Yes, darling, I'm your Holly. Forever and ever."

"You okay?"

"I'm fine," she said, then gently squeezed his fingers to accentuate her point. "You saved my life. Do you remember that? You saved my life."

He frowned. "Bastard . . . had a knife."

"I know. But he's in custody, Bud. It's almost over. He can't hurt me or you or anyone else ever again."

Bud nodded once, then let himself go back under.

Holly didn't care. She would tell him over and over for the rest of their lives, and she would tell their children and their grandchildren, how he'd taken down a madman to save her life.

She was still struggling with how to live with the knowledge that the madman had been her father, but she would put that life and those memories behind her if it took the rest of her life to do it. If Bud had faith in her, then she could do no less than believe in herself. Andrew had believed she was worth saving. Her sisters loved her. It was more to build a new life on than some people had. It would have to be enough.

She glanced down at her watch. Visiting hours were almost over. Detective Carver had left her in the care of a fellow cop and would be picking her up at the hotel later. They'd gotten their search warrant and gone through Harold Mackey's current residence but had found nothing to physically link him to the old murders. He wanted her to walk through it, to see if she could spot something the rest of them had missed.

Holly leaned over Bud's bed and kissed him on the cheek.

"I'll be back," she whispered. "Until then, sleep well, my darling."

As the officer drove her back to the hotel, she was racking her brain, trying to remember everything she could of her life before. There had to be an answer there that would lead her to her mother. All she had to do was find it.

"This is it," Whit said, as he turned off the street and into the driveway.

Holly stared. It was an insignificant house. White. Wood frame. A small porch and a front door in need of painting. There was a chain-link fence around the backyard and no flowers in the front beds. It looked empty — indicative of the man who'd lived within.

"Let's do this," Holly said, and got out, then followed the detective inside.

Holly froze within a foot of the threshold. An involuntary shudder ran through her as she grabbed onto the door frame to steady herself.

"What's wrong?" Whit asked.

"Don't you feel it?"

"Feel what?"

She shook her head, unable to put it into words.

Whit shrugged. He couldn't imagine what this must be like and hated like hell to put her through it, but he had to close the Hunter case, and she was his last chance.

"Why don't you just start walking . . . see where it takes you," he said. "If you spot anything, anything that might help us, let me know."

"All right," Holly said, and then her gaze fell on a framed photo. "Oh, my God! I can't believe he kept this out on display. That's me with my mother."

She picked it up and held it against her chest. "I'm taking this with me."

Whit didn't argue.

"I don't suppose he's doing much talking," Holly asked, as she gazed around the room. She was loathe to touch anything in the dust-ridden house.

"Not a word."

Holly looked down at the photo, studying her mother's face and then her own. *We looked so happy,* she thought. She wished she could remember the moment. It would almost be like having her mother back.

Holly circled the room without speaking, opening drawers in a cupboard, peering into a small cubbyhole in the corner of the room, but nothing spoke to her.

As she moved into the kitchen, the hair rose on the back of her neck. She remembered standing in another kitchen and hearing the sound of a hammer. It was her curiosity that had led to their downfall. The old saying echoed in her head. Curiosity killed the cat. Except it was her mother who had died.

"Anything?" Whit asked, as she dug

through cabinets and drawers.

"Nothing," she said, as she stood on tiptoe to look into the top shelf of the cabinet by the sink, and then suddenly she gasped. "No!"

Whit darted forward. "You found something?"

"My little frog cup," Holly muttered. "He kept my little frog cup."

Whit looked into the cup at the tiny ceramic frog affixed to the bottom.

"Why is there a frog in there?"

"If a child won't drink her milk, what better way than to put a surprise for her at the bottom of the cup? She knows what's there, but she has to drink all her milk to see it."

"Well, I'll be," Whit said, and pretended not to look when she dropped the cup into her purse.

"Where's his bedroom?"

"This way," Whit said. "Follow me."

Holly's nostrils flared when she walked into the room. His presence was strongest here. She didn't linger.

The bathroom proved no better. That left them with one room to go.

"What's in here?" Holly asked, as they paused in the hall outside the door.

"A spare bedroom, with a good twenty boxes of stuff he never unpacked. We went through the boxes but didn't find anything."

He stepped in front of her and opened the door. "As you can see, it's even filthier in here than in the rest of the house."

The imprints of dozens of shoes had been left in the dust. Dust motes danced in the faint light coming through the yellowed window shades as she stepped into the room.

Frowning, she went straight to the closet. Except for a handful of old wire clothes hangers and a mousetrap, it was empty. She stepped back and surveyed the room, frowning and looking for another door.

Whit saw her frowning. "What?"

"I can't believe he would move into this house without a place for his trophies — all his trophies. The ones in the living room are obvious, and so are the mounted fish in his bedroom and the photos of his hunting trips hanging in the hall."

"Are you talking about those scalps you thought you saw when you were a kid?"

Holly spun, and anger was thick in her voice when she spoke. "I didn't *think* I saw them. I *know* I saw them. It got my mother killed."

Whit flushed. "Poor choice of words. Sorry."

"There's no basement here?"

"No."

"No storm cellar door outside? No record of him paying for a storage locker somewhere?"

"No, and trust me, we've looked. The task force has gone through his financial records and every aspect of his life for the past thirty years . . . long before the killings started."

Holly shook her head. "This isn't right. I'm telling you, he wouldn't live in a place where he couldn't have access to all his trophies. There's got to be a cellar or something."

Frustrated, Whit's voice rose in anger, too. "So you tell me where to look next."

Holly turned on him, as angry as he'd been with her. "Down. You need to look down. He was more like the animals he hunted that he was like a man. You know what animals do when they're scared? They go into a hole, under a log, inside a cave. When they're in danger, they do not stay above ground."

Whit's skin crawled. He'd never thought of a man that way before, but it made sense.

Holly spun toward the boxes and began pushing them around.

"There's nothing under here, right?"

"We moved all of them," Whit said. "It's just an old house and an old beat-up hardwood floor." He pushed a half-dozen of them aside to prove his point. "See? Nothing."

Holly shook her head. It didn't make sense. She began walking across the room from one wall to the other and back again, then ran into the next room and measured the distance to see if there could have been a dead space between the walls, but the figures matched up.

Whit watched her pacing, and then she suddenly stopped and turned to look at him.

"How old do bones and body parts have to be for a cadaver dog to smell them?"

Whit blinked. Shit.

"I'm not sure."

"Get a cadaver dog inside this house. He'll find what you're looking for. Because it's got to be here."

"That's pretty far-fetched," Whit said.

"You wanted my best guess. That's it. I'm telling you that the man I remember wouldn't have destroyed those trophies. He wouldn't have packed them away in some storage locker, or tossed them in the Mississippi for fear that he'd get caught. They're in here. I can feel it."

"I'll make some calls," Whit said. "In the meantime, I'll get you back to the hotel."

"I want to be here," Holly said. "When

you bring the dog, I need to be here. My mother might be, too."

Whit nodded. "I'll let you know."

A short while later he dropped her off and drove away. But the closer he got to the precinct, the more certain he was that she might have given them the answer after all.

FIFTEEN

They moved Harold to a holding cell to await his arraignment. He was a pretty sight when they booked him into jail sporting two black eyes and his broken nose bandaged.

He also had a bandage around his head and a couple of stitches in his scalp, with a continuing headache that the doctors had promised would fade with time. The fact that his skull was still in one piece after being hit with a pipe wrench was a miracle in itself, and there was nothing wrong with him that a doctor within the penal system couldn't handle. His days as a free man had just officially come to an end.

He accepted that he was there because of poor judgment. He should have made a run for it. He had no one to blame but himself, but there was one thing that kept bugging him. He was missing his hair. His ponytail was gone.

At first he'd thought they'd cut it off while

tending to his head wound, but they'd told him it had already been gone when he'd been brought in. He still didn't know what had happened to it, and no one he asked had an answer.

Inside the cell, he stretched out on his bunk, then grunted when his feet slid off the end to dangle in midair.

He was too fucking tall for the bed.

He had a court-appointed lawyer coming for a visit, but Harold considered that a waste of time. They had him dead to rights. He had tried to kill his daughter and, for all he knew, *had* killed her man. No one had mentioned the cowboy's condition.

It wasn't as if he could plead insanity. Stupidity was more like it. Disgusted with the situation he was in, he rolled over onto his side and pulled his knees up toward his chin. When he did, half his backside was hanging off the cot.

A miserable fix.

Holly leaned against the wall as she waited for the hotel elevator. It was unusually slow, but there was an obvious reason. From what she could tell, a convention of Mary Kay representatives had checked in. She'd never seen so many women in pink in her life.

While she'd been at the hospital with Bud,

she'd learned that the hotel manager had packed up their stuff and moved them to a suite. It was luxurious compared to the room they'd been in — a room that had suited her just fine until Harold Mackey had invaded it.

By the time she got out on her floor, she felt drained. She felt filthy after being in Mackey's house, and not because of the layer of dust. That was a house where evil abided, and the sooner he was locked up, the better for all concerned.

She locked herself in her new suite and flipped the safety catch, as well. No one was getting into this room without a battering ram. She tossed her purse on the sofa, draped her jacket over the back of a chair and kicked off her shoes, but her steps were dragging as she crawled up on her bed.

She stretched out, exhausted and frustrated and worried about Bud. She fingered her engagement ring, wondering how everything could have gone wrong so fast. Her eyes closed as she rolled over onto her side. She needed to call Bud's uncle Delbert and give him an update on Bud's condition, and she told herself that she would do that in a few minutes.

Delbert Walker had brought her to tears when she'd called him earlier to tell him what had happened, admitting that she felt guilty beyond words that it had happened because of her.

But the old man had been adamant, claiming Bud would be just fine and for her not to fuss. He told her that Bud had done exactly what he'd gone there to do, which was take care of her, and if she was all right, then Bud would agree that the rest of what happened had been worth it. He said that was what men did: take care of the women they loved.

Holly exhaled on a sigh. Bud's face flashed before her eyes, and he was laughing. It was the last thing she remembered as sleep pulled her under.

A phone was ringing. Holly woke with a gasp and then reached for her cell phone, only to realize it was the room phone. She rolled over and reached for the receiver.

"Hello?"

"Miss Slade, Whit Carver. Did I wake you?"

"Yes, but it's all right. What's happening?"

"I found us a cadaver dog. We're going back to Mackey's house this morning. Still want to go?"

"Yes, yes, I'll be ready."

"I'll be there in about twenty minutes."

"I'll be outside waiting," Holly said, and flew out of bed.

With no time for a shower, she stripped out of the clothes she'd slept in, then washed her face and brushed her teeth. Style was the last thing on her mind when she dressed. She brushed her hair, swiped some lipstick across her lips and reached for her shoes. Seconds later she was out the door and on her way to the elevator. With only minutes to spare, she bought two coffees and a sack of doughnuts in the lobby coffee shop and headed for the door, eating her first doughnut as she went.

Five minutes later Whit Carver pulled up. She brushed the sugar off her fingers, then got in.

"Morning, Miss Slade."

"Holly."

He smiled. "Holly."

"That's better," she said, and handed him a coffee and the doughnuts. "Help yourself. I've had all I want."

Whit's smile widened. "Thanks." He set the coffee in the cup holder, dug out a doughnut and took a big bite before driving away.

"So how are you feeling about this?" Holly asked.

"What? You mean bringing in the dog?"

He shrugged. "I'm all for anything that will give me answers. How do you feel about it?"

Holly leaned back against the seat, absently rubbing her engagement ring.

"To be truthful, I can't put into words what I've been feeling. Ever since my dad died — and I mean Andrew, the man who raised me — I've felt like I lost myself. I found out who I really am, and I wish I hadn't. Harold Mackey is an animal. I want him gone. I'll do anything I can to make that happen. But I need to talk to him before I leave St. Louis. If there is a God, He will help me find out what Mackey did with my mother's body."

Whit nodded. "I'll make that happen. And I hope you're right about today. Once we've got enough evidence to convict Mackey as the Hunter, the entire city of St. Louis will be grateful to you for coming back and telling your story. And the families of all his victims will be able to see justice done."

They were silent the rest of the way to Mackey's house, but when they pulled into the driveway, Holly's anticipation rose.

The handler and his dog were waiting on the porch. They turned as Whit and Holly came up the steps.

"Detective Carver, I presume. I'm Ray

Birch, and this is T-Bone."

The German shepherd heard his name and looked up. With his mouth open and his tongue hanging out, he looked as if he were smiling.

Whit nodded. "This is Holly Slade. It was her idea to bring in your dog, and we're hoping it pays off. Miss Slade believes that her father wouldn't get rid of his trophies, which in this case happen to be scalps from his victims. They're twenty years old. I can't vouch for what condition they'll be in even if they're in there. Can your dog work with that?"

The handler patted his dog. "If there's anything here, T-Bone will find it."

"Then let's get started," Whit said, and unlocked the door.

Holly stayed back, watching the handler and his dog sweep through the house.

Ray gave the command that set the dog to working, then he followed, urging the animal on every now and then with a pat or a command. They went through the living room, then the kitchen and utility room. The only thing the dog spotted was a dead mouse in a trap, but he didn't alert on it. Holly thought it was amazing that a dog could be trained to find dead bodies, and differentiate between people and animals.

After the front part of the house, Ray and T-Bone headed down the hall. They went into Mackey's bedroom, going through the closet and exploring every corner before they crossed the hall and went into the second bedroom, which contained nothing but boxes.

Within seconds of entering the room, T-Bone whined. Holly tensed. It was the first sound she'd heard him make. Was that a good sign?

The dog headed for the boxes, and began circling them and climbing up on them, then behind them, over and over.

"We're getting a hit," Ray said.

Whit frowned. "We've already been all through those boxes."

Holly knew her instincts about her father were right. "Move the boxes," she said. "We need to move all of them."

The three of them began shoving and scooting the boxes to the other side of the room, and the more floor space that was revealed, the more T-Bone began to react. He scratched on the floor, as if he were trying to dig.

Ray pointed. "There's something under the floor," he said, then called the dog off the hunt, praising him for his work and giving him a treat as he fastened the dog's leash to a doorknob to keep him out of the way.

Holly was down on her hands and knees, pounding the floor with her fist to see if it sounded hollow, looking for anything that would tell her she'd been right. But the ambient light inside the room was dim, and there was no bulb in the overhead fixture.

She ran to the window and tore down the old shade with her hands. It raised a cloud of dust as she flung it aside, but it also let a bright stream of light come pouring into the room. She turned to look down the length of the room to where the boxes had been stacked, and as the sunlight bathed the floor, she caught a glimpse of something shiny. She moved closer for a better look, then suddenly stopped and pointed.

"Come look! Look at this!"

Whit moved closer. At first it just looked like a nail that hadn't been driven far enough into the hardwood flooring, and then it hit him. Hardwood flooring wasn't nailed down. It was tongue and groove. There shouldn't be nails in the floor.

Holly got a nail file out of her purse and ran it down the same groove, then frowned at what came up with the dust.

"This looks like putty," she muttered, rubbing it between her fingers. She did it again.

"There's more. Here and here and here."

Whit frowned.

"We stop now! I'm calling in the crime scene investigators."

As he stepped out of the room to make the call, Holly got up off her knees and walked outside to the front porch, then sat down on the step. The sun was hot on the top of her head as she waited, but it felt good to be out of that place. At least out here she could breathe easy.

There was a huge knot in the pit of her stomach. Her heart kept fluttering, as if it had forgotten how to keep rhythm. She gazed across the street, eyeing the small frame houses, all of them about as dilapidated as this one, and wondered what went on behind their walls.

The door opened behind her. Whit came out and sat down.

"They're on the way."

She pinched the bridge of her nose to keep from crying.

Whit felt her pain. He couldn't imagine what kind of hell she carried in her head, not to mention the courage it had taken to reveal it.

They sat without speaking as time passed, watching Ray Birch playing catch with his dog in the front yard.

311

Suddenly Whit pointed.

"Here they come."

Holly stood up as he went to meet the crime scene team, then led the way through the house. They began to take pictures. She followed, watching when one of them began tapping on the spare room floor with a big crowbar.

"It sounds hollow here," he said.

It was the same place T-Bone had hit on, and the place where she had spotted the new nail.

Someone began prying up a board. Then another and another, until it became obvious there was a large space beneath the floor.

The knot in her stomach grew tighter as Whit got down on his knees and peered into the opening.

"Son of a bitch," Whit said. "I see stairs."

Holly felt sick. She leaned against the wall and closed her eyes as they removed more flooring until the stairs were completely revealed.

"Give me a flashlight," Whit said, then turned around and looked inquiringly at Holly.

"I need to see," she said, straightening.

"Are you sure?"

"I need to know if he . . . if my mother . . ."

312

She shuddered. "Please."

"Yeah, you've got the right," he said. "Follow me down."

Holly moved past the others without meeting their gazes. She didn't want to see the expressions of disgust and pity on their faces. It was more than she could handle. She braced herself as she started down, focusing on the faint glow from Whit's flashlight, and then halfway down he found the switch and the room was suddenly flooded with brightness.

They stood speechless in the face of what confronted them.

They had been lined up like soldiers — blondes, brunettes, redheads, their scalps all hanging from the walls, silent reminders of her father's insidious deeds.

And suddenly Holly was five years old again, innocently blundering into her father's secret world. She moaned and would have fallen, had Whit not grabbed her arm and steadied her as she descended the last few steps.

Techs from the crime lab quickly followed. Except for a brief gasp of shock or a softly muffled curse, they were silent. The trophy aspect of the macabre scene was obvious. Each scalp dangled from the wooden plaque to which it had been affixed, with an engraved nameplate below it.

Whit was stunned as he counted. Thirteen. They'd only known about nine. Where in hell were the other bodies?

Holly pushed past him and began scanning each name with growing panic. When she got to the last one and realized her mother's name was absent, she groaned, then grabbed her knees and bent over to keep from fainting.

Whit grabbed her arm. "Holly?"

"She isn't here," Holly mumbled, then stumbled toward the stairs, going up on her hands as if she were climbing a ladder, and then crawling out onto the floor on her hands and knees.

"Ma'am?"

Holly looked up. A uniformed officer had knelt beside her.

"Help me," she whispered. "I need to get outside. Get me outside."

He yanked her to her feet, and when she would have walked, he scooped her up into his arms.

Startled, Holly protested, "I can walk."

"No, ma'am," he said, and carried her out onto the porch, then put her down. A muscle jerked near his right eye as he met her gaze. "My mother was one of his victims. I was ten when she disappeared. I became a policeman because I wanted to find the man who killed her. Thanks to you, we've done it."

"Oh, my God, oh, my God, I'm sorry, I'm so sorry," she kept saying, then put her hands over her mouth to keep from screaming.

"You have nothing to apologize for any more than I do. We were children."

He patted her awkwardly on the shoulder, then walked away, back into the house.

Holly sank weakly onto the steps.

"They found what they were looking for?" Ray asked, walking over.

She nodded, then covered her face and started to sob.

Whit stayed on-site with the crime scene investigators while one of the officers took Holly back to the hotel.

Instead of going inside, she went straight to valet parking to get her car. She needed to see Bud. Even if he wasn't awake, she wanted to be in his presence.

Bud woke up with Holly's hand on his arm. She was staring off into space, and even as groggy as he was, he could tell she'd been crying.

"Hey, honey . . ."

She turned and quickly swiped her hands across her face. "Hey yourself, Mr. Man, how do you feel?"

"Alive, which at this point suits me just fine." He touched her face. "You missed one."

She sighed. So what if he knew she'd been crying? "They found the scalps today. They were beneath the floor of Mackey's house."

Bud gritted his teeth as he shifted to a more comfortable position. "Isn't that good news?" She nodded.

"And still you cry."

"You didn't see their faces. I'm his child. They're wondering if I carry the taint that made him what he is."

"Bullshit."

"You know they're thinking it. I know they're thinking it. If we have a child, *you'll* be thinking it, too."

"Unless you've suddenly turned into a psychic, you don't know what the hell anyone is thinking," he said. "As for us having a child, it's not if, it's when."

Holly's chin quivered. She crossed her arms on the bed beside him and hid her face.

It seemed to Bud that no matter what he said, she was ready to shoot it down. It was apparent that the last person who was able to deal with her past was Holly herself.

"All I can tell you is to lean on me, because my love is strong enough for both of us."

Holly lifted her head and saw the truth in his eyes. She threaded her fingers through his and held on, but the pain was too deep to cry.

Mackey was in handcuffs and shackles, and had been waiting for his lawyer to appear for a good ten minutes, when the door suddenly opened. A middle-aged woman wearing a rumpled brown suit and sensible black shoes walked into the interrogation room carrying a briefcase.

Harold gaped. "Who the hell are you?"

She slapped the briefcase onto the table between them and sat. "Myra Finch, your court-appointed lawyer."

"You're a woman."

Myra stifled a snort. "You're more observant than some of my clients. You need to know your situation has changed considerably since your arrest. The police have recovered thirteen women's scalps from beneath a bedroom floor in your house. There have now been thirteen counts of murder and two attempted murder counts filed against you. The police want to talk to you. They said they're short four bodies and wonder if you'd like to explain what you did with them. Also . . ."

Harold held up his hand. Besides the fact that he'd just been sideswiped by the news of the discovery, he wasn't about to talk to her about his case.

"Whoa now! You wait just a damn minute. Why didn't I get a man . . . I mean, a lawyer who's a man?"

"Luck of the draw. Who knows?" She pulled a folder out of her briefcase and opened it on the table between them. "How do you want to proceed?"

"Proceed? I'm not proceeding anywhere with you."

Myra frowned, which caused her eyebrows to run together in a rather impressive uni-brow. Harold couldn't quit staring.

"As I was about to say, you can plead in-nocent, although with your daughter's testimony and the thirteen scalps, it will be a tough sell. You can plead insanity, but no one's going to buy it, since you've been liv-ing a calm, quiet life and holding down a regular job for the past twenty years without another murder to add to your name. Or — and this is my personal favorite — you could plead guilty, save me some time and nightmares, the State of Missouri a butt-load of money, and go straight to jail while awaiting your trip to hell."

Harold stood up with a jerk and yanked at his handcuffs, which were fastened to his chair, while yelling and stomping his feet.

"I want another lawyer! Somebody get her out of here and get me another lawyer!"

Myra slapped the file back into her briefcase and then snapped it shut.

"Totally your call," she said. "I'll let the court know."

She strode to the door and knocked twice, then called out, "I'm through in here!"

The door opened. She walked out without looking back.

Harold's heart began to hammer as he finally processed what she'd said. They'd found them! The trophies were his, and now they were going to become public viewing. Things were spiraling from bad to worse. They would never understand. They would not appreciate his purpose.

A cop entered the room and marched Harold back to his cell.

Bud woke up again. They'd moved him out of ICU. He didn't remember that happening, but he guessed it didn't matter. Holly was standing at the foot of his bed, talking to a doctor, which did matter. He could hear the muffled murmur of their voices as they spoke.

"Holly."

She spun. "You're awake! Hi, honey . . . this is Dr. Larson. He's been taking care of you."

Bud's gaze shifted to the man beside her. The only thing he noticed about the doctor was his eyes. They were kind.

"Thank you."

Dr. Larson smiled. "You're welcome. You're doing fine. The knife blade glanced off your shoulder blade, missing any major arteries, which is good. The downside is, it did cut deeply into the muscles, which are going to take time and therapy to heal. I understand you're both from Montana and will be returning soon. You can easily do your therapy there."

Then he left, moving on to his next patient and leaving them alone.

Holly grabbed Bud's hand. "Isn't that great, honey? We'll be home before you know it."

"Home sounds like heaven."

"Anywhere with you is heaven."

"Kiss, please," he said with a smile.

Holly obliged, taking great care not to touch anything but his lips.

"I talked to your uncle Delbert," she said

a few minutes later.

Bud frowned. "Everything okay?"

"Everything but you," Holly said. "He's fine, and said to tell you to get well."

"By the time I get home, he'll have my job," Bud muttered.

Holly laughed.

It felt good to be happy, if only for a little while.

Bud patted the side of his bed. "Sit," he said. "Talk to me."

She pulled up a chair, then slid her fingers through his.

"Mackey is in custody, and they — we — found his trophy room. Wherever my mother is, whatever he did to her, he didn't take her scalp. That was such a relief."

Bud frowned. "Have they talked to him?"

"Not yet. Detective Carver said he refused his first court-appointed lawyer. They're sending another one."

"What was wrong with the first one?" Bud asked.

Holly grinned. "She was a woman."

Bud chuckled, then winced. "Oh, shit. Laughing hurts."

Her mood shifted. "I asked to talk to him."

Bud's eyes narrowed. He thought of all the reasons why she shouldn't, but he knew they wouldn't trump the one she held.

"Do you think he'll tell you where he hid her body?"

"I don't know. Maybe." She paused, looking down. "No, probably not. But I won't leave without trying."

"I wish I could be with you."

"I need to do this alone. Can you understand that?"

"Some."

She traced the lines on the palm of his hand. "You have a very long life line."

"The better to keep up with you, darlin'," he said softly, then lifted her fingers to his lips and kissed them one by one.

"You're my touchstone, Bud. You couldn't lose me if you tried."

SIXTEEN

Every media outlet in the state of Missouri was running coverage on the arrest of Harold Mackey, aka the Hunter. Old neighbors, acquaintances — everyone who'd ever had access to him — were all being interviewed, and the ones with pictures of him were selling them right and left.

Photos of his victims were also running with the coverage, as one by one living relatives came forward, willing to talk about their personal family stories and the family members he had killed.

The missing persons department was being flooded with calls from people desperate to know if the four unknown victims had been positively identified. Although Mackey had names under the scalps, until DNA confirmation on the four new ones came through, those names could not be released.

Carver's task force was getting calls by the dozen, requesting interviews, and after the discovery of the infamous scalps, even Hollywood had called.

Chief Hollis had issued a gag order and told everyone to refer all calls to his office. Whit didn't have to be told twice. He was still having nightmares about what they'd found. He hadn't been to church in years, but after walking into that bomb shelter, it was the only place he could think to go to absolve him of the feeling that they'd desecrated a tomb.

And he took it as a personal insult that they were four bodies short.

Mackey had never dumped two bodies in the same place, so they didn't have a dump site to go back and check. Whit had stared at that map until his eyes burned, trying to see a pattern, to understand why Mackey had picked the sites he'd chosen, but nothing popped out at him.

And there was a Fed from Quantico wanting permission to interview Mackey. He wanted to know why Mackey had gone dormant so abruptly. But the only request Whit felt obligated to honor was Holly Slade's. All he was waiting for now was a phone call from Mackey's lawyer, but the man had insisted on a new one, which meant there would be a delay in everything, starting with the arraignment. They had the go-ahead from the chief to take Holly to see the man, but that, too, had to wait until he'd conferred with his lawyer. And if Mackey wanted his attorney present when he talked to Holly, they couldn't deny him. All Whit needed was for that phone to ring.

Holly moved from room to room in her suite, pacing, planning, trying to figure out what she would say to Mackey. Exactly how did one ask a murderer to reveal his innermost secrets and make him give up the location of a body?

Carver had said he would call once he'd set up a time, but the phone had yet to ring. What if Mackey said no? What if he wouldn't talk to any of them? How could she live the rest of her life with the question of her mother's fate unanswered?

She moved to the window and looked out at the Arch. It represented an impossible feat of engineering, and yet they'd done it. If only the St. Louis police were as successful with tying up this case.

Suddenly there was a knock at her door. She frowned.

The last time she'd answered a door in this hotel, her own father had tried to kill her. She moved quietly to the door, peered through the security peephole, then gasped and began fumbling with the dead bolt.

"Just a minute!" she yelled, and finally got it to turn, then yanked the door open. "What in God's name are you doing here?"

Bud walked in, grim-lipped and white as a sheet as he headed for the sofa.

"Oh, my God! You shouldn't be here! Are you crazy?"

Bud was already down and stretching out on the cushions. He pointed at her.

"You. Me. Partners for life."

Holly dropped to her knees and ran a hand across his forehead. Except for the sweat of exhaustion, he was cool.

"No fever. I hurt like hell, but I have pain pills."

"Who the hell let you out of the hospital under your own steam?" Holly asked. "What if you start bleeding? What if you get an infection? I'm scared."

"Well so am I. It scares me to see the shock in your eyes and the fear in your face. It scares me that he'll say something to you that you can't face. I need to know as much as you know, baby. We can't get through this unless we do it together."

"Oh, Bud . . . Bud . . . how have I lived this long without you?" Holly whispered, then wrapped her arms around his waist and laid her head on his stomach.

He threaded his fingers through her hair as a fresh wave of pain rocked through him.

"About those pain pills . . . they're in my right-hand pocket. If you'll get the water, I could down a couple right now."

Holly headed for the sideboard, grabbed a bottle of water and a clean glass, and ran back.

Bud popped the pills, then downed them with the water straight out of the bottle.

"Many thanks."

"Come lie down on the bed. It's so much softer." She helped him up and walked him into the bedroom, steadying him with a hand around his waist.

"The pills are likely to make me sleepy."

"I'll be quiet," she said.

He eased himself down on the bed and then very carefully stretched out.

"Ah, God . . . this so sucks."

Holly blinked guilty tears. "This happened because of me."

"No. It was *for* you, not *because of* you. Now quit fussing and lie down beside me."

"Want me to pull off your boots?"

"No, leave 'em on in case they call today. It was too hard getting them on."

"But —"

He gripped her hand, harder than she'd expected. "No buts. I'm here because you're not facing Harold Mackey alone. I won't interfere, but I'll be there, and I'll hear everything he says. It's that or we're on the next plane to Montana and forget we ever heard the bastard's name."

Holly crawled up onto the bed beside him. "I can't cry. I don't want my eyes all red and swollen, so Mackey will think I'm crying because of him, but I want you to know how special you are. I love you, Robert Tate."

Bud fingered her ring. "I love you, too. I think I'm going to rest now. Promise you won't go anywhere without me."

"I promise."

He closed his eyes.

Holly lay facing him, burning every nuance of his misery into her brain. She was determined to remember, when she was in labor giving birth to their first child, that, for the love of his woman, he'd been the first to bear pain.

Edwin Walsh, Esquire, was just coming out of court when his cell phone rang. He saw it was his secretary and answered the call as he headed up the stairs.

"Yes, Bobbie?" he said without fanfare, then realized he was puffing and made a mental note to hit the gym more regularly.

"Mr. Walsh, you got a message about a new court-appointed client. He's in the city jail."

"Give me a name."

"Harold Mackey."

Edwin stopped. Pretty much everyone in the state knew that name now. "No, that's not right. Myra Finch got him. We were talking about it at lunch."

"Yes, sir, but Mackey refused her."

Edwin cursed aloud, then put his hand over his mouth as he remembered he was still standing in the halls of justice.

"Damn it. Hell-fucking-damn it," he whispered. "I know every man deserves legal representation, but this is a career killer."

"I'm sorry, sir."

"So am I. Cancel my next appointment. I'll run by the jail before I come back to the office."

He disconnected without saying goodbye.

His stride lengthened as he headed for his car. "I just had to be a lawyer. Mother wanted me to be a doctor, but no . . . I had to do my own thing."

An hour later he entered the city jail, carrying Mackey's file. He'd been there countless times before, but this time was different. This time he was prejudiced against his client and there was no way to get past it. He believed in the judicial system and that everyone deserved the right to legal representation, but he also secretly believed there were occasional exceptions. By the time he was escorted into the interrogation room, he'd given himself a pep talk. All he had to do was get through this.

Then he took one look into Harold Mackey's eyes and shuddered. He hadn't needed a pep talk. He needed an exorcist.

"Harold Mackey. My name is Edwin Walsh. I am your court-appointed lawyer."

Mackey nodded.

Edwin sat down and began to read off the charges.

Mackey held up his hand. "No trial."

Edwin felt as if someone had just handed him a winning lottery ticket.

"You intend to plead guilty?"

Mackey nodded.

"It's my sworn duty to make sure you understand the charges."

"I'm not stupid," Mackey snapped. "The sooner this is over with, the sooner I settle in."

Edwin frowned. "Settle in?"

"To prison," Harold said.

Edwin couldn't believe what he was hearing. "You *want* to go to prison?"

Mackey leaned forward.

Edwin unintentionally cringed.

Mackey sneered. "No. I don't *want* to go to prison, but I don't see a way out. I am practical man. Facts are facts. So I say no trial."

"I'll get the proper papers ready. You're being arraigned in the morning. You'll enter a guilty plea then."

"Whatever," Harold said.

Edwin shuffled through the file and pulled out a memo.

"There's one other thing. The police want to talk to you about the location of some unaccounted-for bodies, but since you're entering a guilty plea, again I would advise your cooperation. You have no reason not to, and it could get you a life sentence instead of death. Also, an investigator from the FBI wants to talk to you, as well as a woman named Holly Slade."

Harold blinked. That surprised him. It showed guts. And he admired strength.

"I'll talk," he said. "Can't promise what I'll say, but I'll at least hear what *they* have to say."

"I'll arrange it, then. I believe that's all, so I'll see you in court tomorrow, for the arraignment," Edwin said, and shuffled the papers back into the file.

He walked out without looking back.

Bud had slept off the pain pills, and once it got dark and it became apparent that Carver wasn't going to call, Holly helped him undress and get comfortable. He'd traded his boots and jeans for a pair of sweatpants, and decided to bypass a shirt, because it hurt too much to put one on.

Fifteen minutes earlier, while Bud dozed, Holly had ordered room service and found a pay-per-view movie on television that she knew Bud would like. She'd given him the remote and then gotten on her laptop to catch up on email.

There was a message from Maria. It was short but sweet. *I'm out of the hospital. Stuff is happening. Can't wait to see you.*

There were no messages from Savannah, but a lot from friends and neighbors back home, most of which were full of sympathy regarding Andrew's death. She was thankful no one back home knew what was going on with her, or she would never get through explaining the chaos.

She finished answering the messages with the movie playing in the background. Finally their food arrived.

"What's for dinner?" Bud asked, as Holly

followed the waiter in with their meal, and the smells were enticing.

She began lifting the lids. "I wasn't sure what would sound good to you but I thought we should skip the heavy stuff. I ordered a Southwest frittata, hash browns and buttered toast."

"What's for dessert?"

Holly laughed. "You *are* feeling better." She pulled the cover off the last dish. "Apple pie à la mode."

He smiled. "That's what I'm talking about."

She had begun to divide the frittata when he stopped her with a touch.

"Pie first, or the ice cream will melt."

At that point she wouldn't have argued with anything he said. "Spoon or fork?"

He chose a spoon.

She handed him the whole dessert. "Enjoy."

He eased back against the pillows and then took his first bite, rolling his eyes as he chewed and swallowed.

"It's good, but not as good as yours."

Holly smirked. He was so full of it. "You do know how to sweet-talk a woman, don't you?" she said, then served herself some of the egg and hash browns.

They ate in silence, comfortable after

years of sharing the same table, trading bites and then finally stories as the meal wound down.

"I'm so done," Bud said, as he handed her back his plate.

"You ate really well for a man who just had a knife stuck in him."

He winked. "Just keeping up my strength."

Holly wheeled the food cart out into the hall, then made sure the door was locked.

"I'm going to take a shower. You want to watch some more TV?"

"Sure," he said, and she handed him the remote.

She was still in the shower when her cell phone began to ring. Bud started to let it go to voice mail, then saw that the call was from Whit Carver. He answered it.

"Hello."

Whit forgot what he was going to say. "Tate? Is that you?"

"Yes. Holly's in the shower."

"What the hell are you doing out of the hospital?"

"Sticking close to my woman is what I'm doing. What's up?"

"Are you mobile?"

"Is he going to talk to her?"

"Yes."

"When?"

334

"Tomorrow at one o'clock. City jail. Tell her I'll pick her up around twelve-thirty."

"We're both going."

"Can you even walk?"

"He cut my shoulder, not my legs. I won't let her anywhere close to him without me there, too."

"I can promise you he's in chains and shackles, and there will be armed guards in the room and outside the door no matter who he's talking to — except his lawyer, of course. Oh, by the way, tell Holly she won't have to testify in court."

"That's good news, but why not?"

"He's pleading guilty at his arraignment tomorrow."

"That's good to know. When she talks to him, is he going to be in one of those rooms with a two-way mirror?"

"Yes."

"Can you hear what he's saying from the other side?"

"Yes."

"Then that's where I'll be. If there's a spare chair around, I'll take it. Otherwise, I'm good."

There was a long moment of silence, then Whit said, "You are one tough son of a bitch, and I mean that in the nicest way."

Bud smiled. "I'll take it as a compliment.

We'll be ready."

Holly came out of the bathroom just as he ended the call.

"Who was that?"

"Carver. You've got your interview. One o'clock tomorrow at the city jail."

At first she didn't respond. She just stared into space.

"Holly?"

She jerked. "What?"

"Are you okay?"

She shrugged. "I've been trying all day to figure out how to ask him about Mother."

"You'll find your way. You always do."

"Do you need any help in the bathroom?"

"No, I'm good. I'll just sleep in my sweatpants, and settle for washing my face and brushing my teeth. I won't be long."

Holly watched until he had shut the door behind him; then she walked to the windows overlooking the river. The Arch and the riverboats were lit up like Christmas trees. Down below, the streets looked shiny. She was surprised to see it had been raining. There was so much riding on tomorrow, and she was weary of the stress. She pressed her forehead against the cold panes of glass and closed her eyes.

"God help me."

■ ■ ■ ■

At the jail, Mackey was the man of the hour. The agent from Quantico was there, waiting his turn to talk, looking forward to finding out why such a notorious serial killer had quit cold turkey.

Detective Carver was anxious to get locations on the four other bodies, but he wasn't broaching the subject with Mackey until Holly spoke to him first. It only seemed fair, given everything she had done for them. He was on the way to the hotel to pick her up, though he was still anxious about Tate going with her. The will to do something was often stronger than the body's ability. He was hoping they didn't have to call an ambulance to the jail if Tate couldn't hold up.

But to his surprise, as he pulled up at the hotel, they came right out.

"You must have been watching for me," Whit said, as he got out of the car to help Bud in.

"Bud, you take the front seat," Holly said. "It'll be easier for you to get in and out. I'll ride in back."

"Yes, ma'am," Bud said, and eased himself inside. He didn't even argue when she buckled him in before getting in the back.

Whit eyed the couple with something akin to jealousy, wishing he'd found a woman like her when he was younger, then reminded himself that he might have had better luck if he'd been looking somewhere besides a sports bar.

"Ready?" Whit asked, as Holly shut the back door.

She nodded, buckling herself in as he drove away.

"Has anybody talked to Mackey yet?" Bud asked.

"No. Holly gets the first shot." Whit glanced at her in the rearview mirror. It was obvious that she was nervous. "I wish I could guarantee you'll get what you came for."

She shrugged slightly. "There are no guarantees in life, are there?"

"No, ma'am, there are not."

The rest of the trip passed in silence. When they got to the jail, Holly busied herself with helping Bud, so by the time they got to the interrogation room, some of her nerves had settled.

Then Whit walked them through a door and pointed. From where they were standing, they could see Mackey sitting at a table. He was handcuffed and shackled and, to

Holly's horror, staring straight at them. It took her a moment to remember that he was looking at a two-way mirror and couldn't tell who was on the other side.

He looked strange without his ponytail, and it gave her a good deal of satisfaction that, thanks to her, his nose was still taped and both his eyes were black.

The bandage on his nose gave him a macabre appearance, as if he was hiding part of himself behind a mask, which seemed fitting, since he'd shown a mask to the world for years.

Holly frowned. "So he's alone."

"He didn't want the lawyer there when he talked to you," Whit said. "But there will be a guard with you when you go in."

"Nice pair of black eyes," Bud said. "Way to go, honey."

"I slammed the door in his face," she said, but took a step backward just the same.

"He can't see us," Whit reminded her.

"He doesn't have to," Holly muttered. "He knows we're here."

Bud put a hand on her shoulder. "Are you ready for this?"

She turned and buried her face against his neck.

Bud leaned his cheek against the crown of her head as he gave her a strong, one-armed hug; then he pushed her away, forcing her to meet his gaze.

"Holly Slade, you are the strongest woman I know. Don't let that bastard know you're scared."

"I won't." She turned to Whit. "I'm ready, and Bud needs a chair."

"Right, I'll bring one just as soon as I let her in," he said.

Bud watched them walk out the door, then turn a corner. A few moments later the door to the interrogation room opened. A very large armed guard appeared, followed by Holly. Bud's gaze went straight to her face. He knew her better than anyone on the planet and he couldn't tell from her expression what the hell she was thinking. That was when he began to relax.

"Way to go, baby," he said softly.

Whit came back with a stool. "The chair would be too short for you to see in. Is this okay?"

"It's fine. Can we hear what they're saying?"

Whit flipped a switch beside the window. They watched as Holly headed for the table, but instead of sitting across from him, she grabbed the chair and pulled it to the far side of the room before she sat down.

Whit smiled. She was already setting the

340

tone by reminding Mackey that she was the one in charge.

But Bud knew something Mackey didn't. Holly wasn't doing it because she was afraid. She was putting distance between them because of her disgust.

Mackey curiously eyed the woman entering the room. She was tall compared to Twila and didn't look anything like she had as a child. As she moved in front of a barred window, the sunlight caught in her hair. That hadn't changed. It was still thick, and a dark, rich auburn.

There was a moment when the thought ran through his mind that a beautiful piece like that would have been a valuable addition to his trophies, and then his focus scattered when she grabbed the empty chair and dragged it to the opposite wall. The back legs made a loud, screeching noise, like fingernails on a chalkboard. There was nothing subtle about her feelings. No solicitous silence from her.

"Hello, Harriet."

Holly sat. "I go by Holly now. Nice haircut."

It was the studied smirk on her face that gave her away. It was her! By God, she was the one who'd cut off his ponytail. The bitch!

341

Harold waited for her to continue, but she didn't. In fact, the stare she was giving him was so intent it became unsettling. He didn't like being on the defensive and challenged her, his voice loud and angry.

"They said you wanted to talk, so talk."

"I don't intend to talk to you. I have one question to ask you. Just one, and then I'm gone."

"Then ask."

"What did you do with my mother's body?"

The question itself wasn't a surprise to Harold, but the anger in her voice was. It took him a moment to accept that she wasn't scared of him. Not even a little bit. His estimation of her rose even more. She'd fought back in the hotel room. It was part of why he'd gotten caught. Pride swelled within his chest. If he had to go down, it felt right that it was because he'd had a worthy opponent.

"You are a fine, strong woman," Harold said. "You got that from me."

Holly wanted to scream. It took everything she had to stay seated, but she got to him when she laughed. The shock in his eyes was worth the effort it took to make it happen.

"You are so full of shit," she said. "I got

nothing from you. In fact, you *took* every-thing away from me that mattered."

A red flush swept up Harold's neck and face.

Holly glared back. "I repeat. What did you do with my mother's body?"

"Don't you want to know what hap-pened?" he asked. "Don't you care to know that she had to beg for her life because of you?"

Holly stood abruptly. When she came out of the chair, Bud stood up, ready to invade their space should the need arise.

Whit touched his arm.

"She's good, she's good," he said softly. "Let her get it all said."

Holly was livid. She pointed at Mackey. "I didn't kill her. *You* killed her. And I ask again, what did you do with my mother's body?"

In growing rage Harold yanked on the chains anchoring him to the chair.

"You snooped where you didn't belong. I told you not to tell or you'd be sorry. I told you if you did, you'd never see your mother again."

"Son of a bitch," Whit muttered.

Holly was so mad she was shaking. "I was five, you dumb-ass. Five-year-old children know only one thing. If you get hurt, tell

Mother. If you get scared, tell Mother. If someone threatens your life, tell your mother. You did all three to me. You yanked my hair, slammed me up against the wall and then threatened my life, so I told Mother. What did you do with her body?"

Harold's eyes were bulging, and there was a droplet of spittle at the corner of his mouth.

"She came back from that damn church without you. I knew the minute she walked in the door alone that you were gone. She wouldn't tell me where you were. I kept asking, 'What did you do with my kid?' but she wouldn't talk. I tried to beat it out of her, and she still wouldn't talk."

Holly felt sick. Hearing how her mother had suffered wasn't unexpected, but hearing him say it without any emotion other than anger was shocking.

"Where is she?" Holly yelled.

Harold shuddered. He wasn't used to rage. He'd always prided himself on being the one to use anger as a means of control. But he had to admit, his girl was tough. He leaned back in his chair, and just like that, his own rage was gone.

There was a knot in the pit of Bud's belly, but his admiration for Holly had just gone up another notch. Damn, but she was an amazing woman to be able to trade barbs with that animal and hold her ground.

"You know what?" Harold said. "I'm glad I didn't kill you. I'm glad you grew up. I don't even mind so much that it was you who brought me down. You'll carry my blood when I'm gone."

The thought made Holly sick. "Where's my mother's body?"

Harold smiled. He looked like an animal showing his fangs, and still Holly wouldn't give way.

"You know what Twila did that sealed her fate?"

Holly stared.

Regardless of her silence, Harold continued. "I asked her again, 'Where's my kid?' She slapped me and laughed. She said you weren't even mine. I didn't believe her then, and after seeing the guts you exhibit, I know for sure that she lied. You get your toughness from me. But it was that lie . . . that's when I broke her damn neck. There should not be lies between a man and his woman."

Holly stifled a gasp. If even the remote possibility existed that he wasn't her father, it was the best news she'd heard since this nightmare began. But she'd had enough. Her hands curled into fists, and she started toward him.

Again Bud came off the stool. Even Whit got antsy.

The guard in the corner of the room tensed, as if trying to decide to stay put or move forward.

Holly walked across the room. Bracing herself against the table with the palms of her hands, she leaned forward. With only inches between her face and Mackey's, she looked straight into his eyes and screamed the same question again, slapping the table between each word.

"What . . . the . . . hell . . . did . . . you . . . do . . . with . . . my . . . mother's . . . body?"

Harold recoiled, his eyes narrowing. "She's in the basement of our old house, right where our life came undone."

"Thank you, God," Bud said softly.

"I'll be damned," Whit muttered. "I didn't think he was going to tell her."

Holly straightened, then turned around and headed for the door.

"You're one fine woman," Harold said. "You deserve to live."

Holly paused at the door and looked back. "You don't."

SEVENTEEN

Holly was shaking so hard she couldn't breathe. She saw Bud coming through the doorway and all but fell against his chest as she wrapped her arms around him.

"Oh, my God, oh, my God, I feel sick," she said.

Bud was choking back tears. "I've got you, baby. I've got you, and I've never been so proud."

Holly's heart was hammering so loudly that she could barely hear him as she kept her face against his chest.

Whit Carver was in awe. "You are something, lady," he said quietly, patting her awkwardly on the back. "I've got some questions of my own to ask before I turn Mr. FBI loose on him, but after the reaming out you gave him, I think you've softened him up for me. I have four more bodies to locate before I can completely close this case, but the bad guy is behind bars, and he's never getting out until we put him in the ground."

Still held within the shelter of Bud's arms, she looked up.

"Could I ask for one more favor?"

"Anything," Whit said.

"If I give you a DNA sample, can you have it tested against his? If there's even the slightest chance that I'm not his daughter, I have to find out."

"You've got it," Whit said. "I'll have someone from the lab come up and take it, then an officer will take the two of you back to the hotel. In the meantime, I assume you want to be on hand when I take the crime scene team to your old residence?"

"I have to be there. Finding out what happened to my mother is what brought me back to Missouri. She meant to come back for me. I won't let her down."

"I'll pick you up tomorrow. I'll call with a time. You'll be on hand from the start." Whit glanced at Bud. "You look like shit. When you two get back to the hotel, let your woman put you back to bed, and don't get up until you hear from me again."

Within the hour they were back at the hotel and on their way up to their suite.

Ida Pacino was watering her begonias when

she saw a dark sedan turn a corner, then come down the street, followed by three police cars and a big van.

The sedan pulled into the driveway of the house across the street. The police cars pulled in along the curb out front, and the van pulled into the driveway behind the sedan.

People spilled out of the vehicles in twos and threes. When she recognized Holly Slade, she almost called out, wondering what could possibly be going on.

When Cecil Fairfield let them into his house, her confusion grew.

Holly got out of Carver's car and glanced over her shoulder. She saw Ida in her yard but didn't have time to acknowledge her. She was too concerned about Bud making it out of the car. She was worried about him. He hadn't slept well last night and was patently miserable, but she hadn't been able to convince him to stay behind. All she could do was make sure he had his pain pills and find him a comfortable place to be.

For Whit Carver, telling the current home-owners, Cecil and Loretta Fairfield, what lay hidden in the basement of their house had not been pleasant. He was pretty sure from the horrified reaction they'd had when he'd called on them last night that they would be moving before long. He felt sorry for them. The police department was about to make one hell of a mess, for all intents and purposes turning their nice little house into a crime scene.

Cecil met them at the door with a resigned expression on his face.

"Detective Carver."

Whit shook his hand. "Mr. Fairfield, this is Holly Slade and her fiancé, Robert Tate. Holly lived here with her parents as a child, and it is Holly's mother who we believe was buried in the basement."

Cecil paled as he nodded at Holly. "I'm very sorry."

"So am I," she said. "I appreciate how difficult this must be for you and your wife."

"Loretta went to her mother's last night." He looked at Holly strangely. "She remembered talking to you several days ago. Said to give you her condolences." Then he motioned to the people crowding up the porch. "You might as well come in and get this over with."

Within minutes the house was crawling with a crime scene crew, several detectives and a couple of techs from the crime lab. Holly peered curiously down the hallway before following the others into the kitchen.

The house felt different, and yet the basic layout was the same as she had come to remember.

Bud saw the tension on her face and a thin bead of sweat on her upper lip. He feared she was holding on to her sanity by a thread.

"Are you okay?" he asked.

She nodded, but the grip she had on his hand was almost painful.

Carver approached. "As soon as they get all the equipment in, you can go down. Fairfield said when they bought the house from Mackey the basement had a new concrete floor."

Whit glanced over his shoulder as the last of the crew disappeared. "I'll take you down long enough to see if anything stands out as suspicious to you, and then you're free to come back up here or go outside, whichever suits you best."

Holly took a deep breath as they moved to the stairs. She paused at the doorway, and for a moment she was a child again, and something bad was waiting down below.

Bud was behind her. He leaned forward and whispered near her ear, "I'm here."

Holly looked over her shoulder. It was the calmness on his face that got her past the fear.

"Easy does it," Whit said, and went down

ahead of her to steady her descent.

On the first step Holly began to hear the jackhammers, and the farther down she went, the louder they became. It wasn't until she was all the way down and standing beneath the lights that she realized no one had started any machinery. What she'd heard had been in her head.

"So what do you think?" Whit asked.

She set her jaw and looked down. There had been nicks in the concrete and a low spot beneath the stairs, but now everything was smooth and even. It was definitely a newer floor. She turned around, then gasped.

"Wait! That's new, too! It wasn't there before!" She ran to the wall, slapping her hands against the bricks. "There used to be a door here that led to a small room. That was where I saw the scalps. It was me walking into that room that started this whole nightmare."

Bud had to pull her hands away from the wall to make her look at him. "That's bull, Holly. Don't even go there. He started it when he began to kill."

Her eyes were wild, her body shaking from the stress. "All I know is, the door is gone, which means he didn't bury my mother under the floor. I'm saying she's in that room behind that brick wall."

Whit stepped forward, defusing the moment.

"Then the wall comes down."

The news immediately changed the work plan. The men abandoned jackhammers for sledgehammers and pry bars as they attacked the wall with energy. The bricks had been stacked and mortared loosely, as if they'd been put up too quickly and without a great amount of skill. They began falling in chunks of two and three. The wall was definitely coming down.

Holly moved to the far side of the basement, then sat on the steps, refusing to leave. Bud was on the steps above her. She sat between his knees, taking comfort from the pressure of his hand on her shoulder, watching with mounting horror as the bricks gave way to the onslaught of men and tools. Blow by blow, brick by brick, the original wall and the old metal door were soon revealed.

There was a long, awkward moment of silence as the crew stared at the door, each of them struggling with the idea of what was behind it.

"Let's get this over with," Whit said, but when he reached for the doorknob, there was a hand on his arm.

It was Holly.

"Please?"

His first thought was *hell no*. He looked over her shoulder to the man behind her. Tate wasn't happy about it, either.

"No, ma'am . . . Holly . . . you don't understand what's in —"

Holly's chin jutted. "Yes, I do. It's my mother. She's been waiting a long time for someone to find her. It needs to be me."

Whit heard someone in the back of the room blowing his nose and felt like crying himself.

"It might be stuck," he said.

Holly pushed past him without comment and grabbed the doorknob in a quick, frantic gesture, almost as if they were fighting a battle of life and death, when in truth death had come a long time ago.

The doorknob turned, and to their surprise, the door actually swung inward, slowly and with a considerable amount of squeaking hinges, but it was open.

Holly had been in a state of high panic during the demolition, but now that it was done, an odd calm had settled within her.

The interior was as dark as Harold Mackey's heart. She flipped the switch, but nothing happened.

"Flashlight! Someone hand me a flashlight!" Whit yelled.

As they waited, Holly's eyes began to adjust. Even before the flashlight was put in her hands, she'd seen something — something small and crumpled toward the back of the room.

"She's in there," Holly whispered, and then the flashlight revealed the truth. She stared for a moment, her heart breaking with the final proof of her greatest fear, then covered her face and turned away, too devastated to cry.

Bud had seen enough to give him nightmares, and pulled her out of the doorway and away from the room, leading her upstairs and then out of the house, so concerned for her that he barely registered the fact that the media were on the scene.

Apparently someone had tipped them off that the police were at the Hunter's old house, and that they were looking for a body. Camera crews and newsmen lined the street on both sides, interviewing neighbors to find anyone who'd known the Mackeys.

Holly looked horrified.

"Don't look at them," Bud said. "Sit down before you fall down."

There were two wicker chairs on the porch. She sat in one, while Bud took the other. The cameras might be aimed at them, but at least the police were keeping the intruders in the street.

The men filed past the skeleton at the back of the room like mourners at a funeral. The clothing she'd died in was in tatters, while bits and pieces of mummified flesh still clung to the bones. What was left of her hair verged on disintegration, but it was quickly obvious that she had not been scalped.

"Lord have mercy," Whit whispered, and walked away, leaving the rest of what had to happen to the coroner and the techs from the crime lab.

He came out of the basement to find Cecil sitting at the kitchen table staring at a cup of coffee.

"Was she down there?" he asked.

"Yes. But your basement floor is still intact. There was another room he'd bricked off."

"It doesn't matter. We're putting the house up for sale, although after all of this, it will be a miracle if it ever sells."

There wasn't anything left to say. Whit exited the house, then stopped short when he saw the growing media circus.

"Well, hell."

"They're everywhere," Holly said. Her eyes were wide with panic.

"I'll get you out of here, don't worry."

"Do they have to know about me?"

"No, they do not. For all intents and purposes, Mackey confessed to murdering his wife and we just found her body. End of story."

Holly looked at Bud. She needed to get him back to bed, but there was another roadblock she needed to face.

"I can't have her body yet, can I?"

"No, I'm sorry, Holly," Whit said. "Not yet. But you can set everything you need to do in place before you leave, and when the coroner is finished, we can ship her remains directly to Montana, if that's what you want."

"Yes, that's what I want."

"So let's get you two back to the hotel. I'll give you the numbers to call and the names of the people you'll need to see to get this done, so . . . this is where we part company."

Holly stood up, but instead of shaking his hand, she hugged him.

"You have no idea what all this means to me. I can't thank you enough for believing my story and forgiving my blunders. You kept us safe and alive, and we'll be forever grateful."

Whit was embarrassed by her praise. "When it came down to it, you two pretty much kept yourselves safe."

Then they noticed a commotion at the end of the front walk. An elderly woman was trying to reach the house, but the police wouldn't let her.

"That woman is my old babysitter, Ida Pacino," Holly told Whit. "She's the one who gave me the photos, remember? I need to talk to her."

Whit waved at the officers, and they let the elderly woman pass.

Ida was red-faced and wide-eyed by the time she reached the porch steps.

"Come sit down," Holly said, and helped her into the chair she'd just vacated.

"What's going on? Someone said they're looking for a body. Is that true?"

Holly squatted down beside the chair, then took Ida's hands.

"I'm going to tell you something, but I'm going to ask that you never tell anyone else."

Ida gripped Holly's fingers. "You know how much I loved you. I wouldn't do a thing to hurt you."

"You know they arrested my father?"

"Yes! I couldn't believe it. All that time women were dying and the Hunter was living across the street from me."

Holly didn't bother to point out the obvious, that she and Twila had been living *with* him, which was immeasurably worse.

"Yes, and I found out. I was five years old, and I stumbled onto his secret. I told my mother, and it got her killed. We just found her body in the basement."

Shock swept through Ida so fast that Holly thought the older woman might faint.

"Oh, no, no, I can't bear to think it. All these years he led us to believe you two ran away."

"Mother saved my life when she sent me away. I came back to St. Louis to find her. We finally did, and soon I'll be taking her home."

Tears began rolling haphazardly through the road map of wrinkles the years had left on Ida's face.

Holly patted her hand. "This leads me to the favor I need to ask. Please don't mention anything about me, and what I saw and did back then, to anyone. Right now the media doesn't know who I am, and I want to keep it that way. All they know is that the cops found the Hunter's wife. My fiancé and I are leaving soon. We're going home, and hopefully, with time, we'll put this hell behind us."

"I won't say a word. I swear," Ida promised.

Whit frowned. "What are you going to tell

the media? You know they're going to question you when you walk away from here."

"I'll say that the police talked to me because I'm the only one on the street who remembers them living here. End of story."

"Thank you," Holly said, as her focus shifted to Bud. He was tense and sweaty, which meant he was in pain. "Detective, may we please go back to the hotel now?"

As predicted, when Ida left the premises, the news crews waylaid her in the street. Whit walked his passengers to his car. As Holly settled back in the seat, she looked out at the gathering crowd of onlookers and then stifled a gasp as she recognized a face. It was Lynn Gravitt, Twila's friend from the cleaners, and she knew who Holly was.

The woman was crying, and when their gazes met, she lifted her hand once, as if to brush away a fly, but Holly knew she was saying goodbye. Holly put a finger to her lips, as if to beg her for her silence, and the woman nodded, then laid her hand on her heart in a silent promise.

"Who's that?" Bud asked.

"Another angel from Mother's past," Holly said.

Two days later Bud and Holly were packed and in the lobby, waiting for their car to be brought around. When they'd gone to check out, the manager had been waiting with the news that because of the trauma she had suffered under their roof, her entire stay had been comped.

It had been a nice surprise, for which Holly thanked him. As they got in the car to go to the airport, it began to rain.

It had been raining when she began her search. It seemed only fitting that it would end in the same weather.

It was late in the afternoon when they landed in Missoula. To Bud's disgust, Holly insisted that he be taken to baggage claim in a wheelchair, and he was still in it as they exited the terminal to passenger pickup. They tipped the attendant with the chair and the redcap who'd helped them carry out their luggage, then joined the throng of travelers with the same intention as theirs: to catch a ride to somewhere else before dark. They hadn't been there more than a couple of minutes before they heard someone honking.

"There's Uncle Delbert," Bud said, pointing at the black Lincoln Town Car from the Triple S that was coming their way.

"I will be so glad to get home," Holly muttered. "Even the air smells better here."

Bud winced when the car just missed sideswiping a taxi. He should have had one of the ranch hands come get them.

"You drive, okay?"

Holly grinned. "Sure, but we don't want to hurt his feelings."

"I'll tell him I want him to update on what's been happening on the ride home. He won't care."

The car came to a skidding stop fairly close to where they were.

"I think that's about as good as it's going to get," Bud said.

"Do not touch a single bag," Holly warned. "Delbert and I will get them loaded, then you get him in the backseat with you."

"Will do."

The ruse worked. Anxious to talk about everything that had been going on at the ranch, as well as curious about the incident that had put Bud in the hospital, Delbert was grateful to turn the car keys over to Holly.

"Oh, hey, girl, before we get out of here, just drop me by the old folks home," Delbert said. "I had a couple of the hands follow me into the city, one with my truck, the other in one of the ranch pickups, so he could take the first guy home. Figured you

two would want some time to yourselves."
Then he eyed the ring on Holly's finger.
"Looks like my guesswork was right."

Bud laughed. "Yes, we're engaged. Buckle
up and I'll tell you all about it. Holly, honey,
do you remember where Big Sky Assisted
Living is?"

"I think so, but if I get lost, one of you
will tell me."

As she drove away from the airport, it felt
as if she were leaving the weight of the world
behind. After they dropped Delbert off at
the retirement center, she stopped at a
supermarket long enough to pick up some
quick items for dinner and breakfast. Tomorrow she would make a real list and come
back into town, but this would suffice for
now.

Bud waited in the car. He kept wondering
when this was all going to catch up with
her. Obviously she'd already gone into her
caretaker mode by thinking of groceries. But
sometime in the next few days, reality was
going to hit. She was going to have to cope
with her emotions — both ugly and sad. He
would be watching, waiting to pick up the
pieces.

The sun was just setting as they drove
through the Triple S gate and then down
the long driveway toward the ranch house.

Delbert had left several lights on inside. The simple gesture did not go unnoticed.

"Look," Bud said. "The welcome lights of home."

Holly's vision blurred; then she blinked back the tears.

"I wasn't always sure I'd ever see this place again."

Bud heard the tremor in her voice, but he wouldn't let her go there.

"Me, either, but we made it, and I have to say, I am a whole lot happier now than when I left."

It made Holly smile. "Am I going to get any credit for your wonderful change of heart?"

"You get *all* the credit," he said, then opened the garage door with the remote, breathing a huge sigh of relief as the car came to a stop.

Before they could shut the garage door, Monty, one of the hands, headed inside.

"Welcome back, ya'll," he said. "Thought you might like a little help carrying in your bags." He eyed Bud's careful exit. "You okay, boss?"

"I'm good. I'll get better."

The cowboy grabbed a suitcase in each hand as soon as Holly popped the trunk lid.

"Thanks a lot, Monty. I'm going to get

Bud inside and settled. Just put those bags in the hallway. I'll tend to them later."

"Yes, ma'am," he said, and quickly carried in their luggage, then bade them good-night before going back to the bunkhouse.

Holly put away the groceries, somewhat surprised at how neat Delbert had kept the place, then went through the house room by room before locking up for the night.

When she got to her bedroom, she realized Bud wasn't there. He'd gone to his own room, just like he'd done all the years before.

She kicked off her shoes and then padded down the hall in her sock feet, looking for her man. His door was open, and he was sitting on the side of the bed, trying to get his shirt over his head. From the pain on his face and his cursing, Holly could see she wasn't a moment too soon.

"Hey, I lost you," she said, as she eased his shirt over his head.

Bud breathed a quick sigh of relief as he used his good arm to pull her close against his chest.

"You couldn't lose me if you tried."

"So, about sleeping arrangements . . . if you're exhausted and want a bed to yourself, I certainly understand, but if not . . . is it going to be your bed or mine?"

Bud laughed out loud, then swooped, kissing her hard and swift.

"Mine's king-size."

"You win," Holly said. "I'll go get changed."

Bud sat down on the side of the bed. "I'll be right here, waiting for when you get back."

Holly eyed the gleam in his eyes and then shook her head.

"There will be no messing around until you're better."

"I *am* better."

"As long as you have stitches, you are on a sexual diet."

She strode out of the room, leaving Bud with smile on his face. He'd heard of all kinds of diets, but that one was a first for him.

God, but he loved her — every fiery inch of her. He'd seen her face down the devil and come out a winner. He wasn't about to argue about a little sex.

EIGHTEEN

Three days later Savannah called. She and Judd were planning to come home within the next couple of weeks, and they wanted to get married at the ranch.

It was the opportunity Holly had been waiting for.

"It's going to take some planning to make this happen in such a short time," Holly said.

Savannah laughed. "I know, but Judd and I don't want a fuss. We just want to be legal."

"Have you talked to Maria?" Holly asked.

"Not in a couple of days, but I do know that her detective proposed."

Holly squealed. "Oh, my gosh! Do you think she's planning on getting married here, too?"

"We'll have to find out," Savannah said. "Wouldn't it be great if we had a double wedding?"

"It would be even better if we made it a

triple," Holly said.

There was a moment of dead silence, and then Savannah was sputtering.

"What's happened? What's been going on that I don't know about?"

"Bud and I are engaged."

Another moment of silence, and then an ear-shattering scream.

"Are you serious? This is awfully sudden. Why didn't we know?"

"It isn't sudden for me or Bud. I've loved him for a long time, and according to him, he's been in love with me since I turned eighteen."

"You never said a word."

"I know."

"Why would you keep that a secret from us?" Savannah muttered.

"Because *you* can't keep a secret."

Savannah managed a snort. "Whatever. Just wait until Maria finds out."

"If you talk to her in the near future, tell her that if she wants in on the family wedding, she better let me know now."

"I will." Then Savannah started to cry. "I am so happy this is happening for all of us. Daddy would have been so proud to walk us down the aisle. Oh, Holly, who will walk us down the aisle?"

Bud walked in just then, and Holly turned

toward him as a slow smile spread across her face.

"Bud will."

Bud didn't know what Holly had just volunteered him for, but she was smiling, so it had to be good.

"What will I do?"

Holly pointed to the phone. "Savannah's crying because she and Judd are coming home in two weeks to get married and there's no one to walk her down the aisle. I told her you would."

Bud took the phone out of Holly's hand. "Damn straight I'll be walking you down the aisle — and Maria, too, when it comes time to do it."

Savannah was laughing and crying and just the tiniest bit irked that they'd kept such a secret from everyone.

"So who's going to walk Holly down the aisle, Mr. Keeper-of-big-secrets."

Bud grinned. "She finally told you."

"Yes, she finally told me, and you're going to catch it again when I tell Maria about you two."

"Tell anyone who'll listen," Bud said, as he pulled Holly up against him and gave her a quick squeeze. "I'm so happy I've been strutting like a rooster ever since I got back."

"But you didn't answer my question," Savannah said. "Who's going to walk Holly down the aisle?"

"Me. I've been wrangling the three of you a good part of my life. This will be my last shot, and I'm going to give it all I've got."

"Okay, then," Savannah said. "I'm calling Maria. She doesn't know it yet, but there's going to be a triple wedding at the Triple S. That even sounds right, doesn't it? Tell Holly I'll call her with more details later."

The line went dead.

Bud blinked. "Sorry. She hung up before I could stop her."

Holly shrugged. "It doesn't matter. She just wants to be the one to tell Maria first. Hope you don't mind, but you and I are getting married in a couple of weeks."

"Mind? No, darlin', I don't mind a bit."

Ten days later, in the midst of a flurry of wedding plans, Holly got the call that her mother's remains would be arriving at the airport the next day. It rattled the shell she'd built around herself, leaving her to deal with a whole new set of raw emotions.

She and Bud had already planned the actual steps that would need to be taken to get the casket from the airport to the family cemetery at the ranch. She'd contacted both of her sisters to make sure they had no issues with burying her mother there and gotten total support.

Now all she had to do was call the man to come dig the grave, and let the minister and funeral home know. After twenty years of darkness, Twila Mackey was going to be laid to rest beneath the blue Montana skies.

Earlier that morning Bud had driven over to the west side of the ranch to check the grass, to see if it had grown tall enough for him to run some cattle on it. She hadn't been able to slow him down much since his physical therapy had begun. According to him, the therapist's best prescription for regaining full use of the muscles in his back and arm was to use them, which he did every day, and with more and more agility every night when he took her to bed.

When she called, Bud answered quickly.

"Hey, darlin', what's up?"

"I got a call from St. Louis. Mother's remains will arrive at six-thirty tomorrow evening."

His demeanor shifted immediately. "Okay. This is what you've been waiting for. So this is all good, right?"

Holly sighed. She knew Bud was waiting for her to come undone. In the back of her mind, she knew it was bound to happen.

But today wasn't the day.

"Yes, it's all good, and so am I. So you're still okay to call Chet Wheatley to come dig the grave?"

"Sure am. I've got his number in the truck."

"Then I'll call our pastor and the funeral home."

"See you at noon," Bud said. "What are we having?"

"Fried chicken."

"Outstanding," he said. "Love you most."

"Love you more."

Holly called the funeral home, alerting them to the time that a hearse needed to be at the airport, then called their pastor with an update. He promised to be out at the ranch before dark the next evening. They would be burying Twila Mackey at sundown.

She went through the morning with a somber heart. She had the triple wedding event running on schedule. Flowers had been ordered. The pastor had been notified, and the church was reserved. A local bakery was doing all three of the wedding cakes, as well as the grooms' cakes. Measurements had flown fast and furiously between the three sisters until the tuxes had been ordered, but they were picking out their own gowns.

Holly had already chosen hers. It was being altered and would be ready in plenty of time for the wedding.

But this phone call had thrown everything out of sync. Once again there were things left undone. Not until the final shovel of dirt had covered her mother's grave would Holly feel complete.

She hadn't dreamed about her past since she'd come home from St. Louis. But that night, lying within the safety of Bud's embrace, her subconscious brought her one last gift.

Harriet was panicked. Mother was crying as she packed Harriet's clothes in a suitcase, and she was certain it was her fault. She'd done a bad thing, making Daddy and Mother mad. She'd been begging for hours, promising she wouldn't tell anyone else, that she would make her bed every day forever without complaining, that she would always pick up her toys. She would do anything if Mother just wouldn't send her away.

Finally the bag was packed and Mama turned.

"Come here, my pretty baby," she said, and got down on her knees and took Harriet into her arms. "This isn't because you did some-

thing bad. It's because Daddy did something bad. It's his fault, not yours. Not ever yours! You were a brave little girl to tell the truth. You were taught to tell the truth, and you did the right thing, okay?"

Harriet nodded, but she was bothered by the fact that there was only one suitcase.

"Are you coming with me?" she asked.

"No. But I will *come and get you — and soon. I promise. Cross my heart and hope to die, pinky-swear promise . . . Mother will come get you."*

Harriet didn't want to go away with strangers. She didn't know where they lived. What if Mother couldn't find her again?

"But we don't know where preacher's house is. What if you can't find me? What if you never see me again?"

"Look at me, Harriet! Hear my words! I don't know exactly how long this will take, but I promise on my life . . . one day we will be together again."

Someone was shaking her, and then she heard Bud's voice.

"Wake up, Holly. Wake up."

She opened her eyes and then looked toward the window. It was still dark.

"What's wrong? Why did you wake me?" she mumbled.

Bud swept his hand across her cheek.

"Sweetheart . . . you were crying in your sleep."

Holly felt her face, then her pillow. Both were wet from tears. "Oh. I was dreaming about the night Mother was packing my bag to take me to meet Andrew. I thought she was sending me away because I'd told on Daddy . . . because I'd been bad."

"Oh, honey." Bud slid his arm beneath her neck and pulled her close against him. "I'm sorry. I'm so sorry."

"I know, but in a way it's okay, because I also remembered the last thing she said. 'I promise on my life . . . one day we will be together again.' Oh, Bud, this breaks my heart."

"Don't cry, baby. She did what she had to do to keep her child safe. That makes her the most amazing mother ever, and you're just like her. You're always loving and giving and thinking of everyone but yourself. Close your eyes and rest. Tomorrow is a big day. No more bad dreams, just me holding you safe while you sleep."

The sun was sliding toward the western horizon when the plane Bud and Holly had been waiting for finally landed in Missoula. Instead of immediately taxiing toward the terminal, it rolled to a stop a short distance away, coming to a halt a few yards from the waiting hearse.

"She's here," Bud said, and took Holly by the hand. "Come on, honey. Let's walk her home."

They got out of the hearse and moved toward the casket being lowered from the cargo hold. It had taken twenty years for her to be found, but Twila Mackey was no longer alone.

A few minutes later, with the casket secure, they headed back to the Triple S. Holly leaned against Bud's shoulder, calmer that she'd imagined she would be. She'd cried so many tears since this journey began, but today was the true journey's end.

By the time they got to the ranch, it was less than thirty minutes to sundown. The pastor was waiting. The ranch hands stood as pallbearers, honored to be asked. And then the casket was unloaded and placed above the grave.

Bud took Holly's hand as they walked to the side of the grave, standing arm in arm as the pastor began.

"The Lord is my shepherd, I shall not want . . ."

Holly looked up as the preacher continued to read. The sun was sitting on the edge of the world, backlit by a most radiant display of pink and gold.

"Yea though I walk through the valley of the shadow of death, I fear no evil."

She shivered. A fitting verse. Twila Mackey had conquered her fear and faced the greatest of evils.

The preacher's voice faded into the background as Holly stared into the west, watching as the sun disappeared below the horizon, leaving an explosion of heavenly color to mark its passing.

"And I shall dwell in the house of the Lord forever. Amen."

"Amen," they echoed, as the casket was lowered into the ground. Like the sun, it was disappearing below the surface of the earth, but Twila's rest would be complete.

Holly tossed the first handful of dirt into the grave. It scattered silently onto the surface of the casket, as symbolic as the site she'd chosen for her mother's final resting place.

Holly looked toward the tombstone to the right of Twila's grave as the workers began filling the hole with dirt.

Andrew and Hannah Slade — his grave still bearing the mark of recently turned earth, while Hannah's was smooth from the passing years.

Twila Mackey had entrusted her daughter,

her most precious possession, to a preacher named Andrew Slade. Now Holly was laying her mother to rest at his side.

"Daddy . . . you took such good care of me, if you don't mind, I would appreciate it if you'd do the same for my mother. She's been alone for a very long time, but I think you and Hannah will like her. She's a lot like me."

Once the grave was covered, they laid a single wreath of roses at the foot, then walked arm in arm back through the dusk to the brightly lit ranch house. It was symbolic of new beginnings as they walked out of the dark into the light.

EPILOGUE

"Bud! Bud! They're here!" Holly cried, as two cars pulled up in front of the house.

Without waiting, she burst out of the house and then leaped off the porch. Her sisters were home!

Maria got out first, accompanied by a tall, lanky man wearing jeans and a sport coat, but it was the Stetson and the cowboy boots that made Holly smile.

Of course Maria had fallen for a cowboy. Just because he wore a badge, it didn't change the facts.

"Maria! Maria! Welcome home!" Holly cried, and then hugged her sister fiercely before stepping back to give her a once-over. "Are you healed?"

"In body, yes. In spirit . . . I'm getting there," Maria said, then grabbed her fiancé, Bodie, and pulled him forward. "Honey, now is not the time to stand on ceremony. Come meet the heart of our home, my sister

Holly. Holly, this is Bodie Scott."

Holly held out her hand. Bodie grinned, then bypassed the hand and swept her off her feet with a big hug and kiss. By the time he put her down, Bud was coming out of the house and smiling.

That was when the doors of the second car opened.

Savannah was squealing and waving even before she got out of the car. Both sisters headed toward her on the run.

"Be prepared," Bud told Bodie. "These three are bonded like glue. You may as well meet the baby of the family now, so we can get back inside."

Back in the house, Maria and Savannah cornered Bud, giving him grief for keeping his feelings for Holly hidden for so long.

"I can't believe all this happened behind my back," Savannah said. "I'm so happy about these weddings I could die."

All of a sudden there was a hush in the room.

"Seriously poor choice of words, baby sister," Maria said.

Everyone laughed, grateful for the break in the tension, and then Holly began organizing the crowd.

"Since your flights landed so late, you do realize there's not going to be a wedding rehearsal, right?"

"I don't need to practice saying 'I do,' " Bud drawled. "I've been saying it in my heart for years."

"For that you win a prize," Holly said, and kissed him soundly. "So now that that's settled, we'll talk details while we eat. I've been cooking for days."

They bypassed the dining room, gathering instead in the big warm kitchen, filling their plates from the casseroles and platters lining the sideboard, and then sitting down to eat at the long wooden table that had held many a meal.

It had been decided that the men would all spend the night at Judd's ranch, giving the sisters their last night together alone.

Later, after the food had been eaten and the dishes washed and put away, they went into the living room to trade horror stories about what they had gone through. Savannah was holding court with a harrowing story when the phone began to ring.

Maria was closest and answered it without thought.

"Triple S."

"Is this Holly?"

"No, I'm her sister Maria. May I ask who's calling?"

"Tell her it's Detective Carver from St.

Louis. I need to speak to her."

Maria put her hand over the mouthpiece. "Hey! Holly. There's a Detective Carver on the phone for you."

Suddenly Holly looked nervous. "I'll take it in the other room," she said, and bolted before Bud could stop her.

As soon as Maria heard her pick up, she replaced the receiver, but she could tell by the look on Bud's face that all had not been revealed.

"What's going on?"

Bud put a finger to his lips, indicating silence. The room went quiet. In the distance, they could hear the faint murmur of Holly's voice, although they couldn't hear what was being said. Then they heard a sharp cry. Bud got to his feet, but Holly was already coming back into the room.

Her step was light, and there was a smile on her face that went all the way to her soul.

"I just got the best wedding present ever," she said. "The DNA results just came back. There's a 99.99 percent certainty that Harold Mackey is *not* my father. Oh, my God! *Oh, my God!*"

She started to laugh — a high-pitched crazy kind of laugh that, once started, had no place to stop.

Bud flinched. *Here it comes.* He had

known this moment would happen. The wall she'd built around her was coming down. By the time he reached her, she was sobbing.

It was evident to everyone what the news meant to her: no more fear of tainted blood being passed through her to generations to come.

Judd and Bodie left the room, giving her the space she needed to both grieve and rejoice. Holly was prostrate, her legs too weak to stand. Bud got her to her feet and into a chair, then knelt beside her.

"It's okay, baby," he said softly. "It's okay. You go ahead and cry. It's about time you let go."

Maria and Savannah pushed past him and surrounded her chair, touching her hands, her face, reminding her that the family she really belonged to was already here and surrounding her with love.

Holly couldn't quit crying. Even when she tried, a fresh set of tears would well back up. It was killing Bud, and she knew it, but she couldn't stop.

She wrapped her arms around his neck and started kissing his face and neck and lips, over and over.

"I'm fine, Bud, I swear. I'll quit when all the bad stuff is washed from my soul. It's late. You take Judd and Bodie and go. We'll see you tomorrow morning at the church, and I promise I'll have the happiest face of all."

Bud didn't know how he was going to walk out of this house when there were tears on her face.

"I don't want to leave you."

"We'll be with her," Savannah said.

"We're all sleeping together anyway," Maria added. "We'll put her in the middle like always, so she doesn't fall out of bed."

Holly's eyes widened, and just like that, the tears turned to laughter. The first few years of her life when they'd all been small, they really had always put her in the middle to keep her from falling out of bed.

By the time Bud kissed her goodbye and left the room, they were laughing. That was the sound that followed him out the door.

Later, the house was quiet. Outside, the night was broken by the occasional howl of a coyote and an answering yip from another on a faraway ridge.

They'd all crawled into Andrew's bed to sleep. It was the closest they could get to him now that he was gone. As promised, Holly lay in the middle, flanked by the sisters of her heart. They'd been talking and then stopping, swearing they needed to sleep, and then one of them would start a conversation all over again.

But it was Savannah who finally topped the night off with an announcement.

"You know that I'm now sinfully rich, right?"

Holly giggled.

Maria poked her. "Don't brag."

"It's just a fact," Savannah said. "I got both of you a special wedding present. Thomas Jefferson, who is my lawyer and whom you will meet tomorrow, helped me get them for you."

"I didn't get you anything. We all said we weren't buying each other presents," Maria said.

"I didn't get anything, either," Holly said.

"I don't need anything but you two," Savannah said. "Since my grandmother's murder, you two and Bud are all the family I have left. My entire birth family is either dead or in prison because of that money. It's time it was put to good use, so FYI . . . I had a million dollars deposited into each of your bank accounts."

They gasped in unison.

"Savannah! You can't do that! It's too much!" Holly insisted as Maria nodded furiously in agreement.

Savannah shrugged. "I can and I did, and you're welcome. Now be quiet. We need to get some sleep."

Suddenly she was bombarded with pillows, and the house was filled again with laughter.

The John Wesley United Methodist Church in Missoula was packed to the walls, the pews filled with longtime friends of Andrew and his girls. The open invitation to the triple wedding had been announced a week ago in church, and anticipation had been mounting.

The brides had commandeered a Sunday school classroom at one end of the church and were using it as a dressing room, while the men had taken over the pastor's study at the other end.

A florist was running madly from one end of the church to the other, pinning miniature white roses on the men's lapels, and then dashing to the far end of the church with three wedding bouquets. The church was awash in flowers and greenery, but there were no bridesmaids and no best men. By the time the three couples got lined up around the altar, there wouldn't be room left for anyone else but the pastor who would marry them.

The ushers, however, were strangers to the crowd, and whispers abounded as they were being seated.

One was a bald giant of a black man in an elegant suit named Thomas Jefferson, who was in fact Savannah's lawyer and the man who'd helped save her life. The shorter, older man with cropped graying hair and hard, steely eyes went by the name of Whiteside and was the ex-CIA man who'd sacrificed everything he owned to keep her safe.

Coleman Rice, the family lawyer, was the only one who knew the answers to the questions everyone was asking, and he wasn't talking.

Finally the last guests had been seated.

The music began, and the congregation quieted. Up front, two grooms entered and took their places at the altar.

The music swelled, and then the wedding march began.

The congregation stood, watching as Robert Tate escorted Maria, the first of the brides, to the altar. At that point Bodie Scott stepped forward.

"Who gives this woman to this man?" the preacher asked.

"I do," Bud said, then stepped back as

Maria slipped her hand through Bodie's arm.

There was a titter of amusement as the music swelled again and Robert Tate made a beeline back to the foyer. Seconds later, as the wedding march played again, he came back down the aisle with Savannah on his arm. She was still tiny despite three-inch heels, and resplendent in white satin.

When they reached the altar Judd stepped forward, and again the pastor asked, "Who gives this woman to this man?"

"I do," Bud said, and then moved back as Judd Holyfield claimed his bride.

Once more Bud headed back up the aisle, and this time the congregation was laughing aloud.

When the wedding march began again and he came back a third time, it was with Holly. Her hair was down and loose over her shoulders, while the sleeveless ice-white gown she was wearing hugged every curve of her body to perfection. They walked down the aisle toward the altar arm in arm, and when they reached the pastor, again he asked, "Who gives this woman to this man?"

"I'm keeping this one for myself," Bud said.

The congregation roared.

And so it began, the ritual that would bind

these women to their men.

It had begun with laughter.

It ended in vows and promises.

For Andrew Slade's daughters, the end of their wedding was just the beginning of the rest of their lives.

The employees of Thorndike Press hope you have enjoyed this Large Print book. All our Thorndike, Wheeler, and Kennebec Large Print titles are designed for easy reading, and all our books are made to last. Other Thorndike Press Large Print books are available at your library, through selected bookstores, or directly from us.

For information about titles, please call:
   (800) 223-1244

or visit our Web site at:
   http://gale.cengage.com/thorndike

To share your comments, please write:
   Publisher
   Thorndike Press
   10 Water St., Suite 310
   Waterville, ME 04901